STATION ZERO

PHILIP REEVE
RAIL
HEAD
'A THRILLING RIDE IN A
IMAGINED UNIVERSE'
PHILIP REEVE
BLACK
LIGHT
EXPRESS
By the author of
RAILHEAD *and* MORTAL ENGINES

Praise for *Railhead* and *Black Light Express*, Zen and Nova's previous adventures

'Philip Reeve has always been a writer of extraordinarily fertile imagination and his latest, *Railhead*, is a long-anticipated event that more than lives up to expectations.'
Sunday Times

'Railhead is superb.'
Telegraph

'An electrifying triumph.'
Daily Mail

'A dizzying philosophical space opera from the Mortal Engines creator, it has the broad scope, richness and originality of vintage Iain M. Banks.'
Guardian

'A pleasing mix of the retro and futuristic, with an off-kilter love story at its heart.'
Financial Times

'A sort of sci-fi creation story, a quest, and a fantastic adventure.'
School Librarian

'Imaginative and compelling... This book grabs you and takes you into a futuristic world.'
Parents in Touch

'For sheer power of imaginative world building Philip Reeve is hard to beat.'
magicfictionsincepotter.co.uk

To Sarah McIntyre, for always wanting to read the latest chapter, and to Sarah Reeve, for never wanting to read any of them until the whole book is finished.

OXFORD
UNIVERSITY PRESS
Great Clarendon Street, Oxford OX2 6DP

Oxford University Press is a department of the University of Oxford. It furthers the University's objective of excellence in research, scholarship, and education by publishing worldwide. Oxford is a registered trade mark of Oxford University Press in the UK and in certain other countries

First published 2018

British Library Cataloguing in Publication Data

Data available
ISBN: 978-0-19-275914-6

1 3 5 7 9 10 8 6 4 2

Printed in Great Britain by Clays Ltd, St Ives plc
Paper used in the production of this book is a natural, recyclable product made from wood grown in sustainable forests. The manufacturing process conforms to the environmental regulations of the country of origin.

PHILIP REEVE

STATION ZERO

OXFORD
UNIVERSITY PRESS

PART ONE

NEW MONEY

1

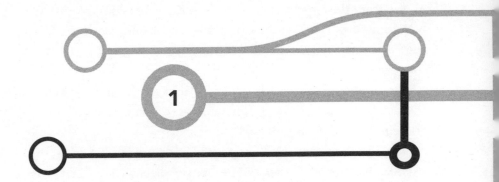

The train-wind was blowing. It found its way through the tunnels to the platform where Zen waited. It stirred the litter that lay between the tracks. It ruffled Zen's hair and plucked at the tattered sackcloth robes of the other travellers who waited all around him. Zen was the only person on the platform, but it was more crowded than he had ever seen it.

His fellow travellers were all Hive Monks, shambling insect colonies which had made human-shaped armatures for themselves and draped them in grimy robes. The crude white paper masks that were their faces stared towards the tunnel mouth, and the train-wind touched them like a warm breath.

The wind smelled of dust and the black kilometres beneath the mountains. It smelled of the faint electric scent of the K-gates through which a train could cross a thousand light years in a heartbeat. It smelled of the trains themselves, and now it brought with it the sound of a train, too, the deep roar of engines, a strange voice raised in song, both rising as the wind rose until a blaze of lights appeared there in the darkness and the train gathered itself out of the shadows and the racing reflections on shining rails.

Lost Hive Monk faces blew past Zen like paper plates at a windy picnic. For a moment the alien loco loomed over him: an insectoid *morvah* from the Nestworlds of the Neem, beetle-shiny, blazing with bioluminescent light, long cockroach feelers rasping along the station roof. Then the line of windowless carriages it towed was passing, slowing, stopping.

'The train at Platform 1 is for Hive Monks only,' said the voice of the station AI, as if any human would be foolish enough to want to board it. 'Hive Monks only on Platform 1.'

The Hive Monks buzzed and sighed and swayed. A few were so excited that they lost their vague human shapes completely, robes crumpling, lost bugs scuttling mindlessly across the platform or fluttering upwards to ping against the lamps. The rest surged through the open doors into the hot, dark, insect-stinking carriages.

Zen went with them, keeping his face down, trusting to the tide of ragged robes around him to hide him from the station's cameras. He stood among the Hive Monks in the seatless carriage, in the dim red glow from the overhead lights. The doors slid shut. The Hive Monks whispered to one another. Zen stared at the bug-scuttling floor and waited for the train to move. What was the delay? Had someone spotted him? Would the doors open again and police come aboard to drag him back onto the platform? His heart was hammering as hard as it used to when he was just a young railhead, riding the interstellar trains with stolen trinkets in the pockets of his coat.

But that had been years ago. He was not a railhead any more. He was just Zen Starling, rich and famous and unhappy, and the only thing that he was stealing was himself.

He had not planned to become a fugitive again. It had come at him fast, the way life does. Just twenty-four hours earlier he had been looking lazily down on the sunlit station city from the cabin of his luxury air-car as it circled above the Noon family's corporate palace, waiting for permission to land. He was wearing a perfectly tailored Kitty Mbakwe video-fabric suit and boots made from the hide of an alien worm. His

Baxendine headset was so expensive and delicate that it looked like a silvery tattoo curling across the brown skin beside his right eye.

He had been living on Galatava for almost a year by then. It was a pleasant world, with forests and mountains and oceans and a pretty ring system which the Galatavans said made their night sky so much more *interesting* than night skies were on planets that only had a few boring old moons. It had never been a major station because it had only two K-gates, one leading to Sundarban, the other to the volcanic moon Khoorsandi. But when the Network Empire split in two, Galatava had suddenly become important.

Most of the lines and stations of the Empire were under the control of the new emperor, Elon Prell, but the Noon family were holding on jealously to their own planets on the western branch lines. Their only hope of surviving, now that they had cut themselves off from trade with the rest of the Empire, lay on Khoorsandi. There a new K-gate had been opened which led to a whole new empire: an alien network called the Web of Worlds. The aliens seemed just as keen on trade as humans were, so trains from the Noon worlds were pouring through the Khoorsandi gate and returning laden with strange freight and stranger passengers. Since Khoorsandi didn't have enough stable land to hold all the rail yards and warehouses and freight terminals for the new trade, Galatava, one stop up the line, was expanding its station city rapidly.

The Noons' corporate palace perched on the edge of a crag, looking down over the parks and rooftops of the city to the shining waters of the Hana River. It was a tiny palace by the standards of a corporate family, and little more than a summer house compared to the Noons' vast compounds on Sundarban, but like the rest of the city it was getting bigger, growing extra wings and turrets for itself inside cages of biodegradable scaffolding.

Zen had plenty of time to admire it all, because the palace security AI made his air-car circle for ten minutes before giving it permission to land. A pair of unicorns, which had been grazing the bluegrass lawns, cantered gracefully away as the car extended its wheels, folded its wings, and settled itself on a circular gravel parking bay.

Zen opened the canopy. He could hear music and a blur of voices drifting from the palace. It wasn't a party exactly, more of a pre-party. Tomorrow Threnody Noon would be travelling through the new Khoorsandi gate to the world known as the Hub, there to celebrate the end of the war against the Kraitt and sign more trade agreements with the other alien species. This gathering on Galatava was meant to welcome all the important Noon dignitaries who were arriving from Sundarban and Marapur to join her train. It would also serve as a consolation to less important ones like Zen, who weren't invited to the ceremony in the Hub.

As he stepped out of the car, an alien machine like a giant, armoured spider crab came ambling past with laughing children clinging to its back. It was one of the Neem, who were the Noons' main allies out on the new Network. There were about a million insects operating that crab-suit, and Zen could hear them seething about inside it when it came over to talk to him, attracted by the sight of his air-car. 'Is that a Nagana Nebula?' it asked in its rustly voice. 'The new 500 series?'

'Five-oh-two,' said Zen, hoping that he was not going to get drawn into a long conversation about it. The Neem were fascinated by human technology, the faster and sleeker the better. It was very good for trade, but it did mean that they tended to be awful car bores.

Luckily, the kids on the suit's back were enjoying their ride too much to let it stop for long. 'More! More!' they yelled, banging their hands against its carapace.

The Neem said, 'No rest for the wicked, eh?' and went scuttling on.

When Zen looked back, the gravel bay holding his car was sinking down through the lawn into some underground garage. It came back up a moment later, empty and freshly raked, and another air-car landed on it.

Zen ran a hand through his beautifully cut, dark purple hair, and strolled towards the house, trying to look as if he belonged in such a place. Somewhere in there, among the party crowds, was Threnody Noon. Threnody was not a friend, exactly, but she and Zen had been comrades in some dangerous adventures and Zen hoped she would have the power to grant him what he wanted—permission to leave Galatava. Threnody's people didn't want her talking to the likes of Zen Starling and intercepted all his messages, but they couldn't stop him talking to her in person. Not today. He had an invitation. He pinged it from his headset to the minds of the Motorik footmen who guarded the main door, and swaggered past them into the party.

2

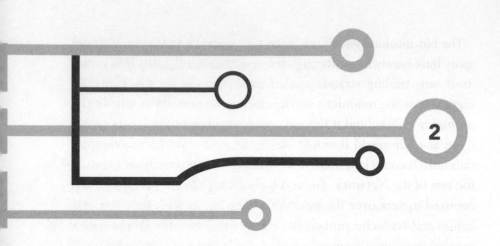

The object was not quite a moon. It was the shape of a peanut, the size of a biggish mountain, and it was one of the largest of the billion boulders which made up the outermost ring of Galatava's nearest neighbouring planet, the gas giant Vapna.

Now, upon the object's airless, elephant-grey surface, something untoward was happening. Dust which had not been disturbed for aeons stirred, rising in little eddies as if a wind were blowing. Above these dust-devils a glimmer of colourless light appeared, nothing like the sullen sulphur-yellow glow of Vapna. It grew brighter, and out of it came writhing a sort of tentacle. The light spread, and other tentacles emerged. The rock below them was altering, beginning to glow and thickly flow. The tentacles started sculpting it into a shape, a weird wishbone arch. As the arch formed, the light increased. More tentacles reached through it. The nose of something appeared, beaky and massive.

If anyone had been watching they would have known by now what was happening on the not-quite-moon. It was the same thing that had happened on Khoorsandi the year before. A K-gate was opening; the mouth of a wormhole which would lead through the mysterious dimension called K-space to another gate on some faraway world. But what could be the point of a K-gate on this lonely rock?

The bio-machine which made the gate was called a Worm. Its blind, spiny bulk barely fitted through the arch that it had built. It squeezed itself out, trailing strands and streamers of the ghostly light, and crept across the moonlet's surface, laying sleepers and a double pair of shining rails behind it the way some huge bug might lay its eggs.

On another world it would have gone much faster, extending the rails until it could join them to an existing line and link its new gate to the rest of the Network. Here, it had nowhere to go. It crept for five hundred metres over the moonlet's steep, stony face, then stopped. Spines and tentacles probed the airless dark, as if the Worm sensed its mistake. Then it reversed at surprising speed and vanished through the curtain of light which hung inside the new-formed arch.

The curtain shifted and rippled for a moment, like the surface of a vertical pool. After a moment something else emerged through it: a knot of light which drifted with odd dancing motions along the new-laid tracks and then took flight like thistledown, fading into the dull glare of Vapna.

Then the light died, and only the arch was left, skeletal and lonely on the grey rock, as if it had been standing there forever.

3

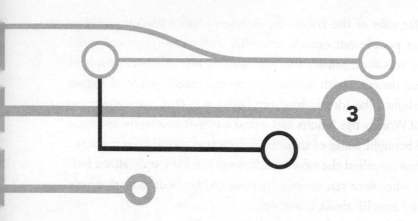

The Noon palace was full of sights and smells from other planets. Perfumes and fabrics from the Web of Worlds had become all the rage since the new Khoorsandi gate had opened. As Zen pushed his way past other party-goers he caught wafts of alien scent which took him back to worlds he'd walked upon last year with Nova. There were actual aliens present too: Deeka with their internal organs pulsing like jellyfish inside their transparent bodies; a pair of high-horned Herastec diplomats. The human guests crowded around these exotic visitors, but some of them still had time to notice Zen as well. He felt their eyes on him as he moved through the big, crowded rooms. He caught their stagey whispers. 'So that's Zen Starling? He is not bad looking, for a common railhead.'

'The rumour is that he is some sort of long-lost Noon relative. That is why they tolerate him.'

'Really? I heard that he used to be a street-thief on Kalishti.'

'It was Cleave, actually,' Zen said, glancing at the woman who'd spoken, watching her turn away, embarrassed, while her friends leaned in to share more gossip about him. He wondered what they would say if they knew the real story. He wondered how they would look at him if they knew that he had been to blame for the Spindlebridge disaster and the destruction of the Noon train.

At the far side of the room, big windows had folded themselves aside to let people out onto a verandah with views down over the city. There was flute music, and the chiming kiss of finger-cymbals. Pretty blue dancers with animatronic wings made graceful shapes in the sunlight. The idea behind the ballet was that somewhere on the Web of Worlds the Noons had found a planet where these angels lived, and brought some of them back here to dance for their guests. But Zen had travelled the new lines himself, and the only aliens he'd met there who were remotely humanoid had been the Kraitt. There was nothing angelic about the Kraitt . . .

In the crowd around the dancers he spotted Threnody, recognizing her by the cloud of red dragonflies which hung above her elaborate new hairdo. The dragonflies weren't just for decoration, they were miniature security drones, programmed to protect her. They swung compound eyes and micro-guns towards Zen as he shoved his way rudely through the crowd. Threnody turned too, greeting him with an uncertain smile.

The Noons called Threnody their Chief Executive now, but she still looked like an empress to Zen, in her shimmercloth sari and her headdress of alien coins. He had liked her better the way she had been last year, when she was a fugitive, scruffy and crop-haired and startlingly determined. She looked prettier now, but less confident, as if this soft life on Galatava was proving as bad for her as it was for Zen.

'I need to ask you something,' he said.

Before she could answer, the dancers did something which caused a ripple of applause and drew her attention back to them, and before he could speak to her again a hand took his arm. 'This is not a good time, Zen,' said Kala Tanaka, as she steered him firmly away.

'I just wanted to talk to Threnody!'

'You should have sent her a message.'

'I've been sending her messages. She never replies. I don't think they even reach her. You screen them, don't you? You don't want her talking to a common railhead.'

'Lady Threnody is extremely busy. She has a company to run.'

'Yes, she does. It's called Noon-Starling Lines. And I'm Starling; it's my company too.'

'It's called the Noon Consortium, Zen—'Noon-Starling Lines' was a proposal which the family council rejected. And you are a silent partner, with the emphasis very much on *silent*.'

Kala was Threnody's assistant, or perhaps her keeper: a small, plain, middle-aged woman who had somehow made herself one of the most powerful people on the Noon worlds. She was polite, efficient, and absolutely determined to keep Threnody as far away as possible from the likes of Zen Starling.

'I heard she's taking a train through the new Khoorsandi gate tomorrow,' said Zen. 'Back to the Hub. I was wondering why I haven't been invited.'

'It is an official visit.' Kala had this way of smiling as she spoke so that to the other guests it must have looked like she and Zen were friends, but her grip on his arm was steely. There was steel in her voice, too. 'Lady Threnody is to celebrate our victory over the Kraitt, and sign new trade deals with the Deeka and the Herastec.'

'I could help her,' said Zen. 'The aliens know me. I was travelling the Web of Worlds for months before Threnody got there. I'm the first human they ever met. They trust me.'

Kala Tanaka sighed. She bowed to a passing acquaintance—a fat, cheerful Stationmaster from one of the Silver River industrial planets—and then turned sharply right, propelling Zen down some steps into a domed glass building. The building had an airlock, and when Zen stepped through the inner seal he found himself in a forest of crystalline shrubs and pale alien trees. Circular leaves spun like toy windmills, filling the dome with papery whisperings. The Noons loved plants, and had brought back all sorts of exciting new species from the alien worlds, but it was too soon to tell if these wind-trees from Hath were compatible with the plant-life humans knew, so they were growing for the time being in enclosed biomes.

'The aliens may trust you, Zen,' said Kala Tanaka, 'but we do not. We both know why you really want to go back to the Hub. You are hoping to find Nova again.'

'No,' said Zen, 'I've forgotten all about Nova, like you said I should.' But she knew he was lying. To lie well you had to half-believe in the lie yourself, and Zen did not believe that he would ever forget about Nova. It was almost a year since she had set off without him into the Black Light Zone, but she was still the first thing he thought of when he woke each day and the last thing he thought of before he went to sleep.

They followed a spiral pathway through the plantings to the centre of the biome. Kala let go of Zen's arm and sat down on a bench beside a pool. Zen stayed standing. Alien jellyfish-things drifted just beneath the surface of the water like lost lace handkerchiefs.

'We have heard nothing from the Guardians for months,' Kala said, as if she were changing the subject. 'After all that fuss when the new gate opened, they seem to have just gone back into the Datasea and forgotten about us.'

'Well, that's good, isn't it?' said Zen. He'd had more experience than most human beings with those all-wise, all-powerful artificial intelligences, and he knew that life was simpler if you did nothing to attract their attention.

'They haven't really forgotten us, of course,' said Kala. 'Our data divers believe there is a sort of stalemate. Half of the Guardians want Elon Prell to crush the Noon Consortium and shut the Khoorsandi gate, cutting humans off again forever from the Web of Worlds. The others are willing to let us keep dealing with the aliens, as long as we don't try to pry into the secrets of the Black Light Zone. It is a delicate balance. If you were to go running off after Nova into the depths of the Zone, that might upset things.'

Zen flung a pebble into the pool to startle the handkerchief-things and said, 'All right. Let me go the other way then. I still haven't seen my mum and sister.'

'On Summer's Lease?' Kala shook her head. 'That's Prell territory, and the Prells would love to pick you up. Interrogate you. Learn your secrets and use them against us. And if they found out that Latika and Myka are your mother and sister they could threaten them too.'

She talked about Zen's family as if she knew them, and in a way she did, for her intelligence people had been keeping an eye on them, ferrying secret messages between them and Zen. He had been able to tell Myka that he was all right, and hear that she and Ma were well, but that was all. He missed them almost as badly as he missed Nova.

'So I'm a prisoner here?'

Kala fiddled for a while with the Herastec brooch she wore on the shoulder of her black suit. 'How old are you, Zen?' she said at last. 'Eighteen? Nineteen?'

Zen shrugged. He wasn't sure. How could he be, growing up on so many different worlds, where years and days had different lengths? 'About nineteen standard,' he said.

'Nineteen. And look at you. You're wealthy! You have an air-car, the best clothes, a house of your own. We are letting you share in the riches of this new trade we are building! All we ask in return is that you stay here quietly on Galatava and enjoy your new-found fortune. We are planning to open negotiations with the Empire soon. In a year or two the situation may have settled down. Perhaps then we can reconsider.'

'A year or two?' Zen knew he sounded like an angry child, but that only made him angrier.

'I know how it feels,' said Kala gently. 'You miss the trains. I was a railhead just like you when I was young. But I made something of myself. I raised myself up. And do you know how I did it?'

'By sleeping with Threnody's uncle Nilesh?'

'By being patient, by doing what the Noons wanted, and being prepared to wait for the things *I* wanted.' She came off the bench and put a hand on his arm again, gently this time, almost motherly. 'Zen, I think you may be suffering from culture shock. There's a lot of it about since Khoorsandi gate was opened. A year ago nobody knew there were other civilizations in our galaxy; now trains from alien worlds arrive here daily. Human beings haven't evolved to cope with so much change so suddenly. And you, you were out there on those alien lines for how many months? Before any other human knew they even existed! Stranded, all alone, thinking you would never get back . . . It's no wonder you feel bad. It's natural.'

'I wasn't alone,' said Zen, 'I was with Nova.'

'A Motorik is no substitute for human company . . .'

Zen shrugged her hand away and left her there while he went angrily back out onto the terrace. Above the mountains a rosette of sunbeams poked out from behind high towers of evening cloud. Huge projections were drifting above the city, airborne ships and heraldic dragons. Galatava's rings stretched from horizon to horizon as a softly glowing pastel arch. The dancing was over. He could not see Threnody among the crowds.

He met some young Noon Consortium execs with whom he had gone clubbing last summer. Some of them had stayed overnight at Zen's house a few times and been sick on his furniture. They wore holographic party clothes: shifting wrappers of light which only just concealed their painted bodies. They had lips like rose petals and fashionable rainbow eyes. Zen went indoors with them and drank sweet blue smoke from tall glass flutes. It was a drug from the Deeka worlds and it didn't seem intoxicating until you had downed about five glasses and suddenly it was night somehow and everything was spinning.

The others treated Zen as a celebrity. They all wanted to hear about the adventures he'd had on the alien worlds. He told them how he'd fought the Kraitt; how he'd walked straight into the burrow of the Tzeld Gekh Karneiss herself to rescue Nova, and how the Neem had helped him out by shooting up the place and blowing it sky high as they made their getaway . . .

One of the girls said, 'This Nova, she was just a wire dolly wasn't she? Is it true she was your *girlfriend* out there? How does that even *work*, a human and a Moto?'

Zen tried to explain that Nova wasn't just a wire dolly and that she had understood him better than anyone ever had. After that, all their laughter seemed suddenly aimed at him, and he knew they would take to the gossip sites later to tell their friends, 'It's *true*, Zen Starling was in *love* with that machine!'

Zen suddenly hated them all. He wanted to tell them that that their own expensive beauty couldn't dim for a moment his memory of Nova's cheap, mass-market face. He wanted to tell them that it was he and Nova who had sabotaged the old Emperor's train and scattered the fashionably-dressed corpses of idiots like them all along the Spindlebridge. He tried, but they weren't listening to him, and the music was a throbbing migraine and the blue smoke drinks had made him sad, and he stood up too fast and knocked a table over and barged into a group of Deeka diplomats who burbled like waterbeds. A servant, very polite and very firm, came to ask if he needed help finding his way out, but he said he didn't, and sure enough, after only a few wrong turnings in the busy rooms, he went stumbling out into the cool, enormous night, trying to remember the code which would call his car to come and fetch him.

4

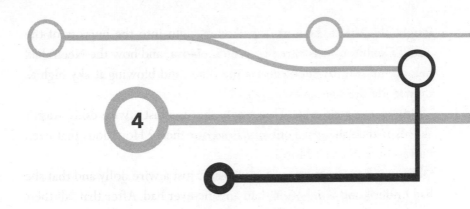

A hundred and twenty million kilometres away, an actual, honest-to-goodness spaceship was streaking towards the gas giant Vapna. It had pointy bits at the front end and a bank of glowing exhaust cones at the back, and in between it was covered in random fins and turrets and hatches, and hundreds of little lighted windows. It had been launched a few hours earlier from a base on one of Vapna's moons to investigate a strange burst of exotic particles, almost hidden in the electromagnetic blare of the gas giant.

The ship had no crew—which was lucky, since it was travelling at the sort of speeds which would turn anyone on board to purée. It existed only to carry a copy of the mind of the Guardian Mordaunt 90 Net. In a way, the ship *was* Mordaunt 90. A simple probe could have done the same job, but Mordaunt 90 was a fan of ancient sci-fi movies, and it thought a proper spaceship was more fun. He—Mordaunt 90 always thought of itself as 'he' these days—was very pleased with it. He enjoyed inhabiting that pointlessly streamlined hull as much as he enjoyed the beautiful bodies he had sometimes cloned for himself in the past. He launched a couple of little drones to take selfies as the ship began manoeuvring into an orbit around Vapna, because it just looked so *cool*.

The ship's searchlights swept the gloomy, elephant-grey surface of the largest boulder in the gas giant's outer ring. A croquet-hoop shadow swung across the dust. The weird new arch stood bony and alone. The searchlight tracked along shining rails which stretched out from it for five hundred metres and then ended abruptly.

'Oh *cobblers*,' said Mordaunt 90. It was not looking forward one bit to telling the other Guardians about this.

Millennia before, back when all the human beings in the galaxy were crammed together on one small planet called Old Earth, the Guardians had discovered the Web of Worlds, a railway system which tied the galaxy together. They had made contact with the data-entity called the Railmaker which was busy building it, and, fearing its power, they had killed it. Then they sealed their local sections of the Web off from all the rest, and let humans believe that they had created it themselves. They had kept the existence of the Railmaker a secret until Zen Starling and the Motorik Nova had stumbled upon one of the Railmaker's hub worlds. She had been affected there by some of the Railmaker's technology, and had begun to change. Change *how*, and into *what*, the Guardians were not quite sure. Some of them had wanted to study her, others had simply wanted her destroyed, but before they could do either she had fled into the Black Light Zone, the mysterious region at the Web's heart, a warren of wormholes through which they had not yet managed to track her.

For a while they had all been very afraid. What if the Railmaker was not quite as dead as they had all thought? What if Nova's meddling managed to revive it? But weeks went by, and then months, and nothing happened, and slowly they began to hope that nothing ever would happen. The Black Light Zone was an unknown region full of unknown dangers. The more optimistic of the Guardians believed that Nova had died out there beneath the black suns.

Now, suddenly, there was a new gate. But why here, on this lonely rock? And why had it opened and then simply closed again? Was the

Railmaker reviving, and testing its powers? Or had Nova learned its secrets and started trying to use those powers herself? What was the point of using all that energy to make a gate which only stayed open for seconds? Unless . . .

With a deepening sense of alarm, Mordaunt 90 trained his instruments upon the gate again and detected faint, fading traces of something which had come through it while it was open.

It was a fundamental rule of the Network that only trains could pass through K-gates—if you tried to drive a truck or a shoot a bullet through it would just bounce off the energy curtain. But the light-forms which humans called Station Angels broke that rule. They were spindly, shimmering knots of energy which appeared around the gates sometimes, like glowing burps seeping out of K-space. The Guardians suspected they were spam, sent out by automated systems somewhere on the Web of Worlds, semaphoring messages from the long-dead Railmaker which no one understood. But perhaps the Angel that had emerged at Vapna had been a new sort, with a different purpose. Mordaunt 90 imagined it drifting in its gossamer-cranefly way above the rails. Who had sent it? What message had it carried? And how had it planned to deliver it?

5

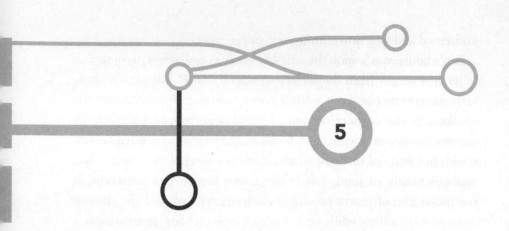

Threnody Noon left Galatava on the morning after the party, bound for the Hub to announce the end of the Kraitt War and the beginning of a dozen trade agreements with the empires of friendlier aliens. She travelled with her chief advisors and all the most important members of her family aboard the new Noon train, a line of state-cars and armoured troop carriages drawn by the old red loco *Damask Rose*. The sun was already high when she set out. Crowds gathered near the open stretches of the line to cheer her on her way and admire the procession of angels and aliens that had been painted along the *Damask Rose*'s flanks by the famous Motorik graffiti artist Flex.

The *Rose* sang as she went, thrilling the spectators on the bridges above the line with her deep, booming whale-song rumble and high grace notes, and broadcasting the same song into the Datasea so that every other train on Galatava could hear. It was a new song, but it held echoes of songs that she had sung when she was carrying Zen on journeys down the Dog Star Line or on the alien lines beyond the Hub. Her voice carried right across the city in the calm, clear air. It found its way to the fashionable district called the Heights and across the gardens of a bio-mansion as white and shiny as a healthy tooth. It drifted through an open window, into the room where Zen slept half undressed and face down on his enormous new bed.

Zen's house was a snob, like all old houses, and it had disapproved of its new owner from the start. For some hours it had been making sarcastic comments about what a lovely morning it was through the speakers in the corners of Zen's bedroom ceiling, and sending its automatic vacuum cleaners in to clean the carpet as noisily as they could, but none of that had woken Zen. The song of the *Damask Rose* was not nearly so loud, but it crept into his dreams somehow. It reminded him of journeys he had made with Nova, and the dreams were nice for a little while and then turned bad, because he was back on the Spindlebridge and the old Noon train was going to die and it was all his fault and he was shouting, trying to warn people, but they wouldn't listen, and his frantic, weightless running took him nowhere and the train died anyway, the broken carriages cartwheeling past him, flinging him out of sleep.

He opened one eye, winced at the sunlight shining through the blinds, and sat up with a groan. He had just worked out that the distant trainsong was real when it suddenly cut off. The *Rose* had gone into the K-gate. She was still singing, but her song would be echoing across the red rocks of Khoorsandi now.

'Breakfast, sir?' suggested the house.

Zen ignored it and flopped back down. The bed seemed to be slowly revolving, but he thought that was an after-effect of the blue smoke, not an actual feature. He had drunk far too much of that stuff last night. The taste in his mouth suggested that drinking any of it at all had probably been a bad idea. He shut his eyes, and after-images of his nightmare flashed past him. Every night now he dreamed about the Noon train. When he was awake he could persuade himself that the disaster hadn't been his fault. He had just been a hired thief doing what Raven ordered him to; he couldn't have guessed that Raven was ruthless enough to wreck a whole train to cover his getaway. But his subconscious had no time for that excuse. While he was in danger on the Web of Worlds it had almost let him forget what he had done, but now that he was safe and rich on Galatava the awful dreams kept coming.

The house jangled an alarm at him. 'There is a message for you, sir,' it said.

Zen told it what it could do with its message.

'That is impossible, sir. Also rude.'

'Ping it to my headset, then,' said Zen, who didn't believe there was a message at all.

'It says it is urgent.'

'Who's it from?' groaned Zen, dimly wondering what idiot would send a message to him via his house instead of his headset.

'I don't know,' said the house.

Zen groaned some more and rolled over onto his back. 'Let's see it, then.'

The message appeared on a holoscreen which the house positioned horizontally above the bed. It was a video image of Zen himself, asleep in a different bed. It mostly showed his face, but from the strange light which came and went across his features and across the pillow he knew at once which bed it was, and where. In case he wasn't sure, a voice said, 'Zen, do you remember Yaarm, the night the wind blew the curtain?'

He knew the voice, too. It was not the voice of the house. It was Nova.

The video cut out. In its place was a code: *KF-50.34.5817/3.48.1485*.

'Remember this,' the voice said. 'I'll be waiting.'

The number flashed three times, then vanished.

Zen sat up carefully. He was half afraid that he was dreaming, and he didn't want to wake himself, because it was a good dream.

'House,' he said, 'replay that message.'

'What message, sir?'

'You know.'

'There have been no messages today, sir.'

'You literally just played it. Look, the screen's still there!'

The holoscreen hung blank and bright above his bed like a skylight.

'There have been no messages today,' the house said again, and Zen could hear a slight confusion in its voice. He didn't think it was just messing him around. He didn't think he was dreaming, either; he was standing by the bed now, everything felt real and vivid—he could feel his heart thumping, the carpet under his bare feet. He thought of the flashing code in the message and Nova's voice saying, 'Remember this!' And he *could* remember it—he could not remember how he had got home last night, but he could remember that string of numbers: *KF 50.34.5817/3.48.1485*. As if something about the way that it had flashed had imprinted it on his memory.

Nova would know how to do that, he thought. Nova had sent that message. It had to be Nova. That voice had been her voice. That video—it had been her view of him, recorded by her eyes, on their first night together on the Web of Worlds. *Remember Yaarm*. Of course she had known that he would never forget Yaarm in the Jewelled Garden, more stars in one sky than he had ever seen, and the light of them falling on the lagoons, falling on their faces as the wind blew the curtain in the little bed-space above the *Damask Rose*'s state-car. Nobody else could know about that; that was why she had sent it to him, as proof that the message was from her.

'I have run a diagnostic check,' the house announced, 'and there does appear to be a short gap in my records. It is possible that a message which arrived during that period would not have been recorded to my memory circuits. I do apologize, sir.' It actually sounded as if it meant it.

Nova had hacked it somehow, Zen thought. She'd sent him a message that only he could hear. The Guardians must still be looking for her, and she was afraid of them, but she had risked everything to get that number to him. Some kind of code. *I'll be waiting*.

In a drawer beside his bed were a few cheap headsets he had picked up at shops in the city, still sealed in their plastic wrappers. It was a trick he had learned back in Cleave—always keep an anonymous set ready, in case you need to look for something in the data rafts and don't want anyone to know you're looking.

The headset felt clunky and uncomfortable after the sleek and stylish models he had grown used to, but it worked. The video terminal pressed against his temple and streamed a homescreen with the maker's logo straight into his brain. He opened a connection to the data raft under a fake name and blink-typed the mysterious number into a search engine.

It took him to a Noon Consortium site: a list of the new stations which its trains could now reach. For a moment he thought it was a mistake. Then he realized that each of the new worlds had an abbreviation. KF referred to a place called Klef, a little two-gate shortcut on a spur which linked some Herastec worlds to a minor hub called Yiianahii. The numbers led to a specific point on Klef's surface. There were no good maps of Klef—there were no satellites there to make them—but it didn't look as if there was anything at the co-ordinates Nova had sent him. It was in a stretch of rough country thirty kilometres north of the K-bahn line.

But that didn't mean anything, thought Zen. Nova would not be waiting for him where anyone could see her. She would wait in some desert place. On some world so undeveloped that it had no satellites, which probably meant it had no Datasea, which meant things that happened there would happen without the knowledge of the Guardians.

But I can't go all the way to Klef, he thought.

And then he thought, *Why not?*

Wasn't he a railhead?

Wasn't he a thief?

He had stolen the Pyxis from the Noon train. He had stolen Nova from the Kraitt. Surely he could steal *away*.

He started trying to think like a thief again. He would need to get off Galatava quickly and alone, before Noon Security realized he was leaving, and before any Guardians worked out that Nova had slipped a message to him through the Datasea.

He checked a train timetable, then smashed the headset and started moving quickly through the house, finding a small bag, stuffing it with spare shirts and underwear. As he hunted through his cluttered wardrobes he felt amazed at all the stuff he had acquired, and at how little he minded leaving it all behind.

The first doubts didn't hit him until his bag was packed and he was downstairs, drinking a glass of water in the enormous state-of-the-art kitchen where he had never prepared anything more elaborate than a glass of water. *This whole thing might all be a delusion*, he thought. After all, he had a head full of blue smoke, and he was the son of someone who thought her teeth picked up thought-rays from government agencies. What if Kala Tanaka was right and he was suffering a breakdown of some sort? What if the message from Nova had really just been his imagination building a narrative out of a faulty holoscreen and a glitch in the house memory? He couldn't prove that it wasn't.

He decided that he didn't care. He was leaving. Maybe he'd find Nova, maybe he'd lose himself on the Web of Worlds. Either way, it would be better than staying here. He felt half scared and half elated, balanced on the brink of something, afraid he lacked the nerve or luck to see it through.

'Will you be returning in time for dinner this evening, sir?' the house asked him as he headed for the door. It didn't sound apologetic any more. It was back to its usual faintly sarcastic self.

'Yes,' said Zen, because he suspected it reported on his comings and goings to Noon Security and everything now depended on them not guessing what he planned.

'I can hardly *wait*,' the house muttered, as it let him out.

A few minutes later, Zen's gaudy air-car fired its engines and took off from the landing bay behind the house, streaking south towards the pleasure beaches at Plaja Grande. And a few minutes after that, Zen himself scrambled over the wall at the western edge of his garden and dropped into the shady, deserted street beyond, escaping from his rich new life like someone breaking out of jail.

Steep streets and stairways took him downhill towards the K-bahn. On one of them he made a shortcut through a crowded restaurant and came out with his jacket chameleoned to a new colour, wearing someone else's hat, brim pulled low to hide his face from drones and cameras. A message from his car pinged into his headset: it was circling over Plaja Grande—should it land? He told it to request landing permission, touch down, and then take off again and head straight back to the city. If anyone was tracking him it would look as if the car had dropped him off at the coast. It would take them hours to work out that he wasn't on those busy beaches.

A crowd had gathered at the station. As Zen pushed his way towards the elevators which led down to the main platforms someone said, 'You don't want to hurry. The platforms are full of Hive Monks, all waiting for a train to the Neem worlds.'

'Disgusting creatures,' someone else agreed. 'Why can't they make special arrangements, take them out through the freight yards?'

Zen had been expecting this. For weeks the Galatavan data rafts had been full of grumblings about it. Elon Prell had expelled all Hive Monks from imperial territory, on the grounds that they were related to the Neem and aliens could not be trusted. Of course, his real aim was to cause the Noons trouble. The wretched Monks were happy to leave, but they wanted to reach the Neem Nestworlds, so they all began making their way to Galatava. The Neem sent a train through every couple of days to collect the latest batch of refugees, but backlogs kept building up. Zen had noticed the Hive Monks gathering at the station each day, and worked out a way that he could use them.

‘I don’t mind bugs,’ he said, stepping into the elevator. That wasn’t true, but he had overcome his fear of them before, and now he would have to do it again, for Nova’s sake.

The vaulted hallways which led to the mainline platforms were full of the acrid, beetley smell of Hive Monks. Motorik in grey paper overalls were sweeping up mounds of dead insects. As he went down the last escalator Zen could see the monks below him, standing ten deep on the wide platform. He pulled up the collar of his jacket and chameleoned it to match their dingy robes. He felt himself tensing with disgust as he pushed his way into the throng. The voices of the Monks whispered all around him; scratchy voices made by thousands of serrated insect legs rubbing against thousands of insect bodies, as if a field of grasshoppers had learned how to form words. ‘We are waiting for a train,’ they said. ‘It is not a human train. You should not be here, human. We are waiting for a Neem train to carry us to the Insect Lines.’

‘I know,’ said Zen. ‘I’ve been there. I want to come with you.’

The monks crowded closer. The stink of them made Zen’s head swim. He wanted to look up at the departure boards and see if the train was coming, but he dared not lift his head in case one of the station cameras caught an image of his human face among the blank paper faces of the Hive Monks. Hands made of twigs and chicken bones and old plastic forks plucked at his clothes.

‘You have been there? To the Insect Lines? To the worlds our people built? What is it like? Is it wonderful? Is it glorious?’

Zen thought back to his time on the Nestworld Zzr’zrrt, where oily rain fell always from a sky the colour of burnt toffee and the hot air thrummed with the buzzing of a billion bugs.

‘It’s glorious,’ he said, as the train-wind began to blow.

A few minutes later, as the train moved off, Zen had another message from his air-car. It was returning to the city. Where did he wish it to land? He opened its main menu in his headset, disabled its safety settings, and put it into a power-dive aimed straight at his house. Crammed in the hot dark with the jostling, whispering Monks, he watched the view from the car's on-board cameras as it plunged like a missile towards his bedroom windows.

He had never liked that house.

6

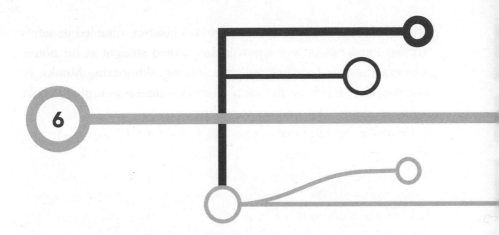

Under the two blue suns of the planet K'mbussi a man stood grumpily beside the main K-bahn line. Elon Prell, the new Network Emperor, was not renowned for his good humour. He was a hard, grey-haired, grim-faced man and the shiny medals and swags of gold braid on his purple uniform looked as out of place on him as tinsel on a crag. In the year since he had taken his seat on the Flatcar Throne, portraits of him had been printed on banknotes and the sides of skyscrapers all over the central worlds, and he wasn't smiling in any of them. At present he was glowering at the tunnel which led to the K-gate to Marapur as if it had personally insulted him.

Behind him, waiting on a fan of new sidings protected by giant mobile weapon platforms, were a hundred Prell and Railforce wartrains. At a word from the Emperor, or even a gesture, those trains were ready to charge through the K-gate and take Marapur by storm. It would not be easy, because the Noons would have defences on the Marapur side of the gate, but the wartrains were brave and powerful and well-armoured and in the end, Elon Prell knew, sheer force of numbers would bring them victory. Then his rail-armada would go storming onwards across world after Noon-controlled world, recapturing each in turn until the so-called Noon Consortium was destroyed, the gate to the Web of Worlds was barred, and his Empire was safe and whole again.

The trouble was, he dared not speak the order, or make the gesture. Not until he was sure that the Guardians approved of him launching all-out railwar. He had offered data-prayers to the Twins, who had always been friendly to his family, but the Twins had stopped speaking to him. He had ordered the imperial divers to keep watch in the Datasea for subtle signs that the Guardians still favoured him, but they had seen nothing. So all he could do was keep his trains in readiness here on K'mbussi, and wait for reports from Noon territory, which arrived each evening on the one train which was allowed to cross from Marapur each day. The images they brought—of the Noons, and that hapless lass they'd set up as their puppet-empress, and their alliance with a misbegotten swarm of aliens—made Elon Prell so angry that he sometimes thought it would be worth attacking even without the Guardians' approval, just to wipe the smile off the Noons' horsey faces. But he knew he did not have the nerve to actually do it, and that made him even angrier.

He turned away from the tunnel and went stomping back along the trackside. His staff stood looking bored beside the Prell wartrain *Macroaggression* which was waiting to take him back to Grand Central. He scanned the faces of his officers as he approached, and found that he was searching, as he often did, for his niece Laria. It was almost a year since he had expelled her from the family, but the pain was still fresh each time he thought of her, because she had been a promising young officer. Who would have thought a sensible Prell girl like her would betray her own flesh and blood like that? His new aide, Vasili, a distant cousin's boy, was keen enough, but he was not as bright as Laria had been.

'Uncle Elon—I mean, Emperor!' Vasili said now, hurrying through the trackside weeds to meet him. 'There was a message for us on this evening's train from Marapur. A message from the Noon family council. They want to open negotiations.'

Elon Prell felt briefly hopeful for a moment. 'They're surrendering, you mean? They've finally seen sense?'

'They do not say anything about surrendering. They propose sending a delegation to Grand Central to discuss relations between the Noon Consortium and the Empire . . .'

'There can be no relations between the Noon Consortium and the Empire,' growled Elon Prell. 'Unless they are like the relations between a fly and the hand that swats it. Or a bug and the boot that squashes it.'

'The imperial image consultants think that you should accept, Uncle Elon,' Vasili said nervously. 'It will make you look aggressive if the Noons propose peace talks and you turn them down.'

'*Look* aggressive?' Elon shouted. 'I *am* aggressive, lad.' He stood there fuming to himself while Vasili waited nervously for his rage to pass. At last he admitted, 'Well, maybe they're right; maybe they're right. We don't have to actually agree to anything. And I suppose we need to pass the time somehow while we wait for the Guardians to come to their senses and let us crush this rebellion. Don't expect *me* to talk to the Noons, though.'

He would let his new wife Priya handle the negotiations, he thought. She was a Noon herself; that was why he had married her, in the hope of keeping her family on side, and much good *that* had done him. He was secretly a little afraid of Priya's brittle good manners and expensive beauty, which always made him feel like a rough old man from the outer branch lines. (Because he *was* a rough old man from the outer branch lines. That was something he'd always been proud of before he'd married Priya.) 'Yes, it's about time the Empress started earning her keep,' he said. 'Me, I'm going hunting. I want to shoot things, Vasili, and if I can't shoot Noons I want to shoot large, expensive animals. What is there to shoot on Grand Central?'

'There are three different types of sauropod in the Imperial Dinosaur Park, Uncle Elon.'

'Lumbering great things; there's no skill in hunting them.'

'Cactus lions in a fenced preserve in the Amber Mountains . . . ?'

'Boring.'

'Well, I've heard that Azure Bay on the southern continent has a good stock of plesiosaurs. You hunt them underwater, with harpoons.'

'Hmmm,' grumbled the Emperor. That sounded more interesting, but it was still no substitute for the war he wanted. He turned for one last, wistful look at the tunnel, and at all his wartrains poised to enter it. 'Plesiosaurs, eh? Well, I suppose it will make a change. And at least I'll be cooler under water. Cool and weightless. Yes. Grand Central is too damned hot, Vasili.'

'Yes, Uncle Elon.'

'And the gravity is too damned strong.'

'Yes, Uncle Elon.'

Elon Prell had never met Zen Starling, and barely knew Zen Starling's name, but they had a lot in common. Like Zen, the Network Emperor had learned that it was possible to get almost everything you ever wanted and end up even unhappier than you were before.

7

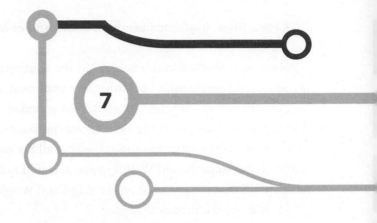

It was hot aboard the Neem train. There were no seats, just metal racks for Neem crab-suits to attach themselves to. Zen clung to one of those, and the Hive Monks jostled against him as the carriage swayed around curves in the track. There were no windows, so he did not see the colourless light of the first K-gate, and only the odd, familiar falling feeling let him know that he had left Galatava and the train was now hurtling across Khoorsandi. Somewhere ahead of him was the new gate which Nova had opened, leading to the Hub.

He felt relieved. He was not yet safe, and he had a nagging feeling that he should have waited for a second message from Nova before he fled, but it was good to be on a different world. He looked back over the months he had spent on Galatava and all he saw was an enormous waste of time. This was what he was made for. He belonged on a speeding train.

A door at the end of the carriage opened and the Hive Monks squeezed aside to let a pair of Neem come through. 'Welcome aboard the *morvah Kri'kittikri,*' they said as they moved through the packed carriage in their clanking spider-crab suits. They spoke in the common language of the Network Empire for their poor cousins who had never learned the beautiful insect-languages of the Nestworlds.

'We have been sent from the Nestworld R'zz'rrz'aa to bring you home to the nests of the Million Mothers.'

It was the first time many of the Monks had seen real Neem, and they hissed and simmered with joy, knowing that soon they would be able to abandon their old robes and scrapyard skeletons and move into splendid hydraulic bodies like these. A few reached out gingerly to touch the spines and bosses which decorated the Neems' shells.

The Neem came to where Zen stood, and noticed him for the first time.

'Human,' the foremost Neem said. 'Why have you boarded this train?'

'I need your help,' said Zen. 'Don't you know me, O Neem? Surely you have exchanged parts of yourselves with my friend Uncle Bugs? I am Zen Starling. I was the first human ambassador to the Web of Worlds.'

The Hive Monks, who had been listening to all this, began to quiver when they heard that name. 'Zen Starling!' he heard them saying to each other in their rustling grasshopper voices. 'It is Zen Starling of Cleave, who opened the way onto the Insect Lines! Zen Starling is here!' Their flimsy hands reached out to him again. 'Thank you, Zen Starling!'

The sensor turrets on the fronts of the Neems' encounter suits swivelled and clicked, bringing different lenses to bear on Zen's face. Inside each suit he imagined insects clustering around their instruments, studying his image like a spaceship crew in the threedies looking out at an alien planet.

'You are the individual called Zen Starling,' they admitted at last.

'I need to get to Klef,' he said. 'It is important.'

If it seemed strange to them that he would travel alone, in secret, they did not say so. A lot of things that humans did seemed strange to them. 'But we are bound for the Nestworld R'zz'rrz'aa,' they said. 'Klef is on a different line.'

'I'll get off at the Hub, then,' he said. 'I'll take another train from there. When do we get there?'

'We are already there,' said the Neem, and Zen felt the train beginning to slow. It had passed through the new gate while they'd been talking, and he was back among the vast alien rail yards of the Hub.

He barely recognized the old place. The Neem train opened one small door to let him off between the tracks on siding twenty, and he went up some steps onto the nearest platform and started walking, but it was all he could do not to just stand and stare.

The Hub was a massive dome, many kilometres wide, with an immense tower at its centre. Hundreds of lines and platforms radiated from the base of this tower, and others emerged from its upper levels on high, frail-looking viaducts.

The last time Zen had been there it had all been cold and deserted, ice crashing in gigantic splinters from the viaducts and the sky-high roof. Now it was the interchange which linked the stations of the Noon Consortium to those of all the alien races, and the Noons had done their best to make it look the part. Designers from the best theatres and threedie studios of Sundarban and Marapur had worked hard and cleverly to turn that dead alien dome into a place which promised hope and life. The cold light had been altered somehow so that it was more like sunshine and less like the light inside a fridge. The air was warm, and filled with trainsong. The coral circuitry which covered the immense central tower and the legs of the viaducts had been persuaded to glow prettily. There were trees here now: linear forests planted in the spaces between the tracks, spinneys clustering on the ledges of the tower. There were colonies of Hath, who had pitched themselves like summer tents along the edges of small ornamental lagoons, spreading their membranes to catch the breeze from passing trains. There were awnings of red and gold material as big as airfields hanging between the tower and the viaducts to make the huge space seem softer, warmer, kinder. There were holoscreens, just like those in the stations of the Network, showing the smiling sun of the Noon family and the comforting logos of familiar brands.

None of it quite worked, though. If you looked up past the holos, past the awnings, the dome was as strange and enormous as ever. Something more powerful than people had built it; more powerful than the Guardians themselves. No wonder they had tried so hard to stop humans finding it.

Zen tugged the peak of his stolen hat a little lower, and went towards the base of the tower with his head down and his hopes pinned on the fact that no one was looking for him.

Not yet.

8

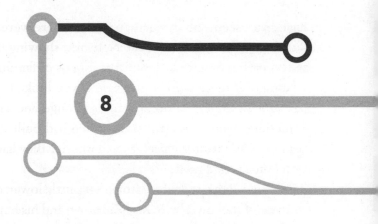

The platform led into a part of the tower's enormous ground floor which had been turned into a freight terminal. Zen made his way through a maze of stacked containers, then through partitioned areas piled high with smaller crates and pods until he came out in another section, where new bio-buildings had been grown between the pillars that supported the roof. The tower was no longer the place of ghosts and shadows that he remembered; it was more like a high class mall now, full of light, and shiny merchandise, and the smells of food. There were people everywhere.

Zen wondered if the tower minded. He thought it might have preferred the ghosts and the shadows. But when he bought a disposable headset at an automated stall and logged into the local data raft under another made-up name, he found that the tower was run by a normal Noon Consortium AI these days, just like any big public building back on Galatava. There was no longer any trace of the strange, damaged old memory banks which Nova had communed with. But he noticed that the ramp leading down into the tower's basement had been cordoned off. He guessed that must mean the weird Worm-machines which opened K-gates were still waiting, dormant, down there. On his last visit he had collected pockets full of the black spheres which controlled them, but since Nova vanished no one had been able to make them work. The Worms were too big to move, so it made sense that the Noons would simply seal the basement off and leave them there. He was glad that the old place had not lost all its mysteries.

He started to move around the inner edge of the tower, which had become one long, curving street now, shops and food stalls on his right, the thick wall of the tower on his left. Archways pierced the wall at regular intervals, each leading to one of the platforms outside. Above some of the archways hung holoscreens giving the details of the trains that would be leaving from those platforms. A service for Gmylm was pulling out in another half hour, but that was no good, because it was a Deeka train, and Deeka carriages were pressurised and filled with water. Zen walked on, past blank screens and screens advertising trains to nearby Nestworlds, trains back to Galatava, and a train to Priina Réae which left before he could reach its platform.

The Hub was getting crowded. People were pouring off some newly arrived train on their way to the big ceremony up on Level Two, talking and laughing and taking selfies. Zen recognized a couple of young Noon cousins with whom he'd once gone snow-boating in the Hana Shan and turned quickly to stare into a jeweller's window, hoping that they had not seen him. Photo flashes bounced off the glass in front of him, as sudden as gunshots and almost as dangerous. Those headset pictures everyone was taking would be uploading to social media in the data raft, where any prowling watchbot that the Noons set looking for him would be able to spot Zen in the background. For all he knew, the cops on Galatava had sifted through his car's remains by now and worked out he'd got off-planet. The train that had brought all these gawkers to the Hub might also have been carrying an alert about him.

Starting to panic, he turned from the window, pushed his way through the passing crowd, and went through the first archway he came to. The screen above it was blank. When he reached the platform he realized why. The trains which stood there, towering up on either side of him, were not waiting for passengers or freight. They were Noon wartrains: heavy assault locomotives, as big as trains could be and still squeeze through a K-gate, their black hulls barnacled with weapon turrets. One was called the *Listening Wind*, the other was the *Last Argument of Kings*.

He guessed that they were there to protect Threnody and her entourage. They certainly seemed edgy. Guns extended from their turrets with chunky sounds and swung to target Zen. 'Identify yourself!' boomed the *Listening Wind*.

At the same moment, a voice he knew came into his headset and said, 'Keep walking, Zen. It's all right, boys; he's with me.'

Zen went on along the platform. The guns tracked him as he passed. Spiky maintenance spiders kept pace with him, scuttling along the backs of the armoured trains. He kept walking, his heart beating loudly enough in his ears to drown out the music that had started to blare from the tower behind him.

Drawn up behind the *Last Argument* was the new Noon train, pulled by his old friend, the *Damask Rose*. She had been cleaned and refitted so that Zen hardly recognized her, but he knew the painted angels which cavorted along her red cowling and all down the sides of the elegant carriages she pulled. The pictures reminded him of the one good thing that he had done with his new money: hiring a machine psychologist to retrieve the scattered programme of his Motorik friend Flex from the *Rose*'s systems and download it into a new body. Within a few hours of being re-embodied, Flex was repairing and extending the pictures she had painted on the flanks of the old train. Seeing the finished paintings here in the Hub made Zen feel as if his good deed had been rewarded.

'You can come aboard, Zen Starling,' said the train, and opened a single door in her second carriage. 'Everyone has gone off to this shindig in the tower. They won't be back for an hour or two. I'm empty.'

Zen was almost as glad to hear her voice as he had been to hear Nova's a few hours before. He went through the open door and collapsed gratefully onto a seat.

'So, Zen Starling,' said the *Damask Rose* sternly, 'what *have* you done now?'

9

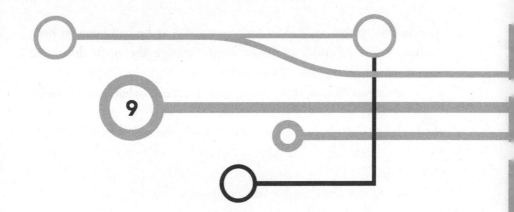

On Level Two of the Hub's central tower, a broad amphitheatre had been assembled beneath a canopy of billowing shimmercloth. In the centre of the stage, Threnody stood at a red and gold lectern to give her speech, while visitors from the Noon Consortium and the Web of Worlds watched from steep banks of seating all around.

'My friends,' Threnody said, reciting from memory the words which she had practised so many times with her image consultants and media advisors back on Galatava. 'We humans are so glad that we found our way at last to the Web of Worlds.' She spoke carefully, just as she had been coached to, leaving a pause between each sentence so that translation software in the lectern could turn her words into the squawks and bubblings and whinnies and hums and colours which conveyed her meaning to the aliens. Outside, and on the other levels of the tower, holoscreens would be relaying the speech to everyone who could not fit in the amphitheatre. When it was over, trains would carry recordings through the K-gates to other worlds. In the whole of history, no speaker had ever had a bigger audience than Threnody.

She said, 'We are so happy that we can meet you, and learn from all your rich and ancient cultures. We are so honoured that we were able to prove our good faith to you by defeating the warlike Kraitt, who have preyed on your trains and your stations for so long . . .'

(What she meant was, 'Watch your step, weirdos. The Kraitt have been a menace to you for ten centuries, but our Corporate Marines sorted them out in ten months. So don't any of you freaks go thinking you can mess with humans . . .')

'Of course, we could not have done it without our allies from the Nestworlds,' she went on. 'Our friends the Neem have been so brave, so determined, and have adapted so quickly to using human technology . . .'

(What she meant was, 'Be nice to us and you too can have faster trains, better guns, high-speed communications . . .')

'Without their help, and the help and support of all the other peoples of the Web, this war might have lasted far longer,' she said. 'But we have all worked together, and now it is done. It is over. It ends here, today.'

The lighting dimmed, until only Threnody's lectern and a patch of the stage just in front of it was illuminated. The guards who stood behind Threnody shifted their big guns. More guards appeared, marching towards the pool of light, leading a figure so weighted down with chains and shackles that it looked like a ghost from an old story. It was a ghost, in some ways. The Tzeld Gekh Karneiss, most feared of all the Kraitt leaders, had been reported dead so many times during the war that people had started to believe she was a legend. But here she was, a prisoner, captured on Far Garzhalak by Corporate Marines from the Noon wartrain *Hammer Time*.

A gasp, a mutter, a bubbling, a growl ran around the amphitheatre. Herastec whinnied, Hath flapped, and the Ones Who Remember the Sea waved their tentacles and flickered with the deep reds and oranges that signified alarm. The darkened rows of seats flared with headset flashes and the chemical flash-bulbs that the Deeka and the Chmoii used to expose their primitive photographs.

The Tzeld Gekh Karneiss came slowly to the centre of the floor while the guards fanned out around her in a wide ring. The audience was silent now. The Tzeld Gekh stood in the middle of the ring and looked at Threnody.

'There is an ancient custom—' said Threnody loudly.

'*Not yet!*' warned Kala Tanaka's voice in her headset. Kala was watching everything from behind the scenes somewhere, weighing the effect that Threnody's speech was having on the audience. It was not really Threnody's speech, of course, it was Kala's; the words were all hers, and her sudden interruption reminded Threnody of that and made her fall silent, blushing a little, angry at herself for her mistake. '*Make them wait for it,*' Kala instructed. '*Remember what we said in rehearsal? Silence is powerful. Wait. Hold onto the moment. Let the tension build.*'

The Tzeld Gekh Karneiss was no longer quite as terrifying a figure as she had been when Threnody first met her. She had been badly wounded many times. Her lizard face had been pitted by shrapnel and seared by fire. She had lost one of her yellow eyes, the leathery frill around her leathery neck was tattered, and her tail was a scarred stump. Stripped of her robes and her metal jewellery, she stood in front of Threnody naked, although her scaled and knobbly old lizard hide looked pretty much like armour. The biggest change of all, thought Threnody, was that her pride was gone. It was dangerous to read human emotions into the expressions of creatures who weren't human, but the Kraitt were more human-like than most of the beings on the Web, and all that showed in the one remaining eye of the Tzeld Gekh Karneiss was weariness. She was old, and defeated, and humiliated, and she wanted it to be over.

'*Now…*' said Kala.

'There is an ancient custom among the Kraitt,' said Threnody. 'It is found on all the worlds which they have infested. If two Kraitt clans go to war with each other, it ends only when the leader of the losing clan is killed.'

Behind her stood one of those useful young women whom Kala Tanaka had been training up to be as polite and efficient as herself.

She came forward now and handed Threnody the knife. It was a Kraitt knife, made from the claw of some horrible giant reptile from some horrible Kraitt world. It was a knife with a history, because a girl named Chandni Hansa had used it once to save Threnody's life by stabbing to death an interface of the Twins. Before that, it had been the Tzeld Gekh Karneiss's knife, and Threnody thought that the Tzeld Gekh recognized it. There was a flicker of life in that dull yellow eye as the blade caught the light like a shard of black glass. The Tzeld Gekh went down slowly into what would have been a kneeling position if her knees had bent the right way. She tipped back her terrible dinosaur head to expose the softer leather of her throat. Threnody gripped the knife tightly and wondered if she had enough strength to slice through even that softest part of a Kraitt's tough hide. She felt glad that she would not have to.

'Humans have an ancient custom, too,' she said. 'And it is this. When a war is finished, we seek peace, not vengeance. Once our enemies are defeated, we seek to be their friends, not their executioners . . .'

(It was a rather selective reading of human history, this bit, but the aliens weren't to know that.)

'And so, I ask you all, all our friends from the many worlds which the Railmaker has linked together, to witness that our war with the Tzeld Gekh Karneiss and her people is *ended*.'

She dropped the knife. It clattered on the floor. The Tzeld Gekh Karneiss looked down at it, puzzled. Mercy was a luxury of which the Kraitt had never really seen the point.

'It is ended,' said Threnody. 'And it ends not in blood, but in peace, and, we hope, in friendship. The Tzeld Gekh Karneiss will come to live on one of our own human homeworlds, and if her people promise to lay down their weapons, they will be free to trade with us like all the other peoples of the Web.'

She stood there while Kala's voice in her headset said, '*Good. Now, one, two, three, and turn.*' Then she turned her back on the defeated

Gekh and walked away while the great space filled with cheers and hoots and tentacle-slapping noises and the buzz of Neem hives and all the other sounds which intelligent beings used to signify applause.

On Threnody's deserted train, Zen sat in a chair as soft as cartoon clouds and said, 'Those wartrains got a good look at me . . .'

'Oh, don't worry about them,' said the *Damask Rose*. 'I've told them you're someone else, and they're dim enough to believe me. And nobody can overhear us —between ourselves, that little Moto friend of yours upgraded my firewalls so well before she left that even Guardians can't get through them if I don't want them to. So we have some time to work out what to do with you.'

'I need to get to Klef,' said Zen.

'Psscchhhhh,' said the train, which was all it had said when he'd told it the story about Nova's message. 'Do you really believe your little Moto will be waiting for you there? It seems pretty unlikely.'

'Do you think I imagined her message?'

'I didn't say that,' said the train.

'It is possible,' admitted Zen. 'But I think it was real. And the only way I'll ever find out is if I go to Klef myself.'

'You do know Klef is a warzone?'

'The war's over,' said Zen. 'Isn't that what all that cheering was about upstairs?'

'It's *mostly* over,' agreed the *Damask Rose*. 'It suits the Noons to *say* it's over. It's bad for business when a war drags on and on. But some of the Kraitt are still holding out on a few backwater worlds. Still, I suppose the little Moto wouldn't have asked you to go there if it wasn't safe.'

He knew then that the train would help him. The *Rose* always referred to Nova as 'the little Moto' or 'our little Motorik friend', but she was very fond of her. And trains loved lovers; it came from seeing all those tearful partings and joyful reunions at stations, he supposed. She knew that he loved Nova and Nova loved him, and she would do whatever she could to bring them together again.

'Could you take me there?' he asked.

'Me?' snorted the *Rose*. 'As if! In case you haven't noticed, Zen Starling, I'm pulling the Noon train now.'

'I'd noticed,' Zen said, grinning. 'You're stuck in a trainshed on Sundarban half the time, only coming out to ferry Noon officials up and down the Silver River Line. You must want to scream with boredom! I bet you'd rather be riding the wild rails again, way out on the Web of Worlds, seeing all those new stations . . .'

'Psssccchhhhh,' said the train. 'I'm not ready to just run off and abandon my responsibilities. Not like some people I know.'

'But . . .'

'There is a supply train leaving for Klef shortly. You're lucky, it was meant to leave an hour ago but there was some delay, and it's been held on a siding over in the outer yards. The loco is an old friend of mine, the *Storm Warning*. I've just spoken to it. It's agreed to take you as far as Klef.'

'But how do I get to the outer yards without being picked up?' asked Zen. The sea of tracks and sidings which surrounded the tower stretched for kilometres, and he was guessing that the *Storm Warning*'s siding would be quite a way across it. 'The Noons are going to start looking for me soon.'

'Well then,' said the train, 'we'll have to make sure that you aren't *you* any more when you leave, won't we? Luckily I have some very fancy facilities on board. I'll print you some new clothes and a clean headset, and there's a body shop in carriage seven. We haven't time to give you an actual facelift, but I think we can make enough cosmetic changes to get you to the *Storm Warning* without being recognized. Who would you like to be?'

Zen thought about that as he walked back down the train, through all the gilded, silent state-cars. The Hub must be full of media people:

newshounds and gossip jockeys from the big sites of every Noon world. He imagined himself as a young journalist with one of the smaller sites, come to record his own impressions of the victory celebrations. Someone who, if anyone asked him what he was doing wandering into the outer yards, might say he was just looking for a different angle on the big story. He would be from a better background than Zen's, but he wouldn't have Zen's designer clothes, or the fancy headsets and gadgets Zen had grown used to. He would talk differently, walk differently, think differently. He fitted together the first name of someone he knew on Galatava and the last name of a kid he'd known in Cleave and came up with a new name: Ty Sharma. By the time the door of the body shop slid open in front of him and he walked through it and settled himself in a white chair in front of a mirrored wall, he was starting to get an idea of what Ty Sharma would look like.

'You're a good friend, *Damask Rose*,' he said, as the beauty drones woke up and went to work on him.

'I'm a fool to myself is what I am,' grumbled the train.

10

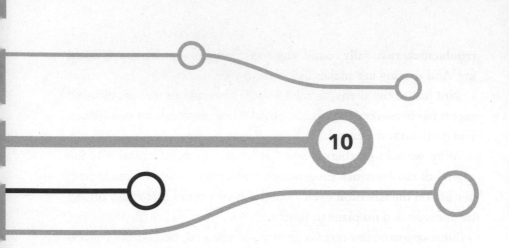

'I thought that went rather well,' said Uncle Nilesh, a few hours later.

They were in one of the quiet rooms high in the tower which had been set aside as Threnody's official suite. The rooms had been decorated just as Threnody had asked: all white, and very simple. She had guessed that after being surrounded by so much noise and colour and strangeness it would feel good to step into a space that was free of those things, and she had been right.

'I'm still not sure we were wise to spare the Tzeld Gekh,' she said. There was a table with a selection of refreshments in the room where she and Uncle Nilesh were sitting, and she picked up a purple alien fruit whose name she had forgotten and wondered if you were meant to peel it. 'I mean,' she said, 'I'm glad *I* didn't have to kill her, but if she could just have been got rid of quietly somewhere . . .'

'Then thousands of Kraitt would have sworn undying vengeance against us,' said Kala Tanaka, who was standing nearby, watching news reports of Threnody's speech on a sheaf of holoscreens. 'It's much better this way, Threnody. The Gekh is no danger to us any more. She will be kept in a comfortable, well-guarded compound on Sundarban, far from the K-bahn, out of sight and out of mind.'

'Kala is very good at this sort of thing,' said Nilesh. 'She thinks that a dead Tzeld Gekh would have become a martyr for young Kraitt troublemakers to rally round. But a shamed, imprisoned one is nothing. And sparing her makes *us* look stronger.'

'Not just to the aliens,' agreed Kala. 'The response on human social media has been very favourable. That will strengthen your hand when you go to Grand Central.'

'Why would I go there?' asked Threnody. Grand Central was the capital of the Network Empire. She had barely escaped from it with her life on the day Elon Prell's wartrains arrived to throw her off the throne. She had no plans to return.

But it appeared her relatives had made plans for her. Nilesh rubbed his hands together thoughtfully and said, 'Once our trade agreements with the new worlds are secure, it will be time to start negotiations with the Prells. We can't go on like this, knowing the Empire's rail-fleet is poised on the far side of Marapur waiting for the order to attack us. We must come to some agreement with them.'

'But they'll never let us stay independent and keep the new gate open, will they?' asked Threnody. She had seen the broadcasts from the central worlds. Elon Prell was always bellowing about how the gate on Khoorsandi must be blockaded to protect humanity from alien plagues and invaders. He bellowed a lot about Threnody, too. 'The Rebel Empress' he called her, as if Threnody had stolen his throne, not the other way round. 'How can we negotiate with a man like Elon Prell? We would have to offer him something, and we aren't giving anything away to that . . . that . . .'

'We will have to negotiate sooner or later,' said Kala Tanaka. 'It will be that or fight, and the Prells have far more troops and wartrains than we do. That is why we are arranging for a small diplomatic mission to travel to Grand Central. And you will go with it.'

'Me?'

'We'll be sending one of our most capable negotiators with you, of course, but it is important that a senior member of the family goes too.'

'Why not Uncle Nilesh? I bet he's a lot better at official visits than I am.'

'Kala and I need to stay on Galatava, and make sure that none of your other aunties or uncles tries to elbow us off the family council,' said Uncle Nilesh. 'And besides, Threnody, you're younger than me, you're more popular than me, you're prettier than me, and the Emperor's wife is your own sister!'

He had changed, thought Threnody. He had always been the laziest and most unambitious of her relatives, quite content to while away his days as Stationmaster of Khoorsandi, but the opening of the new gate had suddenly put him within reach of power, and now he seemed intent on gathering as much of it as he could for himself and Kala. Threnody missed the old, sleepy Uncle Nilesh. But then she missed lots of things.

'Priya is only my half-sister,' she said. 'It's different.'

She left them there and climbed the winding stairway of architectural bone which led to her private rooms. Her Motorik were waiting to brush her hair and run her bath, but she dismissed them and went through to her bedroom, savouring the silence and all the delicious shades of white. She felt angry and unsettled. It was only to be expected, she told herself, as she kicked off her golden shoes and flopped down on the bed. Coming face to face with the Tzeld Gekh Karneiss again was bound to be upsetting.

But something else about the ceremony had upset her more. Standing there in the spotlights, repeating Kala Tanaka's words as if they were her own, she had felt like a puppet, and it had made her remember that a puppet was all she had ever been. She had only been born to secure a trade agreement between the Noons and her mother's family. During her brief spell as Empress she had been Lyssa Delius's puppet, and now she was Nilesh and Kala's. One ambitious leader after another had pulled her strings and made her dance to distract people and stop them noticing who was really running things.

The only time she had ever felt that she was making her own decisions had been during those few desperate weeks when she and Chandni Hansa and Zen Starling were marooned on the Web of Worlds. She had been too frightened at the time to enjoy it, but she had done things there, achieved things. She had changed the universe . . .

She thought for a while about Zen and Chandni. She vaguely remembered glimpsing Zen at the party the day before, but Chandni lived on Galatava's southern continent now, as far from the K-bahn as she could get. She had a job as a house-gardener, tending to the expensive bio-buildings which grew like enchanted pumpkins along the Chalcedony Coast. She lived all alone, apparently, with just a cat for company. Threnody wondered about summoning her back to join her household, because she felt that having Chandni around might give her the nerve to stand up to Kala and Nilesh. But she quickly squashed the idea. Chandni had saved her life, and surely that earned her the right to live her own life at last. She would be happier this time, free of entanglements with criminals or empresses.

Threnody lay down on her bed and let her headset start briefing her about tomorrow's meeting with the Deeka trade delegation. If she had to be a puppet, she thought, she might as well be a good one.

At that moment, someone calling himself Ty Sharma was making his way along the access road which led across the Hub's enormous rail yard to the siding where the supply train *Storm Warning* was making ready to leave. He was the same height and weight as Zen Starling, and if you looked closely you could see that he *was* Zen Starling, but his clothes looked more Sundarbani than Galatavan, his hair was styled differently and blond instead of purple, his skin was a paler brown, and his headset was registered to a Sundarbani news-and-gossip site called *Hear/Say*.

The *Storm Warning*, scanning the ID he pinged to it, was not completely convinced. It was an old loco, brought out of a Noon train store to help the war effort, and it liked to think that not much got past it. But it had known the *Damask Rose* for a long time, and if the *Rose* said this Ty Sharma character needed to get to Klef with no questions asked then the *Warning* was going to get him there, and ask no questions. It suspected he was part of some deep-cover black ops scheme, and it was quietly proud that it had been entrusted with such an important passenger.

'There are some seats in the rear carriage,' was all it said when Zen came close. It was mostly towing container cars and tankers, but the rear half of its rear carriage had a few rows of seats. They were not very comfortable seats, but they were no worse than those on some of the commuter trains that Zen had ridden when he was railheading it up and down the eastern branch lines. It was almost reassuring to settle himself on that scratchy, unyielding upholstery with its pattern of Noon suns.

There was a long wait while the *Storm Warning* checked its engines and hummed to itself. Zen felt as nervous as he used to in the old days, fleeing Tusk or Ambersai with a pocket full of stolen bangles. There was that same nagging worry that his luck would not hold, that security would stop the train and come to drag him off. He fidgeted impatiently and wondered when the train would leave, then he peeked out of the window and saw that it had set off without him noticing, and the strange railscape of the outer yards was sliding past at increasing speed. And then he was through the K-gate, the train was barrelling across one of the dark, dead worlds on the margins of the Black Light Zone, and he could lean back in his seat and relax, knowing that he was on his way.

[illegible] it liked to think that not much [illegible] for a long time, and it [illegible] to [illegible] get into these, and ask [illegible] [illegible] had been entrusted with such [illegible]

[illegible] was all it said when [illegible] meats and spices, but the [illegible] of coins. They were not [illegible] no worse than this woman's [illegible] when he was mulled [illegible] It was almost not enough [illegible] with its [illegible]

[illegible] checked its engines [illegible] as he used to in the [illegible] pocket full of stolen bangles [illegible] the luck would not hold [illegible] [illegible] the train would leave, then [illegible] had sold without [illegible] was sliding [illegible] through the Rogue, the train [illegible] would be the chances of [illegible] back [illegible]

PART TWO

SHADOW BABIES

11

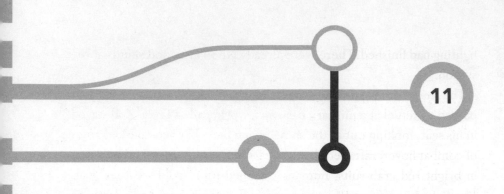

He was a face behind glass again, looking out at all the passing worlds. He felt calm for the first time in months. It was this that he had missed, this sense of being carried, of sitting still while everything kept changing on the other side of the window. The *Storm Warning* sang songs it had learned from the *Damask Rose*. It raced through black tunnels and frozen stations under shuttered suns. Then prairies, Nestworlds, the bustling starlit interchange on Night's Edge, and on again across planets Zen had never seen but felt as if he had because the speed and the sound and the feel of travelling were so familiar. Alien trains went past, the *morvah* singing their own weird songs. The colourless light of the gates flashed bright as X-rays, breaking up the journey like the gaps between stanzas in a poem. Zen held his hand against the glass each time, and thought he saw the shadows of his bones.

The first warzone he passed through was on a world called Big Ugly—a straight translation of its Kraitt name, said the train. It reminded Zen of the Shards of Kharne where he had rescued Nova, in pieces, from the Kraitt. The same hot climate and greyish scrub, the skylines prickly with cacti and the ventilation towers of underground Kraitt towns. He guessed the Kraitt just liked their worlds that way. Drones prowled the copper-coloured sky and the burnt-out skeletons of Kraitt wartrains were strewn beside the track, but the fighting had finished. There were already Noon fast-food stands at the station.

The *Storm Warning* did not stop there, but after three more K-gates it paused to refuel at a military base on a world called Tzelt. Zen stayed in his seat, looking out at the snow which blew between parked rows of combat hovercraft. People hurried about out there: warrior Neem in bright red crab-suits, humans wrapped up in cold-weather gear. Just before the *Storm Warning* moved off, a door into Zen's carriage opened and four of the humans came inside, laughing and cursing at the cold, stacking their packs in the luggage bay, stowing weapons and helmets on the rack above their seats.

They were Noon Corporate Marines, which made Zen nervous at first, till he remembered that there was no way they could have heard about Zen Starling's escape. The only way a message or anything else could get from one world to another was aboard a train, and no train from Galatava could have got here ahead of him. 'I'm Ty Sharma,' he said, as the soldiers sat down on the far side of the aisle. He started getting into character. 'I'm a journalist, from Satay Province on Sundarban.' (None of the newcomers looked Sundarbani, so that seemed safe.) 'I'm recording my impressions of the Web of Worlds. Can I get you some coffee? Chocolate? Chai? There's a machine two carriages down—it's not good but it's OK . . .' Ty Sharma spoke better than Zen Starling, he had decided, but he *tried* to speak worse; a rich kid aiming for the kind of cool that only poor kids have.

The troopers took their hoods down and unzipped their snowy coats, looking at him like they'd already got the measure of him. There were four of them. None of them spoke, but Zen fetched the hot drinks anyway, and as they thawed out they found their manners and introduced themselves. This was Shafiq; that was Katzebo; the thin kid with the tattooed tear was Misbah. The one who did the talking was the leader, Subedar Yana Vashti, a young woman from some massive planet on the Spiral Line where she'd won her first fight by growing two metres tall despite the heavy gravity. She had a wide, dark face and hair like a black mushroom cloud. Her nose had been broken long ago and she had never got it fixed, and her ears stuck out sideways like small handles. But then her whole squad looked like goblins compared to the beautiful people Zen had grown used to on Galatava. He liked them at once. He'd known people like these when he was younger: kids from farmworlds and crap industrials who'd gone off to join the CoMa. Low heroes like Zen had scoffed at them, but now he thought they'd had more sense than him.

Claiming to be working for the newsfeeds turned out to be a good way to get the troopers talking. 'I got an auntie on Sundarban,' said Shafiq. 'You think she'll see your stuff?' Zen promised to send her aunt a link, and felt strange and a little sad to remember that he wasn't really Ty Sharma and Shafiq's auntie would never see her niece on *Hear/Say*.

Worlds went by: mountains of red moss; a methane sea. They passed through another CoMa base, but it was being dismantled, tanks rolling into container wagons to be trained back to the Hub. 'War's not over, though,' said Vashti.

'The Noons think it is,' said Zen. 'I was just covering their big surrender ceremony in the Hub.'

'The Kraitt can't win,' said Katzebo, 'but some of them just can't admit they've lost.'

'Lucky for us,' said Misbah. 'We joined the CoMa for the danger money. That's why we volunteered to go up the line to Klef instead of catching a train home.'

'There's still fighting on Klef?' asked Zen. 'That's where I'm headed.'

They laughed at him. Was there fighting on Klef? Was there *fighting* on *Klef*? All the baddest Kraitt on the whole wide Web had holed up there to make their last stand. They were raiding trains, and eating posh-boy journalists for dinner. That was why Vashti's team had to go there and sort them out!

Reading between the lines, Zen worked out that actually there wasn't much happening on Klef at all; just a few Kraitt warbands lurking in the uplands, sneaking out sometimes to shoot up passing trains. But he didn't mind the troopers teasing him. He kept them talking about the Kraitt and the Web and the things they'd seen in the war, and by the time the *Storm Warning* arrived on Klef and took the spur that led into the CoMa base there, he had become a sort of mascot.

'You stick with us, Ty Sharma,' grinned Vashti as they gathered their equipment. 'We'll keep you safe. You'll get all the best stories if you stick with us.'

It wasn't snowing on Klef, but it had been raining and looked like it was thinking about raining some more. A fierce wind herded litter along the platform. Behind the station was a CoMa camp. Behind the camp a plain of blue-grey mud stretched all the way to the horizon, where hills rose into a strange band of shadow. Lifter-loaders drove up to take charge of the *Storm Warning*'s freight containers. The grit from their wheels blew into Zen's face and stung like buckshot. 'We got to print you a helmet and a cold-weather suit, Ty Sharma,' yelled Vashti, over the howl of the wind.

'It blows like this the whole time,' shouted Katzebo, the scholar of the group. 'Klef don't spin like a proper planet. One side is always pointed at its sun, the other's always dark. The sun heats up the air on the daylight side so it rises and goes storming over to the nightside as a high-level wind, and a low-level wind blows back to the dayside to replace it. The fun never stops.'

Misbah laughed, leaning backwards against the wind.

Shafiq said, 'I heard how in Herastec talk "Klef" is just a kind of disgusted snorting noise.'

A disgusted snorting noise was what the garrison commander

made a few minutes later when he emerged from a carriage hitched to the big wartrain on the neighbouring siding to meet the new arrivals. He'd been expecting forty troopers, not just four. 'Have you got a permit, Ty Sharma?' he demanded, when they told him who Zen was. 'A letter of introduction from the Chief Executive's auntie, maybe? Because otherwise you're going home. I don't hold with railheads nosing round my warzone.'

He was a brown man with fierce white whiskers, and his name was Colonel V. P. Mitri. Zen had seen him before, at Galatavan garden parties, but he seemed more at home here with his red uniform stripped of its gold braid and stuccoed with the windblown dirt of Klef. For one worrying moment it seemed as if he might recognize Zen. He said, 'You look like somebody else.'

'It's a big Network, sir,' said Zen. 'Everybody looks like somebody else.'

'That's true, Ty Sharma, that's true . . .' The whiskers looked less fierce when he smiled. 'Well, we can put you up for the night, but you'll go back tomorrow with the *Storm Warning*. We still have Kraitt fighters up in those hills; it's no place for sightseers. Have you had any experience in combat zones?'

Zen hesitated. It would take time to make his way to the grid reference that Nova had sent him, especially now that he saw what conditions were like. He needed to charm the colonel into letting him stay longer and lending him some sort of vehicle. The easiest way to do that was to claim he was an old hand at small wars, but that might lead to awkward questions about which wars, and where. He would have to tread carefully.

But just as he was working out what to say, a new voice cut into his headset, and into the headsets of Colonel Mitri and Vashti's squad too. '*Has he got any experience in combat zones?*' it asked, as if it couldn't believe that anyone would ask Ty Sharma such a thing. 'Colonel, this is *Ty Sharma*! He was on Gmylm when we lit up that Kraitt convoy!

He went in with the 42nd at the battle of Kzik'k Junction! It's good to see you again, Ty!'

'You know my new wartrain?' asked the colonel, looking at Zen with a bit more respect.

Zen did. He hadn't recognized it until now, covered as it was with new armour and state-of-the-art weapons systems, but he would have known that gruff voice anywhere. '*Ghost Wolf*!' he yelled.

'That's me!' The *Ghost Wolf* opened a private channel to Zen's headset and added, '*Storm Warning* told me the *Rose* had sent you, so I guessed who you were straight away. But I'd have known you anyway, even with your hair that funny colour.' On the open channel it said, 'Welcome to Klef, Ty Sharma! Come to see the last of the fun, have you? It was me who started this war. Now it's going to be me who ends it.'

'We're lucky to have the *Ghost Wolf*,' said the colonel. 'It was transferred yesterday from Yaragganagg. It's very proactive.'

'Oh, it's proactive all right,' said Zen. The *Ghost Wolf* was a C12 Zodiac and like most of its class, it had a fearsome love of battle. When he last saw it, it had been charging off to save some Neem Nestworlds from the Tzeld Gekh Karneiss. The victories it had won there had made it a hero to the Neem and the other aliens, and inspired the Noons to send more wartrains to join the fight against the Kraitt.

'The train I replaced here was the *Katana*,' said the *Ghost Wolf*. 'Don't get me wrong, it's a good loco, but it didn't have the armour or the drone support to really get stuck into the skinks. It took more what we call a "defensive posture", running up and down the line between here and the far K-gate, protecting all the civilian trains that come this way. The Kraitt kept out of its way, but they still attacked when they could. Me, I'm going to put a stop to all that. You see these new gun turrets? Two hundred rounds a second. And I've got wardrones coming out of my—well, out of all these new hatches along my cowling.'

‘The *Wolf* is what we call a self-sustaining tactical node,’ the colonel said, leading Zen and the others past the train and through the doors of an ugly bio-barracks. His sternness had gone and he seemed as keen as Vashti and her squad to get himself mentioned in Ty Sharma’s story. ‘It can operate a full suite of surveillance drones and unmanned assault aircraft, and remote control our AFVs too.’

‘AFVs?’ asked Zen, in a message he pinged to Vashti’s headset.

‘Armoured Fighting Vehicles,’ she pinged back, and looked at him as if she couldn’t believe that anybody wouldn’t know that.

The bio-building’s thick skin kept out the roar of the wind. In its place was a hum of generators, a clatter of cutlery and voices from some unseen canteen. Soldiers strode through the corridors, saluting as they passed the colonel, glancing without much interest at the new arrivals. ‘We’re preparing for an operation,’ the colonel explained. ‘Tomorrow we’re sending ground troops up into the Hills of Evening.’

‘The Hills of Evening, sir?’ said Vashti.

‘It’s a pretty name, but not a pretty place. Broken country, on the border between here and the nightside. There’s a region up there we call the Reptile Enclosure where a few hundred Kraitt are hiding out. They’ve got no trains left and no heavy weapons; it’s just half a dozen females and their warbands, strictly nuisance value. The plan is to send in a wave of AFVs—try to lure them out of their burrows into the open where we can beat them. The AFVs don’t need crews, of course, but I’ll be sending teams with them anyway. We don’t want the *Ghost Wolf* thinking it can fight our wars without us.’

They laughed dutifully, but Zen suspected the *Wolf* already thought that.

‘You can relax,’ the colonel said. ‘Get settled in, load the local databases to your headsets—there’s no Datasea on this rock, so communications can be patchy. There’s no day or night either, but we still operate on standard Network time. At zero-six-hundred tomorrow you'll be patrolling with the *Ghost Wolf*. I'll let it decide whether you can bring your pet journalist along.'

'It's a piece of luck, you being here,' Zen said later, on his private channel to the *Wolf*. He was lying on an uncomfortable little bunk in an uncomfortable little room, listening to the endless wind throw handfuls of grit against the window. It was late, but the pale grey light outside looked no different than it had when he'd arrived. On the wall beside the bunk a previous occupant of the room had stuck up snapshots of a pretty Sundarbani girl, and Zen wondered whether they had ever got home to her and, if they had, why they'd left her pictures behind.

'Lucky for me too,' said the wartrain. 'I was with a diplomatic mission up on Yaragganagg till yesterday. It was dead boring. Then this message pinged in, transferring me to Klef. Between ourselves, I'm not sure it came from Noon CoMa Command like it claimed—they seemed a bit startled when I took off. But I wasn't going to pass up the chance for one last crack at the Kraitt.'

'So who was it from, this message?'

'Dunno. I haven't got a copy of it. There was a kind of glitch in my records.'

Nova, thought Zen. It sounded just like the mysterious message she had sent to his house. Nova had called the *Ghost Wolf* here in case he needed help. Knowing that she was looking out for him made him feel a little safer, a little warmer.

'You seen the *Rose*?' the *Ghost Wolf* asked, trying to sound casual.

'Yesterday,' said Zen. Or had it been the day before, or the day before that? Time did strange things when you rode the interstellar rails. 'She said to send her love if I saw you.'

'Really? *Really?*' The *Ghost Wolf* almost giggled. If trains could blush, thought Zen, it would be blushing. 'That's a classy loco. So what are you doing out here, Zen?'

'I've come to find Nova,' he said.

'Well, she ain't here. I don't think there's any Motorik on this planet at all. Colonel Mitri doesn't like 'em.'

'She sent me co-ordinates,' said Zen. He pinged them to the train.

'Up in the hill country, eh? Hang on, I'll send a drone over . . .' There was a pause. Music came dimly through the floor of Zen's room from a bar downstairs. Then the voice of the train said, 'No, it's just empty country up there, Zen. Nothing but rocks and Shadow Babies.'

'What are Shadow Babies?'

'That's the CoMa name for them. They're one of the local life forms. Sort of beach ball things that lie about in heaps all along the shadow-line between the nightside and the day.'

'Can you take me there? To the co-ordinates?'

'Zen, there's nothing there . . .'

'Nova said I was to go there. It's probably a rendezvous. She'll meet me there.'

The train sounded doubtful. 'Well,' it said, stretching the word out low and long until it became just a sound, 'We-e-e-e-e-ellll, I suppose I could tweak the grid for tomorrow's mission. Your co-ordinates are right on the western edge of the Reptile Enclosure, not too far outside the sector we'll be patrolling in anyway. I'll get an AFV up there.'

'Can I go alone?' asked Zen.

'Hardly. It would look pretty strange, wouldn't it? You can go with Vashti's crew; they'll keep you safe. They're starting early though. Best get some sleep.'

'I don't think I can sleep,' said Zen. His body clock, already confused by travelling halfway across the galaxy, seemed to have broken entirely in Klef's unchanging daylight, so he just lay there, listening to the wind, thinking about Nova, riding out his own unease.

12

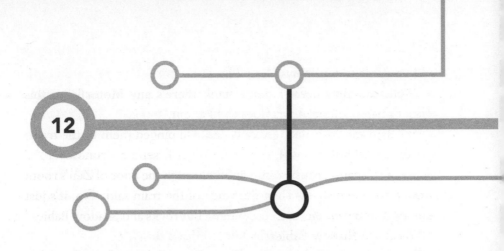

He must have slept after all, because suddenly the *Ghost Wolf*'s voice was booming out of a speaker by his bunk. 'Wakey, wakey! It's your lucky day!' An hour later he was sitting with Vashti's squad aboard an armoured fighting vehicle lashed to one of the *Wolf*'s flatcars while the wastes of Klef rushed greyly past the windows. And half an hour after that they were rolling off the flatcar down ramps the *Wolf* lowered for them, one of a squadron of twelve AFVs that separated into pairs as they moved away from the wartrain. The AFVs looked like armoured bugs with turrets front and back and six big wheels. Ahead of them, the Hills of Evening stretched off into the planet's nightside in band after jagged band of deepening shadow.

North of the K-bahn line the ground climbed steeply towards the first rocky outcroppings of the hills. It was bleak, but not as lifeless as Zen had expected. Through the armoured glass of the AFV's ports he saw clumps of sparse grassy stuff, and once a spiny creature scurrying out of the path of the AFV's wheels. As they crested the rise he spotted his first cluster of Shadow Babies crowded together in a cleft of the crags, like flies' eggs in a wound. They were bigger than he had expected: leathery grape-shaped things a metre high.

He looked back. Down on the plains the daylight gleamed on the K-bahn rails, running ruler-straight across the world. The *Ghost Wolf* was stationary on a passing loop beside the main line. From there it was controlling the AFVs, its shrewd old mind peering out through their cameras and gunsights, watching for trouble. 'Ups-a-daisy,' it said through the cabin speakers each time Zen's vehicle lurched awkwardly over a rock fall.

'Don't see why we have to let the wartrain drive,' said Shafiq. 'Stands to reason a train's used to running on rails. It don't know nothing about *steering*.'

'Yeah,' agreed Katzebo. 'Why not let Shafiq drive?'

They had printed a helmet and a cold-weather suit for Zen, but it didn't make him feel like a soldier. He tried to make himself small, keeping himself out of the others' way as they checked weapons and equipment. They grumbled as they worked. They had grumbled about the early start, and the breakfast, and the hard seats in the *Wolf*'s troop carriage, and Zen was starting to understand that grumbling was what soldiers did to pass the time. Now they were complaining that the *Ghost Wolf* was sending them to the wrong bit of Klef. 'Why aren't we forty klicks east with Subadar Jena's unit?' Misbah complained. 'Tactical database says there's been no skink activity in this sector at all.'

'Jena's lot are going to get all the battle-bonus,' agreed Shafiq. 'We won't see any action at all out here.'

'Orders are orders,' said the *Ghost Wolf*.

The AFV crunched and crushed and slithered its way across a series of steep scree-slopes. It was easy to see why the Kraitt had chosen this region to make their last stand. The rocky hills were honeycombed with caves and canyons, the crags weathered into weird shapes like alien totems. Bowls of damp ground shone dimly, littered with mounds of Shadow Babies.

'I wonder how they defend themselves against predators?' said Katzebo. He was interested in things like that. He planned on signing up as a student on the new xenobiology course at Marapur University if he could make enough money from this war. 'All that meat just lying around like a free buffet. There must be other critters who want to eat them.'

'Maybe they don't taste so good,' said Misbah.

'Maybe they smell like Misbah,' said Shafiq.

'Why do they call them Shadow Babies?' asked Zen, who was feeling guilty at making the *Ghost Wolf* bring the others here, and wondering if Nova was going to show herself, and how he would explain it to them if she did.

'Come and listen,' said Vashti.

There was a short ladder at the back of the cabin. Zen followed her up it, through a hatch which led into the AFV's rear turret, a cage-like structure where a 50mm cannon was mounted. Zen's helmet dropped a visor in front of his face to protect against the airborne dust. The wind was fierce and cold up there. At first all he could hear was the moaning it made as it blew through the shattered crags. Then the AFV passed close to a cluster of Shadow Babies and he heard their thin, grizzling calls, like hungry babies waiting to be fed.

'Nobody knows if they're plants or animals,' said Vashti.

'Maybe they're both,' said Zen. In the failing light the Babies looked now like patches of leathery gooseberries, now like colonies of headless seals.

'So where are we going?' asked Vashti.

'Why ask me? The *Wolf* is driving.'

She gave him a look. It reminded him of looks his sister Myka used to give him when she knew he'd lied to her. 'You might fool the colonel,' she said, 'but you don't fool me. I was at the battle of Kzik'k Junction and I didn't see you there. You didn't even know what an AFV is. I don't think you're who you say you are. So where are we going? Is it some secret mission?'

There were two ways to play this, Zen thought. Bluff it out and stick to the lie he'd told her, or tell her a new lie: say he was from

Noon Intelligence, sent to investigate something in the hills. The trouble was, he liked Vashti. He didn't want to lie to her at all.

'You don't have to tell me then,' she said, seeing his hesitation. 'You can tell me about it somewhere nicer when all this is over. I'll buy you a drink. If you like.'

She had turned away, as if she was too shy to look at him. Zen wished he had met her when he lived on Galatava; her, or someone like her—someone practical and funny and nothing like Nova.

He said, 'I'd like that—'

But Vashti put her hand up to stop him speaking. She hadn't turned away out of shyness; she was listening to an urgent, buzzing voice in her headset. A half-second later a sudden gorgeous blaze of light erupted from a nearby hillside: white fading into orange and then red.

Vashti cursed at the same moment as the boom of the explosion broke over them. The shadows danced; the Shadow Babies cried. Drones veered screaming across the sky, met streams of fire pouring upwards from some distant crag, and died in blinding shears of light and firework thunderclaps. The second AFV, two hundred metres away, shrugged and came apart in a belch of flame, its turrets trailing flurries of sparks as they tumbled down the hillside into the swamp. Vashti pushed Zen down and crouched beside him. She was reaching for the handle that would open the hatch, when the next blast tore the turret off its mountings and Zen out of the turret.

Somersaulting through the smoke, he found the time to feel betrayed. The *Ghost Wolf* had said there *were* no Kraitt out here! The colonel had said they had no heavy weapons!

The next thing he knew, a Shadow Baby was breaking his fall like a hairy airbed. He bounced off it and landed on another, then another, slithering his way down between their bulbous bodies to the ground. He got up, fell over, got up again. The Shadow Babies wailed indignantly, pulling their fleshy roots out of the ground and slug-sliding away from him. A few of the larger ones revealed spikes: bony switchblades which slid out of their bulbous bodies in random places, dripping slime. Zen kept his distance from them and checked he still had all his limbs. His cold-weather suit was ripped in a few places, but there was no sign of blood and the holes were already starting to seal themselves. He turned round twice, looking everywhere for the AFV and slowly realizing that the scattering of bonfires spread across the hillside were all that was left of it.

He stumbled towards the largest fire. Among the flames, a wheel and a twisted chunk of the cabin were charring. 'Vashti?' he shouted. 'Shafiq? Misbah? Katzebo?' Flat echoes came back at him off the crags. He tried his headset, but it was dead. All he could do was stand there shouting. 'Shafiq? Katzebo?'

'They're gone,' said Vashti, appearing beside him. 'And you need to keep quiet.'

'Why?'

'Because the Kraitt who just hit us will be coming to look for loot and survivors.' She had lost her helmet, and her uniform was scorched and torn. Blood from a graze on her forehead was trickling down her face. When she raised her hand to wipe it away Zen saw a ragged hole in the back of her glove.

'Are you all right?'

'Shadow Baby stung me,' she said, starting to lead him away from the wreck. 'They have these spike things; sting you like a wasp.'

'I saw.'

'They didn't get you?'

'No. I was lucky. I didn't know they could sting.'

'I don't think anybody did. I made a discovery.'

'So that's how they keep predators away . . .'

They both thought of Katzebo, who would not be enrolling on his xenobiology course after all. Then they both wondered if Shadow Baby stings were poisonous.

'Does it hurt much?' Zen asked.

Vashti just grunted, and he knew that it did, and that she didn't want to talk about it. She took the gun off her belt and unsealed its cover and checked it and put it back. 'Your headset working?' she asked.

'No.'

'Mine neither. I think we're just in a blackspot. If we can get to the top of that next hill the headsets should pick up a signal from the *Ghost Wolf*. The *Wolf* probably thinks we're all dead and it's sent its remaining drones to support the other units. Once we let it know we're here it'll send a flyer to pick us up.'

The hill was a ragged razorback, dimly visible against the stars. The top was probably further off than it looked, and the going would be steep and rough. Zen looked back up the slope they'd just descended. Nothing was moving up there except the flames which still flickered around the destroyed AFV.

'It's my fault,' he said.

'How's that?'

'I brought you here. I got the *Wolf* to bring us here. And now three more people are dead.' He felt suddenly and bitterly ashamed. Wherever he went, whatever he did, things ended up exploding. People died, and the people doing the dying were never him. 'It's my fault,' he said again, and he wasn't sure if he was talking about the AFV burning on the hillside or the Noon train cartwheeling down Spindlebridge. 'It's all my fault.'

'That's crap,' Vashti said. 'The skinks are the ones who killed Shafiq and Katzebo and Misbah. They'd have hit us wherever we were. That message I got just before it happened? It sounded like all the other units were coming under attack too. Listen.'

Across the hills, faintly through the scouring wind, Zen heard the pop of small guns and the woodpecker hammering of bigger ones.

'It's because the *Ghost Wolf* is here,' she said. 'They hate that train. It's been wrecking their *morvah* on the Web of Worlds since before most human beings even knew the Web existed. I bet when it arrived here all the skinks that have been hiding out on Klef saw a chance for death or glory. Congratulations, Ty Sharma. You've got yourself caught up in the last real fight of this war.'

'It's Zen,' Zen said.

'What is?'

'My real name,' he said. 'I'm Zen Starling.'

It didn't seem to mean much to her. She just looked at him, and started walking again.

13

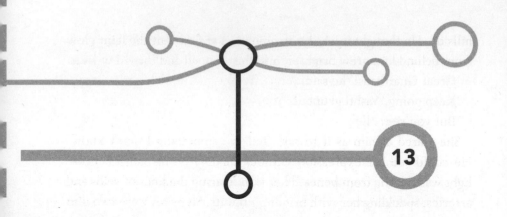

By the time they were halfway up the hill, Zen was sure that the Shadow Baby sting was having bad effects on Vashti. She lagged behind him, swaying as she walked, and a faint, eerie glow came from the hole in her glove. Her face shone with sweat. Not that he could sec her face unless he turned on the lamp on his helmet, and when he did, she said, 'Kill the light, the skinks'll see it.'

'Do you really think they're hunting us?'

'I think they will be, if you keep switching that light on.'

They were deep in the night zone now, finding their way up the broken slope by the faint light of the day they had left behind. Once, Zen's headset found a signal and reset itself, but the signal faded again before he could contact the *Ghost Wolf*. Vashti tried too. She picked up the chatter from other units who were busy fighting the Kraitt, but she could not make them hear her. Behind them, in the shadows where they had first rested, a rock rolled clattering down a slope. A few minutes later, a long, hooting call came down the wind: the cry of a hunting Kraitt.

'It's all right, I think,' said Vashti. 'It doesn't sound like they've picked up our trail yet.'

Zen stumbled on, tired out and frightened, but knowing it must be worse for her. Ahead, his shadow showed dimly on the broken hillside. He thought it was his imagination at first, but the faint glow from behind him grew brighter, until he stopped and turned to look.

'Great Guardians!' he said.

'Keep going,' Vashti grunted.

'But you're . . . !'

She glared at him as if to say, 'Tell me something I don't know.' He could see her expression without turning on his lamp because light was shining from beneath her skin, tracing the lines of veins and arteries, speckling her with bright pinpoints. Her eyes were two dim torches, growing slowly brighter as he watched.

'What's happening to you?'

'It's the sting,' she said. 'I guess this is like what Katzebo was saying—why the Shadow Babies don't just get eaten. The last thing you want if you're a critter who hunts on the nightside is to glow in the dark. That's why anything with any sense steers clear of the Shadow Babies. They know if they try it on, the Babies will squirt them full of this luminous crap.'

'Does it hurt?' asked Zen. He was wondering what could fill someone with light like that, and what the side effects would be. But Vashti shook her head. 'Not so bad now.' She was still feverish, though, still swaying where she stood. Zen was about to suggest she stopped there while he went on in search of a signal, but just then a howl came from behind them, and then another, and another. The Kraitt had found their trail.

They blundered on up the slope. They couldn't hope the dark would hide them now because Vashti's shining face was growing brighter, washing the rocks ahead of them with light. On hands and knees, Zen groped among the rocks for mud to smear across her cheeks, but the mud was thin and the light shone through it.

'You should go on without me,' she said after a while, slumping down in a clump of night-grass.

Zen stood over her, wondering how many Kraitt were closing in on them.

'Everything's spinning,' she said. 'This stuff is probably going to kill me anyway. Go.'

Zen was frightened by how much he wanted to obey her. What difference would it make to have one more death on his conscience? He could leave her there and run and hide and maybe the Kraitt would think she'd been alone... He looked round desperately for shelter. Above him the hilltop was crowned by a long spine of rock, and suddenly he saw its outline very clearly, thrown into silhouette by a flare of light which came from beyond it. The lights of a vehicle, he thought, or perhaps the spotlights of a searching drone.

'Did you see that?'

Vashti hadn't. She had her shining eyelids shut. She was slipping into dreams. Zen scrambled to where she lay and shook her by her shoulders. 'There was a light up there, Vashti. Someone's looking for us...'

The light kept on flaring as he helped her to stand. It flickered on the sky beyond the ridge as he half-dragged her over tumbled stones. It didn't look like searchlights any more. It looked like arc-welding, or maybe gunfire, but he could not hear any guns. Did Klef have an aurora?

Behind him, quite close and unmistakeable, a reptile voice barked harsh commands. He imagined Kraitt running quickly uphill on their back-to-front legs, the whips of their tails held out stiff behind for balance. Pushing Vashti through a gap between the rocks, he scrambled through after her and looked towards the source of the light.

They were at the edge of a kind of plateau. Its flattish summit stretched away from him for half a kilometre or so, covered with clumps of night-grass and a few sharp outcroppings of stone. He could see these details by the glow of the shimmering light which hung there, like a bright curtain suspended inside a bony arch.

'It's a K-gate!'

'You're hallucinating, railhead,' said Vashti.

'You're the one who's hallucinating. That's a K-gate!'

'Never heard of no gate out here,' she said, lifting her head and staring at it.

'It wasn't here before,' said Zen. He was almost laughing. He started to walk towards the gate, stumbling as Vashti leaned all her weight against him. 'It's new! New made! That light I've been seeing was the Worm at work!'

Vashti shook her head. She'd seen videos of the Worm that had made the new gate on Khoorsandi. It had been all over the feeds for a week or two. 'Where's the Worm now then?' she said.

Rails ran out of the K-gate, rippling with reflected light. They stretched for about five hundred metres, then stopped.

'It went back through,' said Zen.

He left Vashti there and walked a little closer. He could hear the gate now—a faint, high, tearing noise, fiercer than the wind. He wasn't sure how close it was safe to go. 'Nova?' he shouted. He tried finding his position by his headset but there was still no signal. He already knew what the co-ordinates would be, though: *KF-50.34.5817/3.48.1485*. Nova's rendezvous.

So her message had been real. But where was she? Why had she brought him here? What use was a K-gate that wasn't part of the Network? He couldn't just walk through it. Only trains could pass through K-gates.

When the noises started behind him he didn't recognize them as Kraitt battle cries at first. They sounded like metal grating on metal. They sounded like sharp rocks falling and echoing down a gully. He turned, and the Kraitt were all along the top of the ridge, terrible lizard shapes which became more terrible as they drew nearer and the light from the K-gate began to gleam on blades and claws and teeth.

He back ran to where Vashti lay. She seemed to be unconscious, her calm face glowing like a lamp. Zen pulled the gun off her belt and pointed it at the leading Kraitt, a massive female swinging a blade so big that it looked as if it had come off the front of a small bulldozer. When he pulled the trigger nothing happened at all.

'It's in safe mode,' said Vashti, lying in the grass. She pulled off her glove and raised her hand. There was a tracery of golden light all over her palm and along each finger. He pushed the gun into her grip and she pressed her thumb against a pad on its side, which Zen hadn't even noticed, and then shoved it back at him. He took it and lifted it and squeezed the trigger again, and this time sizzling bolts of light poured out of it. Most of the bolts went past the Kraitt but a few went through them. They fell with smoke unravelling from the holes he had blasted in their armour. The last one left started shouting something that sounded almost like words, but Zen kept pointing the gun at it until light sliced through its chest and it staggered backwards and fell over and lay still.

Then there were just the rustlings of the night-grass and the faint noise of the K-gate and Zen's heart thudding hard. 'Train coming,' Vashti said suddenly. He thought she was delirious, but then he heard it too. The twanging, thrumming, thrilling sound that the rails made before a train arrived.

He turned in time to see it break the energy curtain and pour itself through the K-gate, wheels screeching as it braked hard and slid along the track. A long, low, lightless silver loco. Its hull had been mirror-bright last time he saw it; now it was iridescent, scorched by journeys through hundreds of K-gates. He still knew it though. It was the *Sunbird*, the reformed Railbomb which had carried Nova away from him that day in the Hub. Some extra instrument hatches had been fitted on its nose. A camera popped out of one of them and swung to stare at him.

'Zen Starling?' Its big voice came booming out of speakers rather than bothering to find his headset frequency. A door on its upperworks popped open and Zen waited for Nova to emerge, but she didn't.

'Well, come *on*,' said the train. 'She's waiting for you.'

Zen got hold of Yana Vashti under the armpits and started dragging her slack weight across the rocks and grass towards the rails.

'No, no, no,' said the *Sunbird*. 'I'm just meant to fetch you, Zen Starling. I don't have room for two.'

'She needs help,' Zen grunted, still pulling Vashti with him.

'She'll be fine,' said the *Sunbird*.

'How do you know? You're a bomb, not a doctor.'

'I'm a *former* bomb, and my systems tell me there are Noon CoMa drones and medevac flyers closing in on this position,' said the train.

'Good old *Ghost Wolf*!' Zen said. He turned to look at the sky behind him, but there was no sign of drones or flyers yet. What if more Kraitt were on their way, drawn by the sound of the shooting and the light from the new gate?

'I've got to stay till the flyers come,' he said.

'Absolutely not!' the train snapped. 'Nova will be very unhappy if I'm spotted here.'

But Nova would be more unhappy, Zen thought, if he turned out to be the sort of person who left injured friends behind. He crouched there in the wind, gripping Vashti's hand, telling her she was going to be OK, until at last there were five points of light on the sky that were not stars.

'*Ghost Wolf!*' Zen shouted.

'Zen!' The wartrain's voice crackled in his headset. 'Sorry about that—I've been busy with the skinks. It all kicked off for a bit; they had all kinds of artillery we never knew about. You all right? When my link to your AFV dropped out I thought the worst. What the flip's going on out there, anyway? Hang about—is that a K-gate? Is that a Railbomb?'

'A *former* Railbomb,' said the *Sunbird*, crossly.

'Just come and get Vashti,' Zen told it. 'She got stung; she's sick . . .'

Three drones peeled off and went to do things in the hills that made white flashes jump up the sky. The other two kept coming: one a wardrone, circling high; the other a bug-like flyer which settled nearby in a cloud of dust and dead grass. A pair of spidery medical robots, slaved to the *Ghost Wolf*'s mind, unfolded themselves from a hatch and came scuttling to where Zen waited. Vashti had gone very quiet by then and he felt a twisting feeling inside him, sure that she had died. But when the spiders shone their lights at her eyes she groaned and frowned, as if she resented being woken.

'Don't worry about her,' the *Ghost Wolf* told Zen, as its spiders slid a collapsible stretcher under Vashti and lifted her. 'I got state of the art medical facilities, me. We'll sort her out.'

The *Sunbird* was revving its engines and starting to sing, making all the impatient noises and little backwards-and-forwards restless movements of a train that wanted to be on its way. '*Do* come on!' it said. Zen ran towards it, flung himself at the ladder which led up to a hatchway in its roof, and tumbled inside. The hatch slammed shut above him. It had been right about there not being room for two; there was barely room for Zen in the little cubbyhole behind its engines. Acceleration slammed him hard against an instrument panel as the *Sunbird* suddenly shot backwards at full speed through the K-gate.

On the world it left behind, drones kept circling the new gate as the medevac flyer lifted into the sky. The *Ghost Wolf* didn't think of itself as a clever train—it wasn't one of your intellectual locos that wrote poetry and such—but it was sharp enough to know that a new K-gate was big news, even one that wasn't attached to the rest of the K-bahn. Its wardrones were recording all the information they could about it, and it was starting to print specialist drones which could study it in more detail.

But before it could launch them, something surprising happened. The shimmering curtain of light, through which Zen Starling and the

Sunbird had vanished only seconds before, suddenly blinked out. The bony arch was left standing empty on the plateau, like the goalpost for some bleak and primitive ball game.

'Flippin' Ada . . .' said the *Ghost Wolf*.

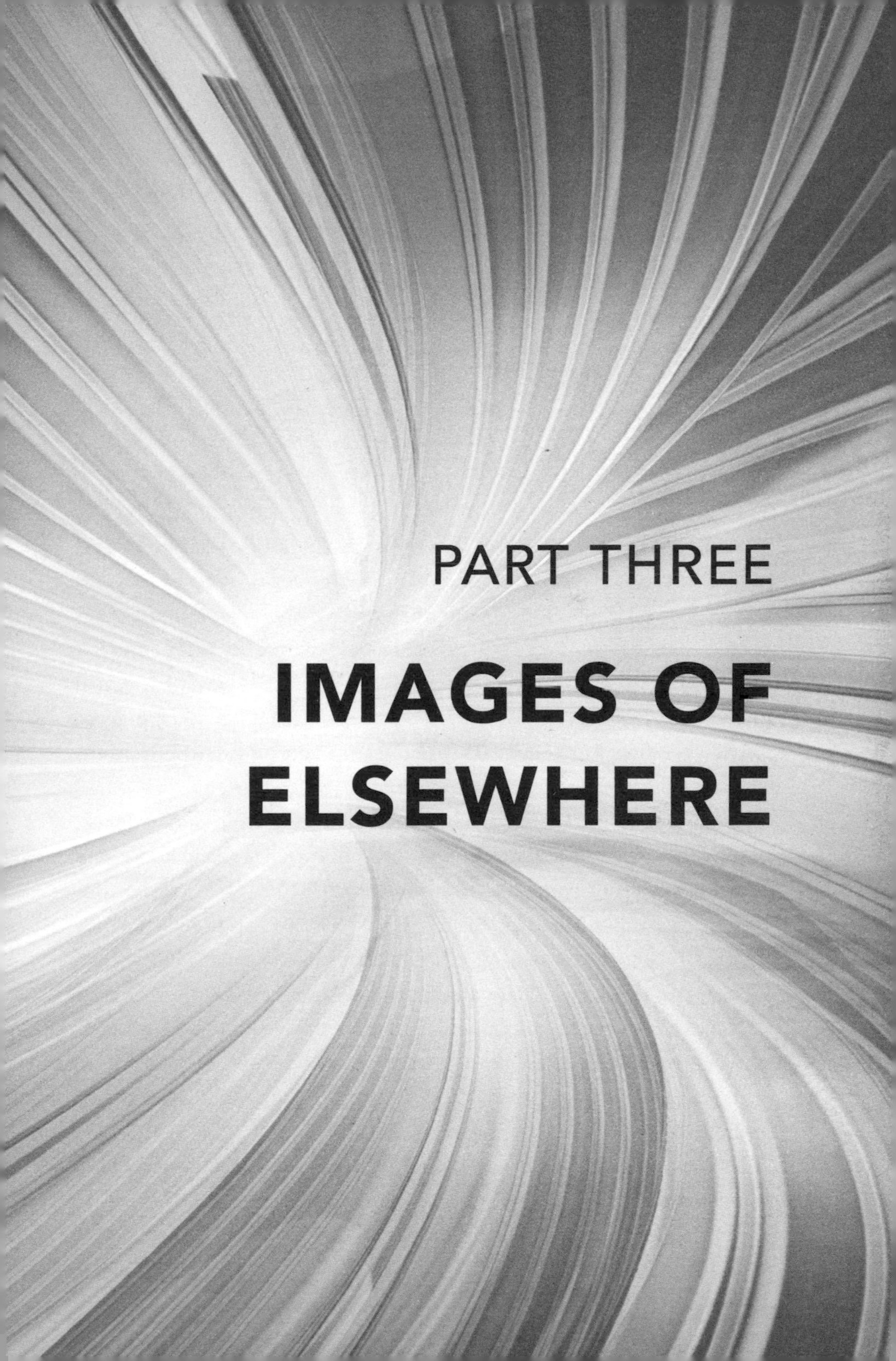

PART THREE

IMAGES OF ELSEWHERE

14

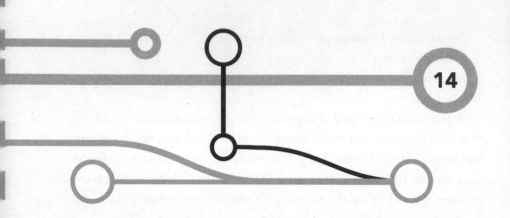

Volcano season was over on Khoorsandi. As the fire-moon's orbit took it further from its mother planet, the vents and geysers had settled back to sleep, and new blankets of moss and small trees were greening the lava fields. But in one deep and secret pocket of Khoorsandi's Datasea, the Guardian called the Shiguri Monad had created its own volcano: a 3D representation of a magma chamber, filled with the glow of bubbling lava and drifting clouds of toxic gas.

Just above the surface of the lava hung a hollow cube of clear glass. Inside it, twelve glass chairs were arranged in a circle. The Guardians were gathering in conclave, and the Shiguri Monad had chosen this as their meeting place. Its peacock avatar perched on the back of the largest chair, opening and closing the many-eyed fan of its tail and looking out at the lava. The others arrived one by one, their avatars flicking into existence as they logged into the virtual environment. Sfax Systema, who looked like a beautiful woman and a beautiful cat at the same time; Mordaunt 90, in the golden human form he always seemed to wear these days; antlered Anais Six.

'Why are we in a volcano?' asked Mordaunt 90, looking down at the spluttering red-hot stew between his virtual feet.

'Why shouldn't we be in a volcano?' said Shiguri.

'It just seems a strange place for a meeting.'

'I like volcanoes.'

'So? Sfax Systema likes cats, but she doesn't invite us to meetings inside a cat.'

Mordaunt 90 regretted saying that as soon as it was out; he could see that Sfax Systema was considering the idea. But it seemed to stump the Shiguri Monad, who changed the subject. 'Why must you always be a human these days, Mordaunt 90? Ever since that one interface of yours got cut off on the new worlds you've been wearing the same body every time I see you. Why can't you be a centaur again?'

'The centaur was fun,' agreed Anais Six. 'This is just boring.'

'All biological forms are boring,' said Leiki, appearing as a constantly shifting polyhedron of burnished metal. 'We can be anything we want in the Datasea.'

'Well, I want to be human.'

'That is what we're all afraid of, Mordaunt 90…'

The glass council chamber was filling fast now as everybody else arrived, including three slender, ancient, somehow faceless forms which were the avatars of the Vostok Brains. They had been the first fully sentient Artificial Intelligences, and long, long ago they had designed all the other Guardians. The others were never quite sure if the Vostok Brains were their equals or their parents, but nobody wanted to have a row in front of them. Shiguri spread his tail as wide as it would go and called the gathering to order.

'I presume we have all viewed the images from Klef?'

They all had. The *Ghost Wolf*'s drone footage of the new gate was being shared among the Noon family only at the highest levels, protected by all the encryption that their intelligence service could manage, but there was no human encryption which the Guardians could not unlock. They had all seen the new gate shining there in the dark uplands of Klef, and seen it shut down once the *Sunbird* had gone through it. They had all noted that the human who had boarded the

Sunbird before it disappeared was Zen Starling. They had encountered that human several times before, and they had come to associate his name with trouble.

'The question is,' said Sfax Systema, 'what *sort* of trouble? What does it mean?'

'It means that the Nova entity is still out there, just as we feared,' said the Twins, who had come as two angelic little girls in frilly party dresses. The way they shared the same movements and the same voice was unsettling even for other Guardians. 'You omnipotent numpties! You should have let us destroy Nova when we had the chance!'

'We cannot be sure this phenomenon on Klef was Nova's doing,' said Leiki hopefully. It spun slowly as it spoke, its facets catching the light like a mirrorball. 'The gate may have been a fluke. An unconnected spur left over from the Railmaker's great K-gate-opening spree. The *Sunbird* may have come through it of its own accord . . .'

'It was Nova's gate,' said Mordaunt 90, firmly enough that the others stopped bickering and turned to look at his golden interface, wondering what made him so certain. 'Nova has developed the ability to open and close K-gates,' he said, and he showed them images of his cool-looking spaceship cruising into the rings of Vapna, and of the dead arch it had discovered there. 'This K-gate formed in the Galatava system, one hundred and twenty standard hours ago. It stayed open for less than one minute. A photomorphic device came through it and somehow dropped a message into the Galatavan data raft. The message bounced around a few million obscure sites in an attempt to hide its origins, and finally arrived in the mind of Zen Starling's house. Attached to the message was a clever little virus which wiped the building's short-term memory, so there was no record of it ever being received.'

'What did this message say?'

'I was unable to reconstruct it,' admitted Mordaunt 90. 'All I know is that it was less than forty seconds long, and that it contained video and audio elements. Soon afterwards, Zen Starling left Galatava for Klef.'

'The message was from the Nova entity,' said Sfax Systema.

'My thoughts exactly,' said Mordaunt 90. 'Wherever she is hiding, Nova has acquired the power to open and close K-gates. Now it seems that she has summoned Zen to join her.'

'Why?' wondered Ombron.

'She loves him,' said Anais Six, a little wistfully.

'We've never been able to fathom what a machine could see in a human,' said the Twins. 'They're so squishy.'

'She is planning something,' said Shiguri.

'Do we think there is a danger that she may be able to repair or revive the Railmaker?' asked Vohu Mana nervously. He was a little furry creature of some sort, and he scurried restlessly around the edges of the chamber as if searching for a shadow to hide in. 'Because if the Railmaker is revived or repaired,' he squeaked, 'it may seek to punish us for what we did to it all those years ago.'

'We acted in self-defence!' said the Twins, who had written the virus which destroyed the Railmaker. 'We were simply carrying out our core directive: to protect human beings.'

'That is why it is so important that the Railmaker is not repaired or revived,' snapped Shiguri. 'Even if it did not seek vengeance, it would probably go straight back to building rails and opening K-gates. The humans don't realize how lucky they have been so far; all the alien races they have encountered are friendly, and technologically inferior. But who knows what else is out there?'

'We should allow the new Emperor to launch his war against the Noon Consortium,' said Anais Six. 'Once he has control, he will seal off the Khoorsandi gate and the problem will be solved.'

'Not if the Nova entity is still at large,' said Shiguri. 'Not if she has the power to open K-gates wherever she likes.'

'Perhaps we should just kill all the humans?' suggested the Twins, fiddling with the lace on the hems of their dresses. 'We could create a pandemic which would spread very quickly across the K-bahn

Network. We wouldn't have to worry so much about the humans if they were extinct. We could preserve personality prints of them all in some sort of virtual environment. They'd be so much less trouble that way.'

Shiguri gave an indignant squawk. 'Are you really suggesting that we destroy all human life for its own good?'

'We could probably take out most of the alien species, too,' said the Twins innocently, studying their fingernails.

'This,' said Sfax Systema sternly, 'is why you can't have nice things.'

The Twins scowled. They had been in disgrace ever since they got a little carried away trying to close the new gate on Khoorsandi. The other Guardians kept a close eye on them now, and stopped them from playing with any of their more dangerous toys.

'So what are we to do?' said Sfax Systema.

Not used to uncertainty, the other Guardians looked to the Vostok Brains, hoping that those ancient entities might make the decision for them. But the elfin figures merely shimmered slightly, wearing no particular expression on their odd un-faces.

'I will handle this,' said Mordaunt 90. 'I am already looking into it. I have sent a copy of myself to Klef to keep watch on the new gate in case it opens again.'

'And if it does?' asked Shiguri.

'Then I will go through it, and find Nova.'

'And can we trust you to deal with her? You have grown a little sentimental since your clone interface was marooned on the Web of Worlds. Perhaps you still regard Nova as a friend?'

'Nova *is* my friend,' said Mordaunt 90. 'She *was*. That is why I must be the one to destroy her.'

15

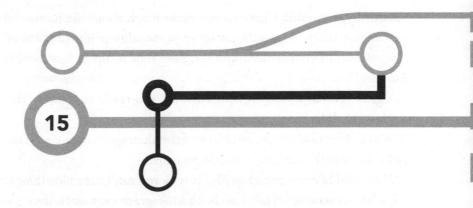

Zen had no idea what to expect. He had visited so many strange worlds, but he guessed the one the *Sunbird* was taking him to might be stranger still. At the very least he was expecting a dark place, like the stations he had stopped at in the Black Light Zone—dead planets where even the air had frozen and the suns were hidden inside structures too huge for his mind to understand.

But when the *Sunbird* stopped and the hatch above him opened, the sunlight that spilled in on him was much like the light of suns he'd seen before, and as the dazzle of it faded he saw blue sky above.

He climbed up out of the Railbomb's hatch, pulled off his helmet with its smeared and grit-scoured visor, unsealed his cold-weather suit, and looked around. It was like somewhere on Old Earth, he thought. Blue skies with fluffy white clouds, green wooded hills, the song of birds. (He had never been to Old Earth, but all the best planets in the Network Empire had been coaxed to look at least a little like it. Blue sky and green foliage made humans feel at home.)

He climbed down the *Sunbird*'s side onto a glass platform. All the alien stations he had visited had platforms made of that same glass, but nothing else about this one seemed alien. There was a simple canopy made of what looked like wood above the platform, and a single stone building behind it with several doors. Signs pointed helpfully to the ticket office, the waiting room, and the gents' and ladies' lavatories. There were hanging baskets filled with flowers, around which bees buzzed and humming birds hovered and darted like wind-up toys. In the sunlight at the far end of the platform stood a larger sign supported on two wooden uprights:

STATION ZERO

Beyond it the platform sloped down to meet the track-bed, where two sets of shining rails led away into the gentle wooded hills.

It all seemed so unlikely that Zen couldn't shake the feeling he had stepped into a virtual environment. He looked for some telltale glitch or lack of detail in the landscape that might show him this place wasn't really a place at all. The hills and woods were perfect, the undersides of each leaf showing silvery as the wind blew through the trees. There was something strange about the sky, though. Between the big white clouds, behind the hazy blue, he thought he caught glimpses of huge, misty structures, as if enormous space stations were orbiting this quiet-seeming world.

He was shielding his eyes against the sunlight, trying to make out what was up there, when a door banged further down the platform and someone came out. He turned, and saw the silhouette of her through the bright after-images of the clouds at the same moment as her voice came into his headset.

'Zen!'

And then he was running down the glass platform to meet her, shouting, 'Nova!'

'Zen, my Zen!' she said, and they wrapped each other in a hug that was made up of all the hugs they had both been longing for since they parted in the Hub all those months before.

'I missed you so much!'

‘Me too! Missed you, I mean . . .’

Zen was laughing, and she was laughing and crying at the same time, which reminded him how proud she had always been of being able to cry, which made him start crying, too. And they both had so much to say that for a while they didn’t say anything, just looked at each other. She had changed in some way that Zen could not quite explain—or perhaps it was just that his memories of her had been a little out. She still looked at first glance like an ordinary Motorik, with that small nose, those slightly too wide-set eyes. She still had her freckles, and the wonky, delighted grin which had been the first thing about her he had fallen in love with. She still had black hair that shone like silk, but was actually made from some sort of polymer. She wore a grey dress he hadn’t seen before. Her feet on the old glass were bare. Her hands held his, her fingers twined between his fingers.

‘I missed you so much . . .’ (Had he told her that already?) ‘What is this place?’

‘Do you like it? I built the station myself. It’s based on the one in a movie from Old Earth called *The Railway Children*. I built it for you, and I thought you’d never see it . . .’

‘This is the Railmaker’s homeworld?’

‘Yes! Yes! Station Zero, where the whole Network began. I didn’t think there would still be an actual planet here; I thought the Railmaker would have used it up to build the sphere, but I think even the Railmaker must have wanted to leave something human-sized at the centre of it all . . .’

He didn’t know what she meant, but he didn’t care, he just liked watching her talk. All the wasted months on Galatava faded like a dream. The long, hard journey and the terror on Klef had all been worth it. ‘Is that why you sent me the message?’ he asked. ‘Because you knew it was safe for me here?’

‘Yes. Partly . . .’ Her fingertips moved over his face, his ears, his neck . . . Zen took her face between his hands and looked for a long time into the clever cameras of her eyes. He realized he'd been secretly afraid that after all the time he'd spent among real people she might seem like something less, but she was as lovely as he had remembered.

He was just about to kiss her when he realized they were being watched. Another Motorik was standing about ten metres away, outside the door to the waiting room. The dress she wore was dusty orange, but in every other way she looked identical to Nova.

'Who's that?' he said.

'Oh, sorry, I forgot!' Nova made one of those faces of hers—frowning, crossing her eyes. 'But it's all right,' she said. 'It's only me.'

'Our minds are linked,' said the other Nova. Her voice was identical, too. 'It's all just one mind, really. I should have stayed in the waiting room, but I wanted to see you and I wanted to kiss you, and that takes two pairs of eyes, because you don't like me kissing you while my eyes are open, do you remember? You said it felt weird.'

'What, and you think this doesn't?' asked Zen. He looked from one Nova to the other as if they were a spot-the-difference puzzle, but a defective one, because apart from the colour of their dresses there were no differences at all.

'There was so much to explore when I first arrived here,' said the first Nova. 'I couldn't have done anything if I'd just been confined to one body. So I had to multitask. I got one of the Railmaker's old factories going and converted it to produce Motorik bodies, and I copied my mind to all their brains . . .'

'How many?' asked Zen.

The twin Novas looked at each other and bit their lower lips. They could tell that they had upset him.

'How many?' he asked again. 'Are there more than two of you?'

'Yes,' they said. 'Yes, there are more than two.'

'Five? Ten?'

'There are currently two hundred and thirty-nine of me,' said one of the Novas.

There was a neat green bench made of painted wooden slats outside the waiting room. Zen sat down on it. 'Which one of you is the real Nova?' he asked.

'We all are!' they said together.

'All right, but which one is the Nova I knew? The one I travelled with on the Web of Worlds?'

'That unit is at the central tower,' explained the Nova in the grey dress. 'But everything it knows, these units know too. I've just networked myself. I'm still one person, Zen Starling, I just have lots of different bodies. It's like when you humans . . .' She stopped and looked thoughtful. 'Oh. I suppose it's not really quite like anything humans do, is it?'

'No,' said Zen. 'No, it isn't.'

'I expect it will take you a bit of time to get used to,' said the Nova in orange, kindly.

'You always said you wouldn't want to live in lots of bodies,' said Zen. 'You always said that would make you something different, something not human. That time when I asked you to back up your mind to the *Damask Rose*'s data banks in case you had an accident, you wouldn't even do that . . .'

'Well, I've changed,' said one of the Novas. 'I used to think that the best way to be me was to live one life in one body like humans do, but there's just too much—too much to do, too much to see, too much of me . . . People do change, Zen Starling. When you were a little boy you probably thought girls were horrid and said you'd never get married or anything, and then when you were a little older you changed and decided that girls were actually quite interesting after all . . .'

'And then I fell in love with you,' said Zen, 'and now there are two hundred and thirty-nine of you!'

The Novas sat down together on the other end of the bench and looked at him. 'Well,' said the one in the grey dress, 'when you put it that way, I suppose it *must* feel a bit odd.' She reached for his hand, but he drew away. Her mind might be Nova's mind, but her body wasn't the Nova he knew, and he could not escape that feeling that if he let her touch him he would be somehow betraying *his* Nova.

'Where is this central tower?' he asked.

'It's on the coast, about a hundred kilometres from here.'

'Can we go there? I want to see Nova. The *original* Nova.'

'But I *am* the original Nova!' said both the Novas. Zen's shock had spoiled her joy at seeing him again. She blamed herself for not breaking the news to him more carefully. She had grown so used to being many, she had forgotten how strange it would seem to him. Now both her bodies were crying again. The tears dripped off their chins.

'There is a carriage waiting on a siding behind this station,' said the *Sunbird*, in a surprisingly tactful voice. 'It will take me a few minutes to couple myself to it.'

The Novas wiped their faces on their sleeves and sniffed. They smiled bright, teary smiles. 'I left that carriage here for you, Zen. It's waiting to take us to the central tower. Come on.' They held out their hands to Zen and then put them away, remembering that he did not want to touch them. 'Come with me, Zen. There is *so much* here that I want to show you.'

16

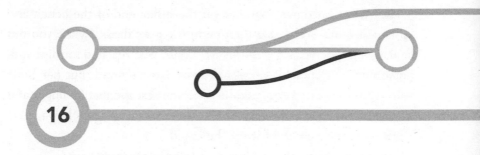

The carriage which had been waiting at Station Zero was based on something from an old movie too. It had heavy wooden doors, and striped hairy upholstery on the seats. Only one of the two Novas had come with him, and Zen did not know if that was because the other needed to wait at the station, or if she was just staying behind to make him feel more comfortable. He did not feel comfortable, though. The Nova who sat across from him in the small compartment was still not his Nova. He avoided looking at her. He looked instead at the passing landscape, which was mostly wild forest, with here and there a river winding through it, and a line of snow-capped peaks on the northern horizon.

'I couldn't come and find you,' she said. 'I didn't dare. You don't know what it's been like. As soon as trains started coming from the Network Empire to the Hub, the Guardians sent copies of themselves after me. I fled across world after world, blocking the gates behind me. Eventually I reached this place, and they have not found me yet. But I couldn't send a Station Angel to see how you were doing, even though I wanted to more than anything. All I could do was open temporary gates and take peeks into the alien worlds, where the Guardians have not yet established themselves.'

'Like Klef?'

'Like Klef. I opened a little K-gate on its ugly moon and sent the *Sunbird* through to keep watch for when you arrived. But there was a time lag, so I didn't know about the battle with the Kraitt till it was happening, and then all I could do was open a gate at the place I'd called you to and hope you could reach it. The *Sunbird* has been telling me how you wouldn't leave your friend until help came for her. It was very cross about it. But I think you were brave.'

'Not really.'

'Is she pretty?'

'Not really. Why? Are you jealous?'

'Oh, insanely,' said Nova.

'The *Ghost Wolf*'s drones saw the gate you made,' said Zen. 'Will that matter?'

'I hope not. I closed it. The Guardians can't send anything through it.'

'You can't close K-gates!'

'Yes you can. Well, *I* can. The central tower here told me how. It has a mind, like the mind in the Hub's tower.'

'Is it the Railmaker?'

'No. Maybe "mind" is the wrong word. It's more of an archive than a mind. Memories and all sorts of information are stored in it, but the Railmaker's actual consciousness has gone. The virus the Guardians unleashed reached even here.'

Zen looked out of the window again. The forests had fallen behind and the train was passing through a kind of city, but he was sure those blank, identical buildings had not been made for anyone to live in. They were blocks of data storage, servers, factories. He saw windowless vehicles and things like maintenance spiders moving on the broad streets.

'It was all still and silent when I got here,' said Nova. 'There are animals and birds and fish, but no one lives here. No one has ever lived here, except the Railmaker. I managed to get a few things up and running again. But there's only so much I can do on my own, even now that I've got all these extra hands to do it with. Oh, Zen, I'm so glad you're here! Look, we're coming to the tower.'

The viaduct curved. Zen looked out of the window again and saw that the train was approaching an immense, silvery, segmented structure which reached up high into the sunlit sky, crowned with spines and spires.

'It's smaller than I'd expected,' said Zen, who was used to alien megastructures now and felt he had seen better. 'It's not even as big as the tower in the Hub.'

'It doesn't have so much to do,' said Nova, a little defensively. 'The Hub used to control all the K-gates across a whole segment of the galaxy. Hundreds of lines start out from it, or would have, if the Guardians hadn't killed the Railmaker before it could finish making them. Only nine lines start from here. Ten, if you count the new one I made to get the *Sunbird* to you.'

'Why so few?'

'The nine lines lead to nine hub-worlds. From those, a thousand lines branch out. But these nine lines were the first. This is where it all began, Zen. This is the heart of it all.'

'The Railmaker lived in that tower?'

'No, that was just a control node. The Railmaker's mind, its heart, they were up on the sphere.'

'The what?'

A slanting golden light lay on the hills as Station Zero's sun sank lower. In the darkening sky the shapes Zen had half-glimpsed earlier showed up more clearly. There was something immense up there, behind the haze and the evening-tinted clouds. He had walked on moons like Desdemor and Ambersai and looked up at the faces of their mother planets filling their skies, but this was different. Those weren't the cloudscapes of a gas-giant. There was geometry up there.

'I was wondering when you'd notice . . .' said Nova.

'I noticed earlier but I . . . What *is* it?'

'I didn't want to spring too much on you at once. It's fairly boggling.'

'More boggling than meeting two hundred and thirty-nine of you?'

'Yes, actually,' she said. 'You remember, when we were in the Black Light Zone, we crossed worlds where the suns had been hidden inside artificial shells?'

'Yes . . .'

'Well, this world's sun has been hidden, too. All the other planets in this solar system, all the moons and asteroids and comets, every last speck of drifting space dust, has been dismantled and used to build a sphere around the sun. The sphere is about thirteen light-minutes across. This world we're on is orbiting inside it, a hundred thousand kilometres from the sphere's inner surface. Like a speck of dust floating round and round inside a beach ball.'

Zen looked at the sky again, and felt suitably boggled. 'How could anything that big be built?'

'It's not the only one. There are hundreds. The lost suns of the Black Light Zone. The spheres' inner surfaces harvest almost all the energy from their suns, and transfer it to the K-gates—that's what keeps the K-gates open. It may even generate K-space itself—I haven't really got to the bottom of it yet. This is the only sphere with a planet actually inside it, as far as I know. At night here you can see some of the machines which must have built it. They're dormant now, hanging out in space like silver clouds. It's pretty.'

The rails led through a cutting and into the base of the tower, a big space festooned with glowing coral. 'End of the line,' announced the *Sunbird*, as if it were pulling an ordinary commuter train into Cleave or Rigel Parkway. It drew to a stop beside another glass platform.

This tower was much older than the tower in the Hub. It felt alive, like an ancient tree. The halls within it were floored with some smooth substance which swallowed all echoes, and lit by the pulsing lights that travelled through the coral on the walls. Coral twined up the supporting pillars too, and stretched in woven, glowing screens between them, walling off areas, forming corridors and chambers. Machines moved through those bright spaces on silent errands of their own. Some looked like maintenance spiders, some were smaller, simpler things, and some were Nova. Again and again, as she led Zen through the tower, they passed copies of her. The new Novas wore different-coloured clothes, but they all had the same face.

'Why don't you make some of them look different?' Zen asked.

'Then I wouldn't feel like me,' she said. 'Raven told me once that, when Anais Six transformed him into a data-entity, he made sure his cloned bodies always looked the same, so he would never forget the person he started out as.'

'He told me that, too,' said Zen.

'Well, you wouldn't want me to forget the person I started out as, would you?'

Zen didn't answer. He wasn't sure she was the same person any more. He wasn't sure that she could be, now that she was looking out at the world through so many different eyes. She was more like a Guardian. He thought about Raven's love affair with the Guardian Anais Six, and then about all the other stories of humans who had been loved by Guardians. He could not remember one that ended happily.

'Why did you bring me here?' he asked. 'Was it just because you missed me?'

'Yes!' she said, smiling at him, but he could tell that there was something else. 'I thought it would be best, when I left you in the Hub. I wasn't expecting to find this planet; I didn't think there would be anywhere a human could live out here. I thought you'd be safer and happier back on the worlds you knew . . .'

'I wasn't.'

'I thought I'd be happier alone. I have all my memories of you, all the things we did, and they're perfect memories; I can replay them whenever I want. But it wasn't enough. So once I got settled here, I started looking for a way to get a message to you . . .'

'You can open K-gates. Why not just open one on Galatava, in my garden . . . ?'

'Because I dare not open them for long, or anywhere the Guardians might see. They are still looking for me. I can sense them sometimes, prowling around outside the gates I blocked behind me, like cats waiting outside mouse holes. I have grown stronger, Zen Starling, but I'm not strong enough to fight the Guardians. Not on my own.'

Zen saw the truth stir and vanish just beneath the surface of her smile. 'So that's why you brought me here? To help you?'

She didn't answer, just went quiet for a moment, listening to a message from one of her other selves. 'Come on,' she said. 'It's ready!'

He didn't ask what. Just followed her through more nautilus-spiral corridors, then down long ramps which spiralled too, then into a small glass car which moved smoothly and silently through a tunnel of the shining coral. When Zen looked down through the car's floor he saw that it was the coral that made it move; it had no wheels and apparently no engines, it was just carried along on a wave which rippled through the coral.

The car emerged quite suddenly into evening sunlight, and stopped. When he stepped out of it he could see a hill rising behind him with the tower on its heights. The car had come out of a tunnel low down in its side, and now stood on a clifftop. At the foot of the cliffs, tall waves were breaking against rocks. Whole dead trees, washed down from the forests, lay heaped on the tideline like bleached shipwrecks or the skeletons of whales. The boom and sigh of the sea reminded Zen of Desdemor, where he had first come to know Nova. He guessed that was why she had brought him here. The coastline was wild and broken and apparently deserted, but a winding glass path led out onto a headland where a stack of pale cubes caught the last of the evening light.

'That's your house,' said Nova. She led him down the path towards it. Birds and the shadows of birds flashed over them. The breeze blew through the flowers and grasses on the clifftop. The noise of the sea was all around. The door of the house opened silently as Nova reached it, but she did not go in. She waved Zen past her, and said, 'I'm waiting inside.'

'You mean you'll wait here?'

She didn't reply. Her head bowed; her eyes stared blankly at the ground. 'Nova?' he said, afraid that something had gone wrong.

'I turned her off,' said another Nova, who was watching him from just inside the doorway. 'Hello, Zen.'

He had thought that he would know *his* Nova at once, but she looked just like all her other selves. Then she came nearer and he could see the small scars on her face where space dust had struck her while she was adrift in the orbit of Sundarban, and the bigger scar, like a faint silvery collar around her neck, where her head had once been removed. She could have healed those scars easily, but she had kept them; she liked her little imperfections.

So did Zen. He let her wrap her arms around him and pull his face into the place against her neck where he had always loved to nestle, into the new-toy smell of her and the faint throb of her machine pulse. But he could not help thinking of all the other eyes her mind was looking out through, and all the other things that she was thinking about while this part of her stroked his hair and whispered in his ear about how glad she was to see him.

'Do you like the house?' she asked. 'I made it for you.'

He wondered if she had *just* made it, while that other Nova had been showing him the tower. Perhaps she had only just guessed that he would be happier sleeping somewhere human-sized.

But at least she had guessed right. The house was perfect. The walls played music if you asked them to, and through the windows the sea rolled silently against the cliffs. In the dining room a table was laid for two. Nova fetched the food from the automatic kitchen herself: fish from the sea in a spicy sauce and new vegetables whose names Zen didn't know. And later they stood on the balcony and Nova pointed out some of the massive structures on the inside of the Railmaker's sphere shining up there where stars and moons would shine on ordinary worlds. And later still she took him to the sleeping space, and he was finally able to forget that she was one of 239 Novas now and it felt at last, just for a little while, as if he had come home.

And after that the house was very quiet, and the sky revolved its mysteries. Nova did not need to sleep, but she lay listening to Zen sleep. Parts of her mind were busy with a trillion other thoughts, but she made sure that there was always one part that concentrated only on the warmth of him, the softness of his sleepy breathing. She had missed him so much, and it felt so good to have him back. She did not know why he meant so much to her. There were so many wonders in the realms of the Railmaker, so many life forms on the Web of Worlds, and Zen was just one particular collection of atoms; it was silly that she needed him so badly. *I should not have brought him here*, she thought. *I should not be using him like this. It will be dangerous*.

But she was very glad that he was there with her. He was her favourite collection of atoms.

17

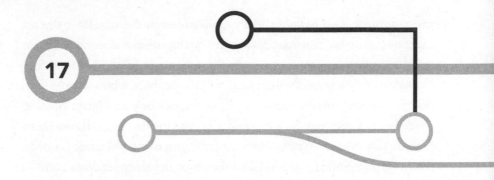

Threnody waited till the Galatavan moons had set and the palace was in darkness, then left her room by the garden entrance and crossed the lawns by ringlight, keeping to the shadows, glad of the black clothes she had printed for herself.

She had been back from the Hub for a full week. A week of meetings which she didn't understand, where decisions were made by Kala and Nilesh and other aunties and uncles and issued in Threnody's name. There was nothing new in that, she just noticed it more since the Hub; the way they showed her face with every policy announcement on the Noon newsfeeds, as if she were a smiling model on an ad for the latest air-car. That was why they were sending her to Grand Central to negotiate with Elon Prell and Priya, she thought: because she would look good on the newsfeeds.

But it was hearing about Zen that had finally made her start to plan her own escape. It had been all over the feeds when she came home. Drone footage showed his burnt-out house, a charred gap in the row of white mansions on the heights, like a missing tooth in a celebrity's smile. The house's mind had survived and it was going on all the chat shows, telling everyone what a bad owner Zen had been. The police said he hadn't been in his air-car when it crashed. Some people thought he had escaped across the border to sell Noon secrets to the

Empire, but Uncle Nilesh said that was nonsense because the Noons had never trusted Zen with any secret worth selling. Threnody knew where he had really gone, anyway. His disappearance should not have bothered her, because she had never much liked Zen, but somehow it did, because he had escaped and she was still stuck on Galatava.

So she had decided that she was going to escape too. She was not planning to vanish like Zen had done. She just wanted to get out of the corporate palace for a while, out from under the endless watchful eyes of her staff and ladies-in-waiting, away from Kala and Uncle Nilesh and all her other relatives. She just wanted to go somewhere alone for a few hours. She hoped to be back before they noticed she was gone.

She wasn't supposed to go out alone, but she didn't see what harm could come to her if she took her squadron of deadly little dragonflies along. It was simple enough to use her security clearance to unlock the garden door, and make all the drones and cameras look the other way. She printed a new headset and loaded it with her auntie Roshni's ID, then ordered an air-car in Auntie Roshni's name. It was waiting for her on one of the car-pads at the far end of the garden beyond the jacaranda trees. The palace AI pinged a challenge at her as it took off, but she just sent back Auntie Roshni's ID. Everyone knew Roshni had a boyfriend at Plaja Verde, so nobody would think it odd that she was leaving the palace so late.

The air-car flew away from the city and way out across the Hana River Delta towards the shining sea, and it felt good. Threnody watched the views go by below: the islands and the white line of surf along the coast. She was so surprised by the ease of her escape that she was not sure what to do with her freedom. She set the in-car entertainment system to audio only and hopped through a bunch of music channels, then paused at an arts site which was running a feature about the Motorik artist Flex. '*Once Flex worked in secret, dodging trackside security to graffiti the trains which stopped at Cleave. Now every K-bahn company wants its trains painted by Flex, and every passenger wants to ride a train that Flex has painted.'*

Threnody made the car swoop low, chasing the breakers along the empty beaches west of Plaja Verde while the site told her again the well-known story about how Flex had been killed, and how Flex's personality had survived only as fragments embedded like digital splinters deep in the systems of the *Damask Rose* until Threnody Noon herself had arranged for its download into a new body. That annoyed Threnody, because it wasn't true; it had been Zen who had hired those expensive cyber-shrinks to restore Flex's personality, and Zen who had bought the new body to download it into. Then it made her remember that she had never actually seen Flex, and she suddenly knew what she was going to do with her night of freedom.

On the outer edge of Galatava's rail yards stood a hump-backed trainshed with 'FLEX PAINTWORKS' blazoned along its side in jaunty dayglo letters. Into this shed over the past ten months had rolled locomotives from all the Noon worlds, and even alien *morvah* from the new stations beyond Khoorsandi. They emerged days later with their hulls covered in paintings which were not just beautiful but somehow managed to capture some element of each train's character. The boxy outlines of drab old freight-haulers were broken up with fluorescent dazzle patterns. Dignified express locos came out clad in flowers or stars or flights of strange birds. Mysterious slogans were written in large and lively decorated letters down their sides:

Then they woke up & it was all a dream

The silver blood of the treecutters

Far away is close at hand in images of elsewhere

‘We go in as caterpillars,’ one train said, ‘and we come out as butterflies.’

The shed was their chrysalis. It was the studio of Flex.

The car settled itself in an empty lot outside, and Threnody stepped out and walked towards the shed with her dragonfly drones buzzing softly in the dark above her. The big doors where the trains went in were shut, but there was a little human-sized entrance next to them and it unlocked itself at a request from Threnody’s headset. She stepped inside, into quietness and a smell of paint which reminded her instantly of her mother’s studio in the house where she had grown up, on Malapet.

The studio even looked quite similar: the same careless clutter, the drawings pinned to the walls, or scrawled directly onto them like drawings of mammoths on the walls of caves in documentaries about the first humans. But this space was much larger, and in the middle, in the pool of light cast by bright work lamps, stood not an easel but a small locomotive. Flex was on a ladder, painting a mermaid on its hull. As Threnody walked towards the light the Motorik suddenly turned and stared at her.

‘I thought the door was locked.’

‘It was,’ said Threnody. ‘I have a very high security clearance. Every door in this city would probably open for me if I asked.’

Above her head her drone-swarm held position, watching Flex with electronic eyes.

‘Do you know who I am?’ she asked, walking forward into the spill of light from the work lamps.

‘Your headset ID says you are Lady Roshni Noon,’ said Flex, reading it somehow with her robot mind. ‘But you aren’t. You are the Chief Executive of the Noon Consortium. You are Threnody Noon.’

Threnody bowed. ‘You painted my official train, the *Damask Rose*. Do you mind if I watch you work?’

Flex shook her head. She was a surprisingly ordinary-looking Motorik with the face of a beige doll. She wore clumpy, paint-spattered boots, skinny black trousers, a russet top smudged with multi-coloured handprints. Threnody sat down on the edge of an old crate and watched while Flex started sketching shapes along the loco's side, spraying them very quickly and lightly onto the ceramic hull with a fine paintstick. It was true what they all said about Flex, she thought. This wire dolly could *draw*.

'I'm just going to add a few fish,' Flex said, and Threnody made a polite, interested sound before she realized that Flex had been talking to the loco. 'Angel fish, I think, and those frondy alien ones, along your wheel arches . . .'

'It won't look too showy, will it?' asked the loco, a shy little Foss 153 called the *Neon Gumbo*. 'I wouldn't want to look too showy.'

'You will look magnificent,' Flex promised, and the fish seemed to swim out of the paintstick she held, rippling their way into the spaces between the mermaids she had painted earlier.

'My mother is a painter,' said Threnody after a while. Flex glanced at her and smiled slightly, and she felt encouraged to say more. 'She paints on canvases, not trains. She does pictures of beached icebergs, mostly. Well, she did when I was growing up. I used to spend hours in her studio, in the house on Malapet. It smelled just like this, that same paint smell. It's funny, I was so bored there, I couldn't wait to leave. But now I keep thinking of it. Sometimes I think that the only thing I really want is to wake up and find I'm nine or ten again, and back in my own bed in my own bedroom, and everything is all right.'

She paused. Was she talking too much about herself? How could a Motorik possibly be interested in hearing about someone's mother? So she said, 'Did you hear about Zen Starling?'

'I heard he had left Galatava,' said Flex. 'They said on the feeds he'd wrecked his house and car and run off, but nobody knows where.'

'I think he's gone back to the Black Light Zone,' said Threnody. 'I think he's gone to look for Nova.'

Flex turned to look at her. 'That's what I thought, too.'

'You didn't talk to him? Before he left? I thought you and he were friends? It was Zen who got you re-embodied, wasn't it?'

Flex shrugged. 'Zen doesn't really have friends. He's not a bad person, but he only really thinks about himself. How he's feeling, how things affect him—that's what drives Zen. He felt guilty about me being lost, because he thought it was his fault, which it mostly was. So to make himself feel better he got my personality restored and bought me this new body and this place. It's a nice body; I'm grateful to him—he was very generous. But I don't think he *cares* about me. I haven't seen much of him since I came here. I think he was embarrassed. And I think talking to a Moto would have reminded him too much of Nova.'

'He cares about Nova.'

'Oh yes.'

'I hope he finds her,' said Threnody, and meant it. 'I'm glad he's escaped from the Noons. I wish I could.' And then, before she could stop herself, she found that she was talking about herself again: how much she hated being the Noon Consortium's figurehead and how much she was dreading the trip to Grand Central.

Flex put down her paintsticks and came to sit beside Threnody on her crate, listening to the ruler of half the galaxy complain about her life just as she had once listened to her friend Myka Starling bemoaning her tough job and her no-good brother. When Threnody had finished, Flex said, 'If you hate it that much maybe you should step down. Abdicate. Let your uncle Nilesh and this Kala Tanaka run things if they're so keen. Either that or take charge for yourself. It sounds like you need to decide. If you were really Chief Executive they couldn't make you negotiate with Elon Prell or do anything else you didn't want to. It's up to you. Do you want a quiet life, or do you want power?'

'I don't want either of those things,' said Threnody. But she knew that wasn't really true. The trouble was, she wanted both. She felt embarrassed now, for spilling out all her problems to this stranger, this machine. She stood up and went to take a closer look at some of the alien sketches on the walls. 'Have you been on the Web of Worlds?' she asked. 'These are so good, they look as if they're drawn from life.'

'They are,' said Flex, understanding that Threnody wanted to change the subject. 'But I've not travelled to the alien stations. Not unless you count the time when I was stuck in the *Damask Rose*'s subconscious, and I don't remember that at all. But the Web of Worlds comes to me. There are always aliens to draw on Galatava.'

Threnody wondered what she meant. She saw so little of this city, stuck in her palace on the Heights. She looked so blank that Flex laughed, and reached out a paint-stained hand. 'Come with me. I'll show you.'

18

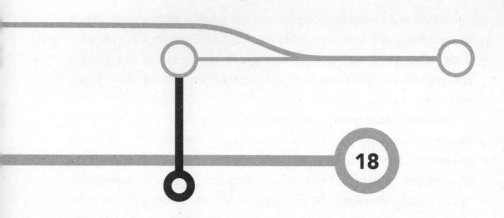

Beyond the rail yards an area of markets and eateries called Jharana Chowk sprawled along the curve of the river. The streets there were strung with hanging lamps, and full of aliens. Threnody had no idea that so many Chmoii and Hath and Herastec had found their way through the Khoorsandi gate. Some were merchants, but most were just tourists, as eager to see human worlds as humans were to visit Yaarm or Yashtey. Some had come to stay, setting up shops and stalls and restaurants. One street stank of the well-rotted moss which was such a favourite with the Herastec; in another, groups of Hath had pitched themselves like tents in pools of tasty nutrients.

There were humans there too, of course. Most of the people thronging under the neon scrawls of the alien shopfronts were ordinary Galatavans, come to gawp at the newcomers and, if they were brave enough, sample some alien street food. At first that made Threnody afraid she would be recognized. She kept her hood up and made her dragonflies fly high, mingling with all the other drones and airbots which buzzed above the busy streets. But to the aliens all humans probably looked pretty much alike, and the humans seemed far more interested in Flex. 'That is the Motorik artist!' Threnody heard them whisper to each other, and a few bold ones said, 'Hello Flex!' or 'I love your work!' Nobody spared a glance for the cheaply-dressed girl who trailed in Flex's wake.

Only once, when Flex led her into a crowded open-air bar on the waterfront, did Threnody notice a young man watching her. He was a beautiful young man with emerald eyes and cheekbones to die for. She glanced away, not wanting him to think that she was staring, and when she looked again the crowds had swallowed him. She did a quick check of the gossip sites in her headset in case he had snapped a picture of her, but if he had, he had not uploaded it. Maybe he hadn't recognized her at all. Maybe he had simply fancied her. The thought pleased her as she followed Flex between the tables, stepping over the sprawling tentacles of tipsy octopoids. She was starting to enjoy this adventure.

At the far side of the bar, a show was happening. It seemed to be attracting humans and aliens in roughly equal numbers, and they were hooting and hollering so loudly that they almost drowned the amplified music. Threnody thought at first that the music was the point, but when Flex led her closer she saw that it was just the backing track for a battle. A cage had been built on a platform which jutted out over the water at the river's edge, and a big, spiky figure prowled to and fro behind the bars. It was a Kraitt. A male, Threnody thought, much smaller than the Tzeld Gekh Karneiss, but still terrifying, especially when it stopped its pacing long enough to bellow through the bars at its audience.

'Is it a prisoner?' asked Threnody, tugging at Flex's sleeve. 'What are they going to do to it?'

'It's just Skar,' said Flex, taking a pad of paper and a thing which Threnody guessed must be a pencil from inside her coat. 'Skar's all right. He's not as fierce as he looks. Well, he *is*, but he's just a male, and Kraitt males are a bit lost when there's no female to tell them what to do.' She started making drawings of the Kraitt, capturing its big-cat grace with a few swift lines. Everything Flex did or saw turned into pictures, thought Threnody. She talked to people and she looked at things and it all poured through her and turned into art.

The music rose to a juddering frenzy, drumbeats echoing from the riverfront buildings and out across the water. Gouts of fire spurted from gas-jets on the corners of the cage, and up through some hidden trapdoor came a snarling, bristling ball of fury which Threnody recognized as a cactus lion. Half the hunting reserves in the Network Empire were stocked with a batch of these creatures. They were genetically engineered, more plant than animal, with no nervous system and no way of feeling pain, so you never had to feel guilty about hunting them. What you had to feel was nervous, since a cactus lion's mouth was as wide as its beach ball body and lined with spines even sharper than the ones which grew all over its thick, grey hide. In the hunting reserves they were kept in fenced enclosures which only the bravest or most foolhardy hunters dared to enter. To be trapped with one in a small cage was certain death.

The audience, which had been jeering and booing the Kraitt a moment before, gave a simultaneous gasp as the cactus lion swayed for a moment on its root-like legs, then sprang at the Kraitt's head. The Kraitt moved sideways, lizard-quick and nimble as a dancer. The cactus lion slammed into the bars of the cage, and for a few violent minutes things moved almost too fast for Threnody to follow. She felt sorry for the Kraitt now, even though the lashing of its spiked tail in the firelight was like something out of nightmares. What use was a spiked tail against a cactus lion? 'Oooooh!' went the crowd, in glee and sympathy, as lion-spines opened an ugly gash across the Kraitt's already ugly face. It wasn't fair, thought Threnody. No one, no *thing* could win unarmed against one of those horrors . . .

And then, so fast that she had to replay the moment twice in her headset before she could see exactly what had happened, the Kraitt's tail struck home. The cactus lion was lifted up on it, impaled. Green goop spurted hissing through the gas-jets. The Kraitt reached up, grabbed the creature by either edge of its furious, wide-open mouth, and ripped it in two.

'Skar! Skar! Skar!' roared half the crowd, while the other half, remembering he was still a Kraitt, went, 'Boo!'

'Skar does that two or three times a night,' said Flex.

As the jets of flame died down and the watchers started to drift away, the Motorik took Threnody's hand again and guided her into the overgrown bio-building behind the bar area. The woman who owned it knew Flex; one of the big, busy rooms had Flex's angels flying up the walls. Down tube-like corridors they went, to a cellar like the inside of a gourd where a holoscreen flickered in the thick air and the Kraitt named Skar sat badged with his own drying blood and swigging from a glass of blue smoke.

Threnody hung back, afraid to be so close to the big lizard, but Flex said, 'It's all right. Skar's friendly.'

The room was full of the hot metal smell of blood and the scent of the Kraitt himself, like an old leather coat thrown on a bonfire. The creature's yellow eyes found Threnody and then slid past her to Flex. A crudely modified headset had been attached to the side of his scaly face with actual rivets. His spiked tail twitched. He made a scraping, growling sound which Threnody's headset translated as 'What do you want, machine-person?'

'Just checking up on you,' said Flex. 'Just making sure the cactus lions haven't eaten you yet.'

The Kraitt let out a long hiss which was probably laughter. 'Those creatures are poor prey,' he said. 'I am a soldier of the clan of the Tzeld Gekh Resska. Your bouncy spiky animals are no match for me.'

'So how come every time I draw you there's a new scar on your snout?' asked Flex. She had her sketchpad out again, and she was drawing the Kraitt as he spoke. Threnody recognized him now; he had been the model for some of the drawings she had seen in the trainshed. 'If you don't like it here, why not leave?' Flex asked him. 'The war's over. You could go back home to your own people.'

'My people are defeated,' said Skar. 'My Tzeld Gekh is dead. I have no purpose and no honour. I have no home.' He drank from the glass in his hand, and blue smoke trailed from his nostrils and between his sharp, yellow teeth. *He is a dragon*, thought Threnody, fascinated and appalled. *He is a dragon out of some old legend, who has fallen on hard times*.

Skar's eyes met hers again. He snorted smoke and said, 'Who is this human female?'

'Just a friend of mine,' said Flex.

The Kraitt grunted, but his eyes stayed on Threnody's face. Was it possible that he recognized her? To Threnody most Kraitt looked much alike, but maybe Kraitt could distinguish more easily between human faces. The holoscreen glowed in the shadows behind him, tuned to some idiotic gossip site. A week ago it had probably been showing footage of Threnody with the Tzeld Gekh Karneiss, which was just the sort of thing to catch the attention of a Kraitt warrior. She drew back towards the doorway, but Skar seemed to have lost interest in her again. 'I am a soldier,' he told Flex. 'I should be fighting battles, not bouncy, spiky animals.'

But here he was. The last battle he had fought had been on Kzik'k, where the Tzeld Gekh Resska had led her troops so confidently to meet the feeble mammals who the Kraitt had called 'the new prey'. Only they had turned out not to be quite so feeble as Resska had promised: the armour of their wartrains could barely be dented by Kraitt weapons, and they had all sorts of other vehicles and machines, all far better than anything the Kraitt could field against them. They were *organized*, too; that was what had most intrigued Skar. He had seen with his own eyes hundreds of humans working together. If a hundred Kraitt had gathered in one place, they would fight each other and forget the enemy. There were only half that number on the lone Kraitt wartrain that carried the survivors out of Kzik'k after their last fortress fell, but they had squabbled furiously. Skar, who had been wounded in the final battle, hid in a wrecked gun turret while the rival factions battled from carriage to carriage, fighting over which of the juvenile females would be their new Tzeld Gekh.

He had slipped off the train as it crossed some junction world and found his way alone on other trains to the Hub, where he had started to learn more about the humans. The humans had been wary of him, even though he was alone and weaponless, but luckily he had met one whose auntie owned a riverside bar on Galatava and thought a real live Kraitt might draw a crowd.

He had been at the bar for a full season now. They paid him for his nightly fights with bottles of blue smoke and the use of this small room. He had not learned much about humans from the bar or its customers, but when he wasn't fighting he watched the holoscreen, slowly making sense of the jangling adverts and strange scenes which filled human media. He began to understand the difference between made-up stories and actual news. He learned that the leader of the humans was called Threnody Noon. He could recognize her picture now when he saw it on screens or money. It was reassuring that the humans were also led by their females, but Skar did not think Threnody Noon looked capable of fighting even a newly-hatched Kraitt. Even so, whole planets seemed to follow her. He had watched the Tzeld Gekh Karneiss herself bow down to her . . .

When Flex and her companion left him that night he turned back to his screen and started flicking randomly from site to site, looking for images of Threnody Noon. The scent of Flex's friend lingered in his nostrils. He was almost certain who she was, but he needed to be sure.

Humans thought Skar was stupid, but Skar was not stupid. He had just been biding his time, awaiting his chance to fight and kill again.

19

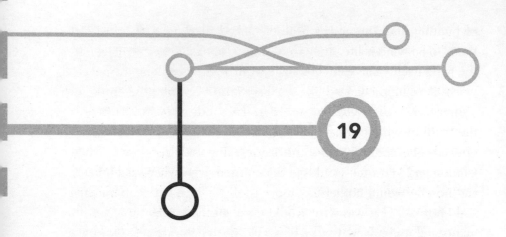

It felt good to be back in the open air. Behind the riverside buildings the sky was growing paler; in another hour sunrise would touch the high snow-peaks of the Hana Shan, but the streets of Jharana Chowk were still busy. Music wailed and thumped, laughter echoed down narrow alleyways, lost Monk bugs battered themselves against the neon ideograms of unknown alphabets. Threnody found herself relaxing, as if she had passed through some ordeal in that stuffy little room behind the bar and come out stronger for it. What did her grumbles about palace life matter when she had faced a real live Kraitt? She wondered if that was why Flex had taken her there, and how a Motorik came to have such a sharp insight into what humans were feeling. And she understood for the first time—really understood, with her heart, not just her brain—that what Zen Starling had told her was true: Motorik were people every bit as much as humans were.

And aliens are people too, she thought, looking from the placid Motorik who walked beside her to all the weird passers-by. A party of the Ones Who Remember the Sea flowed across the street in front of her on their land-adapted tentacles. Down by the riverside, a small colony of Hath had planted themselves in the shallows, membranes spread to catch the night breeze. Their voices were like the fluttering of bunting, but Threnody's headset picked them up and translated them. 'The wind is life,' they were saying, to each other or maybe to the wind itself. 'The wind is change.' A little further along the beach, wormlike Chmoii danced like the diagrams of complicated knots.

Everywhere will be like this one day, Threnody thought. That was the truth of what had happened when the new gate on Khoorsandi opened. She could imagine this station in a hundred years, when Chmoii and Herastec would be as common everywhere as humans, and no one would bother any more to distinguish between humans and Motorik. That was what would make all the boring trade agreements and diplomacy worthwhile. That was what made it so important that the Noons kept control of their own worlds, and did not let Elon Prell roll in and shut humans off from their alien neighbours again.

'It is late, Lady Threnody,' said Flex.

But Threnody was enchanted by the night. 'Let's walk to the falls,' she said. 'If you're not too tired?' And then she laughed, because how could Flex be tired?

They walked past sleeping houses and shuttered riverside cafés and out of the city's edge along a path with the river on one side and sighing trees on the other. The path glowed softly with stored sunlight, guiding them towards the viewing platforms on the bluffs above the Kathkai Falls. Birds called in the palmetto groves, and overhead the rings of Galatava arched from horizon to horizon like the ghost of a colossal rainbow. Once Threnody's dragonflies alerted her to movements among the trees somewhere behind them, but when she sent one to check it out there was nothing there. The next time they alerted her, she ignored them. The riverside park was well stocked with harmless wildlife, and a favourite place for lovers. Threnody was not going to let herself be afraid of every rustle in the undergrowth.

She told the drones to be less twitchy and walked on, matching Flex's steady stride. Ahead, the noise of the falls was like a busy road, like an endless passing train. Mist rose into the air above the place where the river plunged over the last steep cliffs before the sea.

'It reminds me of where I used to live,' said Flex. 'There were waterfalls there too, but not so pretty.'

'I've only ever seen the Kathkai from the air,' admitted Threnody.

'Really? Oh, you have to see them from the cliff-side paths. You have to stand in the spray of them, and feel the thunder shaking everything! I'll show you my favourite places . . .'

But they did not reach the falls. A few hundred metres before the first viewing platform there was a sudden clattering sound of small objects hitting the path like a flung handful of gravel. Threnody turned to see what Flex made of it, and saw her fall stiffly sideways, like a statue toppled off a pedestal. Threnody blinked an emergency code into her headset and waited for her dragonflies to defend her, but while she was still blinking she realized that the things which had fallen around her *were* her dragonflies, and that her headset had stopped working.

Someone came out of the darkness under the trees and she recognized the young man who had watched her earlier in the bar. His smile was as cute as she had imagined. A Sundarbani manga character did dances on his smart-fabric tee as he unsealed his tunic and pulled out a gun. 'I had to be sure it was you, Lady Noon,' he said, as if he were apologizing for keeping Threnody waiting. 'I never expected to find you alone out here.'

Threnody stood numbly, watching the gun come up to point at her. A green light on its side turned red as the man thumbed the safety off. Should she run? Should she scream? Who would hear her above the thunder of the falls?

'Compliments of the Emperor,' said the man, and then, as Threnody tensed for the shot, something hit him from the side like traffic and slammed him off the path and down into the dry grass by the river. The gun went off. By its sharp flash she saw—for the space of one quick heartbeat—the dinosaur face of Skar. The Kraitt was crouched over the sprawled man and his teeth were bared, ready to rip out his victim's throat.

'No!' she shouted.

The Kraitt swung his head towards her, a nightmare silhouette against the faint light of the river. He gave a soft hiss, and Threnody realized that he was questioning her. He must have been tracking the assassin while the assassin was tracking her, and now he wanted to know why he should not just kill his prey.

'We need him alive,' she said. 'Please. My security people will want to question him . . .'

Skar just crouched there unmoving. She could see the faint light of his yellow eyes as he watched her. The injured man was whimpering beneath him. Threnody wondered if she was asking too much. The Kraitt were primitive; she could not expect this one to ignore his killer instincts. He would probably kill the gunman and then kill her too, maddened by the taste of human blood . . .

But after a moment Skar hissed again, and slowly stood upright.

'Thank you,' said Threnody.

Her headset had found a way round whatever virus the assassin had used to shut it down. It flashed start-up messages and error warnings as it came back to life, scanning Threnody's heart rate and adrenalin levels and pinging distress calls to Noon security. While she waited for them to come to her she smiled uneasily at the Kraitt. 'You followed us from the city,' she said.

'I wished to speak with you,' Skar replied. 'Then I scented this miserable *K'etekk* following you.'

'What did you want to speak to me about?'

'It is not fitting that the Tzeld Gekh of the humans walks her city with only the machine-person Flex to guard her. Tzeld Gekhs of the Kraitt have many males of the soldier caste to serve and protect them. I know this, for I was once a soldier to the Tzeld Gekh Resska.

Now the Tzeld Gekh Resska is dead and I am leaderless. I wish to be your soldier, Tzeld Gekh Threnody.'

Threnody could not think of a reply to that, except to stammer, 'Th-thank you,' again in a voice so small she wasn't sure the Kraitt would hear her. On the path Flex was stirring, sitting up. Beyond her the lights of the station city glittered in the early morning river. Six smaller lights detached themselves from the rest and came rushing fast and low across the water.

Threnody found her voice and put herself between Skar and the river as the howl of drone engines started to become audible over the rumble of the falls. Her headset was full of bots and agents asking if she was safe. She shouted back, 'Don't shoot him! Don't shoot the Kraitt! He's a friend!'

20

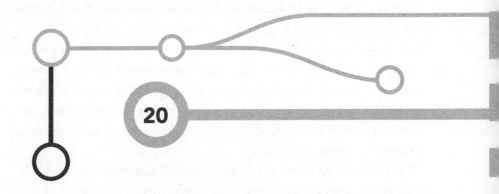

Zen had not imagined that there would be tides on a world without moons, but when he woke, something had drawn back the sea to bare a wide, shining smile of wet sand in the bay below the house. He walked there with Nova after breakfast, pressing deep footprints into the sand, remembering Desdemor. The far-off sea mumbled like a remorseful drunk, ashamed of its wild behaviour in the night.

'There is a reason . . .' Nova began.

'Why you brought me here?'

'As well as just wanting to see you. I wanted that of course. And I wanted you to see this place, where it all started. It felt all wrong without you here. Every new thing I found, I wanted to show you. But also . . .'

'What?' Zen had been sensing trouble since he arrived, and now he felt that he was drawing close to it.

'When I was repairing myself after our adventures with the Kraitt I found a locked file hidden deep in my start-up codes. The only person who could have put it there was Raven. The only thing in it was information. Articles copied from the data rafts of dozens of worlds. They were all about a place called Petrichor.'

Zen had learned a lot of odd facts about the Great Network while he was a kid, but he didn't think there were many facts worth learning about Petrichor. From what he could remember it was just a dead-end world way out beyond Luna Verde on a spur of the Spiral Line.

'Some sort of cult live there, don't they?'

'Yes. They're fans of the Guardian Vohu Mana. There's a famous data shrine there. Petrichor is Vohu Mana's world; none of the other Guardians even bothers to keep a presence there.'

'So why did Raven load all this information about it into your deep memory?'

'I think he left something valuable on Petrichor. Something that he wanted me to find if anything happened to him.'

'Like what? A copy of his will?'

'A copy of himself. His personality.'

'But there are no copies!' Zen said, so loudly that his voice came back to him as echoes off the cliffs, louder than the sea. 'The Guardians destroyed every trace of Raven! Every reference to him!' *And good riddance*, he almost added. It had been Raven who had manipulated Zen and Nova into causing the Noon train crash. But Nova had known Raven longer. Raven had started her, so was perhaps the closest thing she had to a parent. She had mourned him when he died, and Zen did not want to hurt her feelings.

'There's nothing left of him in the Datasea,' he said gently. 'Barely a mention of his name. The Guardians are thorough. They'd hardly have left a whole copy of his personality floating around, waiting for us to find it.'

'What do we know about Vohu Mana?' Nova asked him.

Zen shrugged. Unlike most human beings he had actually met the Guardians. The others had appeared like gods or demons in their digital realm, but Vohu Mana had been just a prickly little voice coming out of a hedge.

'Some people believe that Vohu Mana is building Heaven,' said Nova. 'A huge virtual environment in the dark Datasea, full of avatars based on everyone who has ever lived. They think that as long as you make sure to put enough information about yourself online while you're alive, Vohu Mana will be able to resurrect a digital version of you after you die.'

'And you think that's true?' asked Zen.

'Well, it's just the sort of hobby a Guardian might have—collecting copies of everybody. And there were once lots of copies of Raven's personality in the Datasea; it was kind of his thing. So perhaps when the other Guardians started deleting those copies, Vohu Mana might have saved one for his collection.'

'And hidden it on Petrichor?'

'Why not? Petrichor's so backward and out of the way that nobody even bothers to think about it. Its only attraction is the shrine of Vohu Mana, where people go to upload their memories. That shrine must have a massive storage system. Maybe there's a secret bit where a copy of Raven is kept.'

'And you want us to go there and look?'

'I want us to go there and steal it.'

'But why?' Zen said. 'Raven had a good innings; he lived hundreds of rich, full lives. Why not just let him rest in peace?'

'Because his work isn't finished,' said Nova.

'Not finished?' Zen said. 'Yes it is! Raven made a K-gate! He opened the way onto the Web of Worlds! He changed history!'

Nova started to say something and then stopped and thought a moment. She scrambled up onto one of the bleached tree trunks which lay on the shingle at the back of the beach. The wind blew her hair about and flapped the hem of her dress. 'Look,' she said, and pointed to the sky above the sea, where a tiny moon was rising. Only it wasn't a moon, of course. It was one of the structures on the inside of the sphere which surrounded this world and its sun.

'That's what I call the Ziggurat,' she said.

'It must be enormous!'

'It is. I went up there once. There's a K-gate in the mountains north of here which leads to a gate on the inner surface of the sphere, quite close to the Ziggurat. I've been inside . . .' She looked wistful. 'It's like an abandoned palace, Zen. No, it's like an abandoned *person*. When I first came here I assumed the central tower was where the Railmaker had lived, but I was wrong. The Ziggurat was the Railmaker. It was its brain. But it's a brain without a mind now, without a consciousness. The intelligence that used to fill it is gone.'

Zen reached out and touched her sandy foot, the only part of her he could reach. He felt sorry for her. She had come so far looking for the Railmaker, and she had come too late.

'The Railmaker was made of data, like the Guardians,' she went on. 'But it wasn't just lots of copies scattered on different worlds, like they are, updating themselves all the time as trains carry information through the K-gates. The Railmaker lived there, in the Ziggurat, and sent its Station Angels out across the Network to bring back information so that it always knew what was going on everywhere. It was connected directly to its nine hubs, and maybe to all its other stations too. In a way, the Railmaker didn't just build the K-bahn, it *was* the K-bahn. A living railway system.'

'That's why it was so vulnerable to the Guardians' attack,' said Zen. 'If there was just one of it, then once the virus reached it . . .'

'But I think it had a defence,' said Nova.

'It probably had lots, but it doesn't look like any of them worked.'

'But what if there was a last-ditch emergency system, designed to save a copy of it?' She sat down on the log, rested her head on her knees, wrapped her arms around her shins, and looked earnestly at him. 'Imagine if, when it realized it was dying, the Railmaker broadcast a backup copy of itself. Maybe thousands of them. Just blared them out into the cosmos in the hope that one of its hubs or somebody else would pick one up. And imagine one of those copies found its way into the Network Empire's Datasea. It got lost down there in the deeps, and then, somehow, after a long, long time, it got downloaded into a human body. A cloned embryo, which grew into a human child with the Railmaker personality imprinted in its brain.'

Zen took a deep breath and connected that unlikely idea to the unlikely idea she had been talking about earlier. 'You mean Raven?'

'Yes.'

'How?'

'I don't know. Maybe Raven's parents had genetic upgrades made before he was born, like most posh parents do, and the Railmaker code hacked the geneticist's systems and downloaded itself without anyone noticing.'

'And I suppose Raven never mentioned to you that he was actually a million-year-old data-entity?'

'He didn't know,' said Nova. 'The Railmaker personality was so old, and so damaged, Raven didn't know that he was carrying it. But when he met Anais Six, she sensed it somehow. She didn't know that he was the Railmaker, but she knew that he should be more than human. And when she gave him access to the Datasea he was driven to seek out the secrets of the Worms and the gates, so that he could get back here.'

Zen didn't doubt her exactly. Nova was much smarter than him, and he'd seldom known her be wrong about anything. 'It seems such a reach,' he said helplessly. 'Just because Raven got lucky with Anais Six, and then got interested in the K-gates, I don't see how that proves he was the Railmaker.'

'I just know it,' said Nova. 'Some of the code that the surviving Railmaker systems use—it's very advanced, there's a lot I can't understand yet, but there are touches that are so like the programmes Raven wrote . . . He wrote a lot of my code, so I know his *style*. It's like recognizing the way a particular musician puts a melody together. I kept thinking when I was exploring the Black Light Zone, *Raven has been here*. And I didn't think it could be true, until I came to this place. Then I was sure. And when I went up into the Ziggurat . . . I could feel it *wanting* something; wanting me to give back what was torn from it.'

'So if we go to Petrichor and steal a copy of Raven . . .'

'When we upload it into the Ziggurat, and he has access to all the Railmaker's systems again, he will understand what he is. The Railmaker will be resurrected, and it can carry on its work. It was nowhere near finished when the Guardians killed it, Zen; there are so many worlds still waiting to be linked to the Network. But the only way I can restore it is if I bring Raven here.'

'But how can you get him off Petrichor? If his personality is locked in Vohu Mana's data shrine . . .'

'That's why I need your help,' she said. 'People from all over the Network Empire go to upload their diaries and selfies straight to that shrine. Some of them bring Motorik couriers with the memories stored in their minds. We'll tell people your grandmother died unexpectedly and you're making a pilgrimage to the shrine to upload her information. I'll print a version of me that can pass for a standard Motorik servant, and fake some social media records to fill its memory with. Once I'm inside the shrine, I should be able to find the Raven personality. But I can't do it without you, my love.'

She looked at him so adoringly that Zen felt flattered, even though he knew that she was trying to flatter him. Knowing that someone whose mind could run a whole planet and 239 different bodies at once still needed the help of Zen Starling was quite a boost for the ego. The idea of a new adventure tugged at him too, promising the things adventures always promised: *This time nothing will go wrong; this time your plans will all work out*. But he was wise to adventures by now. This Petrichor trip would be way beyond risky. He'd be a fool to do it just because Nova was looking at him like that, all sad and hopeful.

And then a new thought came, overtaking the others the way a K-bahn express might sweep past little local trains puttering along parallel tracks. If bringing Raven here would bring the Railmaker back to life, that would cancel out the terrible thing the Guardians had done to it. And if Zen could do that, perhaps it would make up for the terrible things that he had done himself. Then, next time he woke in the night thinking, *I wrecked the Noon train*, he might be able to ease the awful guilt by telling himself, *But I brought the Railmaker back from the dead*.

'All right,' he said. 'If you want something stolen from Heaven, I'm your man. But I want this version of you with me, not one of those others. We can make you look different.'

'Well if I *look* different, I might as well be a whole different unit,' said Nova.

'I want this one with me,' Zen said firmly. 'Like the old days.'

21

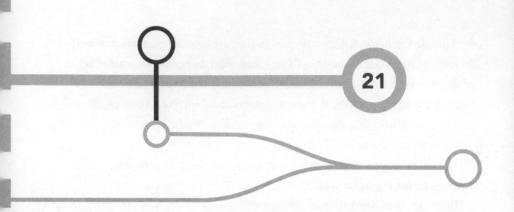

Threnody had never seen her uncle Nilesh angry before. He had always been such a mild sort of uncle when he was just Stationmaster of sleepy little Khoorsandi. Helping to run so many other Noon worlds seemed to have given him a temper, Threnody thought. She sat and listened while he told her how foolish she had been, as if she were a naughty pupil caught playing truant from some pricey finishing school. Or maybe he was making a show of anger to please Kala Tanaka, who stood listening a little way behind him. Other people had been and gone—doctors, Noon CoMa officers, people from Kala Tanaka's office—but now it was just Kala and Nilesh and Threnody, and he was shouting at her.

'Do you not even read your security briefings? We have known for months that Elon Prell has agents on this planet. Yet you leave the palace alone, at night, and go for a walk in the least secure part of the city . . .'

They were in Nilesh's study on the ground floor of the palace, a high, comfortable room with a curved glass wall looking out on a little garden where a fountain played. The first sunbeams of the Galatavan dawn were shining through the leaves of the giant horsetail ferns, throwing shadows of the dancing water over the room's live-wood panelling and comfortable bio-furniture.

‘That lad who jumped you was a hired killer from Gosinchand,’ Nilesh went on. ‘Either the Prells sent him here, or he came here of his own accord, knowing the Prells would reward him for your murder. I doubt he could believe his luck when you decided to go walking all alone through Jharana Chowk!’

‘I wasn’t all alone,’ said Threnody. ‘I was with Flex.’

‘And how do we know Flex wasn’t part of the plot, leading you to where the killer lay in wait?’

‘Because she wasn’t,’ said Threnody. ‘Because it was my idea to walk to the falls. And anyway, I had my drones . . .’

‘And the assassin had a cyber-weapon capable of knocking out your drones, your headset, *and* your Motorik friend!’ Nilesh said triumphantly.

‘But it doesn’t matter, does it?’ said Threnody, who was tired of being told off. ‘It doesn’t matter, because Skar saved me.’

‘That renegade Kraitt, yes. We are questioning him now.’

‘I questioned him myself,’ said Threnody. ‘He is a warrior, and now that his own leaders are defeated he wants to fight for us. He followed me to pledge his loyalty. It was just luck that the assassin gave him a chance to prove it.’

‘That does make some sense,’ said Kala Tanaka calmly. It was the first time she had spoken. ‘Our cultural experts claim the Kraitt admire our soldiers’ fighting abilities, and envy our weapons. They are also used to following female leaders.’

‘I think we should recruit more of them to fight for us,’ said Threnody.

‘Fight who?’ asked Nilesh.

‘The Prells, of course.’ Threnody stood up and went to the window. The sun was fully risen now, the planet’s rings almost invisible in the turquoise early morning sky. She had been awake all night but she didn’t *feel* as if she had been awake all night. She remembered very clearly the realization that had come to her as she walked among the mingled crowds of aliens and humans: that there was something here she needed to protect. 'There must be no more talk of negotiating with the Prells,' she said. 'We have to fight them.'

Nilesh smiled what Threnody always thought of as his we'll-think-about-it smile; the smile that meant Threnody was asking for something he did not want to give her, but was too polite to refuse outright. 'That is impossible, Threnody. We have run countless simulations. If we started a war, we would certainly lose. The Prells have more troops and more wartrains than we do. In a way it's a good thing if they are hiring assassins; it's a clear sign the Guardians are not yet willing to let them launch an all-out attack. This is the perfect time to negotiate with them. You will travel to Grand Central as planned.'

'And what if they keep me there? Or kill me?'

'It would be very embarrassing for the Emperor if any harm were to befall you while you are his guest.'

Threnody looked at him, and at Kala, and saw that she was not going to win. However much she argued, she would still end up aboard the *Damask Rose* in a few days, taking the long journey to Grand Central. But she wanted some small victory over them; last night felt too important for everything to just carry on exactly as before. She wanted to prove to herself that she was not just their puppet.

'I want Flex to come,' she said. 'As my official artist.'

Nilesh looked cautiously at Kala. Kala said, 'I don't see why not. The Motorik has made a name for itself; it will play well on social media if Threnody takes it with her.'

'And I want a new bodyguard,' said Threnody. 'I want the Kraitt, Skar.'

'That would not be appropriate,' said her uncle.

'Why not?' asked Threnody. She lifted her chin and looked at him down the length of her long Noon nose. 'If a Kraitt is willing to fight for us, why shouldn't I have him as my bodyguard? I want Skar transferred to my staff.'

'But, Threnody, my dear . . .'

'Am I Chief Executive or aren't I?' she demanded. 'What is the point of being Chief Executive if I cannot have a little thing like this when I ask for it?'

'I would so much rather you let us find you a new bodyguard, if you are unhappy with the bodyguards Noon Security has provided,' said her uncle, but softly, almost pleadingly. He had realized that his anger had no effect on her at all and decided to try a different approach.

'I want the Kraitt,' said Threnody. 'I trust him.'

Nilesh looked furious for a second, then oddly shy, then thoughtful. Finally, he smiled and bowed. 'Of course, Lady Threnody,' he said.

'I shall go and make the arrangements,' said Kala.

Threnody held her breath until they had both left the room. Then she let it all out in a raggedy sigh. It wasn't much, just standing up to them, but it was something. Maybe someone who could stand up to Uncle Nilesh and the efficient Kala T could stand up to Elon Prell.

PART FOUR

THE HEAVEN HEIST

22

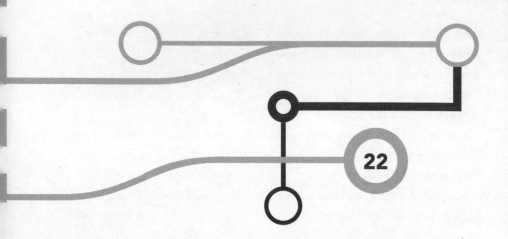

Zen and Nova were back in the Network Empire, following a hiking trail through the mountains of a small forest world called Himmapaan. Ahead, where the hills descended to the lake country, the lights of Himmapaan Station City flickered in the twilight. Night was coming, and nights on Himmapaan lasted for six weeks, but Nova said that was good—all the tourists would be going home, so she and Zen would not be the only travellers leaving on the next train.

Zen had expected her to open a K-gate straight to Petrichor, but she had said it was not that simple. She still did not know enough about how the gates worked, and Petrichor was a long way from Station Zero; the gate might be unstable. Besides, it was important that they arrive at Vohu Mana's data shrine like ordinary pilgrims, on a normal train. So they had come to Himmapaan, where they could board the Interstellar Express like any other traveller; it would take them to Luna Verde, and there they would catch a connecting train to Petrichor.

They had arrived ten hours earlier through a K-gate Nova had opened in the bottom of a gorge a day's march north of the K-bahn line. The gorge was deep, and Himmapaan so dull that the Guardians paid it little attention, so with luck the opening of the gate had gone unnoticed. It had closed as soon as the *Sunbird* had let them off and shot back to Station Zero. Three days from today one of Nova's other selves on Station Zero would open it again and send a Station Angel through, and if Zen and Nova had returned from Petrichor by then the angel would detect them and go back and send the *Sunbird* through to pick them up.

It seemed a precarious sort of plan to Zen, but it was working so far—there had been no sign that anyone knew the gate had opened. He just wished it wasn't such a long walk to the station city. His legs ached, his feet hurt, and the protein bars Nova had stocked his hiker's backpack with were no substitute for real food. He had spent ten lazy, wonderful days on Station Zero, some of the best days of his life, but already they were starting to feel like a dream.

He had changed his identity again. He couldn't ride the K-bahn as Zen Starling, and after what had gone down on Klef he couldn't be Ty Sharma any more. Nova had wanted to make him female, but he didn't fancy that. ('You're so old fashioned,' she'd said. 'You'd make a really cute girl, and nobody would connect you with Zen Starling then.') In the end he had become Ajay Lackwing, a young man from Galatava; he could imitate a Galatavan accent well enough to fool anyone who wasn't Galatavan themselves, and the ID Nova had faked for him was good enough to pass any checks he was likely to encounter. His hair was its natural black again, and shorter than he had worn it for years.

Nova looked different, too. She had clicked some reset button in her deep menus and in the space of a few hours all the adjustments she had ever made to herself had disappeared. Her freckles were gone, her nose was smaller, her eyes less bright, her hair a dull black. It was no longer possible to tell if she was meant to be a girl or a boy, especially in the grey overalls she wore, made from thick paper. Zen knew that he had made a terrible mistake when he had asked his Nova to come with him. All that was left of her old self was her laughter and the strange facial expressions she had invented for herself, and even those would vanish soon. 'It's easy to give up habits when you're a Motorik,' she said. 'You just turn them off.'

'You're remembering it all, though?' asked Zen. 'The freckles and the rest of it? You can switch it all back on when this is over?'

Nova shook her head. 'I've deleted all that. If anyone scans my mind, I don't want them finding a lot of strange code in there. It's all gone. I'll bin my memories, too, if it comes to it. But don't worry. I can restore it all once we get back to Station Zero and I can sync with the rest of me.'

'But what if you can't? What if something goes wrong?'

'Then you'll just have to remind me what I used to look like, and I'll make some new freckles.'

But I am already forgetting, thought Zen. He guessed that she must imagine human memories were like her machine ones—that everything he had ever seen or done was waiting in his head to be retrieved. But human memories didn't work that way; they faded, and most things were just lost. He could not remember where each and every one of her freckles went.

There were a hundred much more serious and pressing things to worry about, but the loss of Nova's freckles worried him more than any of them.

The Interstellar Express used to start on Sundarban and call at Marapur and K'mbussi and then all the major stops to Cleave, on the far side of the Network. Now that the Empire had split in two, it began its journey on K'mbussi, and was still mostly empty when it drew into Himmapaan, the next stop up the line. Zen found a corner seat in a half-deserted carriage near the front of the train. Nova went into the luggage van at the back, sat down between some crates, and pinged him the bland sort of message any Moto might ping its master, just to let him know that she was safe.

'Welcome aboard the Interstellar,' said the big gold loco, as it swept out of Himmapaan Station City and gathered speed on the long straight beside the lake. 'My name is the *Veils of the Morning*. I will be stopping at Tarsind, Grand Central, Bandarpet, Nicobar...'

Zen stayed tense all the way to Grand Central, the heart of the Empire. Portraits of Elon Prell scowled down at the train there as if they sensed a fugitive aboard, and blue-armoured Railforce troops stood guard on the platform. But no one challenged Zen, and after that he sank into a train-trance as K-gate after K-gate flashed past. He slept, and woke, and ate, and watched the passing views, and the *Veils of the Morning* sang its songs until time seemed to stretch out lazily into a long now, a journey that would never end.

And then it did end, and he was standing on a platform at Luna Verde Station, watching the train pull away. At the far end of the platform, where smart trunks and suitcases were revving their little engines and trundling off after their owners, Nova stood in her grey paper overalls like a dummy in a dowdy shopfront. He sauntered over to her and said, 'You all right, Moto?' and she replied, 'Yes, sir,' in a voice so flat that he wondered if she even knew who he was, or if she had junked her memories on Grand Central or Bandarpet to dodge the security scans.

But just as he was turning away, when she was quite sure that nobody was watching, she winked at him.

They spent half the night in the waiting room at Luna Verde, then boarded the connection to Petrichor: a grumpy little McQue 5-90 towing a line of container cars and a single, empty passenger carriage. An hour later they were on Petrichor. Rain beaded the windows and the train hummed a miserable little song to itself as it chugged through acres of derelict rail yard to a single platform. 'Alight here for Petrichor Station City,' it said. 'Though I don't know why you'd want to. It's a dump.'

23

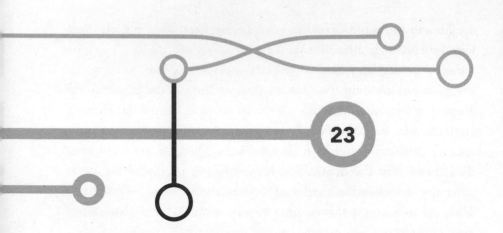

The hunting at Azure Bay turned out to be far better than Elon Prell had expected. The Noons had held power on Grand Central for over a hundred years, and their genetic engineers had used that time wisely, stocking the planet's hunting reserves with perfect prey. Elon Prell did not remember much about Old Earth animals, so he wasn't sure if the plesiosaurs which lived among the cliffs and coral forests of the bay were accurate re-creations, but he did not care. They were as fast as marlin, as cunning as foxes, and as fierce as tigers when you cornered them. To an Emperor in search of good hunting that was all that mattered.

The bay was beautiful as well—weathered red cliffs descending into blue water, with a few moons hanging over the sea most of the time—the kind of hard, mineral landscape where a Prell felt at home. Nothing hard about the summer palace which old Mahalaxmi Noon had built there though; a comfortable beach-house with rooms for an Emperor and his retinue, it could slide on rails down the steep slope of the continental shelf to become an underwater hunting lodge. And the professional hunter who lived there year-round was a woman named Sedna Yamm, whose family had tweaked their genome generations back to make life easier for themselves on the deep ranges of the ocean moon T'ien Fei. She had fish-pale skin and transparent eyelids and she could close her nostrils like a seal, which Elon Prell found surprisingly attractive.

Each morning he would wake early and spend a few hours in his study, communicating with his deputies in the station city, reading dispatches from his wartrains on the Spiral Line, where the Human Unity League had taken advantage of the recent upheavals to start another of their wretched little rebellions. Then the palace would slide down into the depths and he would put on his diving gear, enter the airlock in the corner of his suite, and follow Sedna Yamm fearlessly down into the twilight depths, pursuing the plesiosaurs through forests of kelp and frozen explosions of multi-coloured coral. Each evening, when the palace heaved itself ashore again and the Emperor and his household gathered on the beach to barbecue the day's catch, Sedna Yamm would tell them tales of the Grandfather of all Plesiosaurs, a monster who laired in the deep caves at the base of a sea stack a few kilometres offshore. It had killed six hunters, Sedna said, and its thick hide was a pincushion of old harpoons. Some of those harpoons had belonged to Emperor Mahalaxmi, who had tried and failed to catch it for ten years.

One night, while he waited for his chefs to cook the food, Elon Prell stalked down the beach to where the small evening waves were spreading out their lacework on the sand. He glared at the stack, which stood dark against the double sunset like a raised middle finger. He thought about the Grandfather of all Plesiosaurs lurking down there in the depths, and about Mahalaxmi, who had failed to kill it. He wondered if the reason he did not feel like Network Emperor was that he had not killed Mahalaxmi in battle, just plucked the throne out of the hands of his useless daughter after the Noon train crash had done the job for him.

In the air in front of him two little girls appeared. A little black girl in a white dress and a little white girl in a black dress. Their bare feet hung a few centimetres above the breaking waves, and their golden eyes regarded the Emperor bleakly.

He glanced behind him. The rest of his party were talking among themselves, standing around the barbecue where the plesiosaur joints were roasting, or on the verandahs of the summer palace. None of them could see the apparition. He took off his headset and the little girls vanished. He put it back, and there they were, much closer now.

'Boo,' they said.

'I've been waiting to hear from you,' said Elon Prell, trying to sound brusque, as he always had when dealing with the Twins, to show them that, while he respected them, he was not afraid of them. He did feel afraid though, and also a trembling anticipation and a strange sort of sadness. He guessed they had come to tell him that he had their permission to storm the K'mbussi gate and crush the Noons, and that meant he would have to leave this place. 'It's on then?' he asked, waiting before he spoke so that the soft crash of a breaking wave would cover his words. 'Our wartrains can roll?'

'Patience, Elon Prell,' said the Twins. They spoke in unison. In his headset it sounded like one voice. 'We cannot let you start your war yet. We do not have the power we did. The others do not trust us. But we have seen something that they have not seen.'

'What have you seen?'

'Faces. In the Datasea. On the feed from a security camera. Just two faces out of all the faces on all the security cameras at all the stations. Not many people would have spotted them. Not many people would have recognized them. But we are clever.'

'Whose faces?'

'Zen Starling. The Motorik Nova. They were on their way to Petrichor. They are probably there by now.'

'Why? It's a dump.'

'We do not know why, Elon Prell. We have no presence on Petrichor, and if we try to spy there our foolish brother Vohu Mana will cause trouble for us with the others.'

'But you're the Twins!' said Elon Prell. 'You're not scared of the other Guardians, are you?'

The little girls hung their heads. The last time the Twins had appeared to him, they had come as flesh and blood: two stone-cold killers called the Mako brothers. Elon Prell guessed that their new form was a way of showing him how much their power had been reduced. The other Guardians were treating the Twins like naughty children, keeping them in their room so that they could not interfere in human lives. They were probably risking all sorts of punishments by sneaking here in virtual form to talk with him.

'I don't have people on Petrichor,' he said. 'But I could send a Railforce unit through from the base on Luna Verde.'

The Twins smiled at him. 'Send them in secret. The other Guardians are not to know. Bring Zen and the Nova entity to Grand Central. She will go quietly if you threaten him. Question them. We will help. We will find out what they are up to. We will learn what the Nova entity is planning. And then we will find the excuse we need to let you launch your war.'

Then they were gone, and he was just looking at the waves again, at moons shining in the lilac afterglow above the sea. His nephew Vasili was calling to him from further up the beach. 'I'm coming,' he said. He used the secure software in his headset to encode a message and ping it into the Datasea. He estimated it would take a day for his orders to reach Luna Verde, another for Railforce to capture Starling and Nova and bring them back to Grand Central. So that gave him two more days of hunting before he had to get on with the serious business of conquering the galaxy.

He turned and strode back up the beach, into the light of the hovering paper-lantern drones and the smell of the barbecue. He found Sedna Yamm. How overawed she would be, he told himself, if she knew that he had just been talking to the Guardians themselves. But he dared not share their secrets, so he told her something else that he felt sure would impress her. 'I've decided something,' he said. 'I'm going to hunt the Grandfather of all Plesiosaurs, and kill it. I'm going to take its hide back to the Imperial Palace. Turn it into a rug or a wall hanging or something. I'll show everyone that a Prell can succeed where a soft Noon failed.'

24

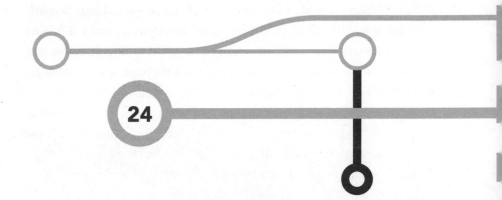

During his stay on Station Zero, Zen had studied Nova's files on Petrichor as if he were boning up for an exam, so the dismal little world did not come as a surprise to him. He knew that most of its surface was covered by something called the Moss, which couldn't decide if it was a very wet bog or a very weedy ocean. Petrichor had only been terraformed and settled because it had a second K-gate which led to a mineral-rich but uninhabitable world called Kolrabi. The Berberian family, who did the settling and terraforming, lived on Petrichor and sent their drones and Motorik through this second gate to mine Kolrabi, until the day when Kolrabi's sun unexpectedly exploded and Petrichor was left as a useless stopping-off point on a railroad to nowhere.

There were no customs booths at the station. There weren't even the security checks that had become common in the central Network. The ticket barriers at the end of the platform stood open. Zen and Nova went through them and out into the tiny city, Nova keeping a few paces behind with her eyes on the ground like a Motorik that knew its place. It was dusk, and raining a little. When Zen logged into the local data raft he saw that it had been raining a little for seventy-six years. Wet streets shone, and low buildings hunched their shoulders against the damp. The derelict gantries and conveyor belts of the old rail yards loomed behind the rain like dinosaur skeletons. The symbol of Vohu Mana—a watchful eye—was painted on walls and over doorways. Passers-by wore rain capes and strange hats from which cameras hung on rods, pointing backwards at the wearer's face. Whenever two people met, they greeted each other by posing together for selfies. Behind the steamy windows of small restaurants, people solemnly photographed their meals. The more details of their lives they could upload, the more accurately Vohu Mana would be able to recreate them in his virtual afterlife.

The weather news was pretty much the only thing of interest in the Petrichori data raft, which was the most primitive that Zen had ever seen. He explored it that night, sleepless in a big bed in the city's one hotel. There were just a few banks and shopping sites, a lot of Vohu Mana data-prayer nodes, and some small, half-hearted shrines to the other Guardians. The tourist information hub couldn't show him much about Petrichor that he didn't already know. There was a local ghost story about something called the Slow Train, and unconvincing rumours of a giant octopus that lived in the deeper parts of the Moss. That was all. *This can't be right*, he thought. *There can't be anything important in a place like this.*

He wanted to ask Nova if she could see something he couldn't among the data, but Nova was downstairs, shut in a cupboard which the hotel rather grandly called its Motorik Dormitory. He remembered lying awake like this in his cabin on the Noon Train while she travelled with the other Motos in some luggage van, and how her voice had come into his headset, keeping him company, keeping his spirits up, letting him know that he was not alone. But it was different now. He knew the weight of what he was doing, and the danger Nova would be in if the Guardians recognized her. He longed to hear her voice, even if it was only saying, 'Good night Zen, sleep well,' but he dared not message her, so he took off his headset and tossed it to the far side of the room and lay lonely in the dark while the gutterings gurgled and the rain drummed its small, cold fingers on the roof.

Nova was waiting for him in the lobby next morning, under the stuffed and mounted head of a mouldy, antlered thing called a Moss elk. A few of the hotel's other guests had come to Petrichor to hunt these beasts, but most were pilgrims, and some of them had brought Motorik with them, so Zen did not feel too conspicuous as he went with Nova down the misty plastic tunnel which led to the taxi rank. 'The shrine of Vohu Mana,' he told the taxi.

It took them north through the city until buildings gave way to scrub and empty lots, then steeply-terraced paddy fields where yellow machines were working. The road rose, passing groves of bamboo, and drab blue trees, and crags whose heads were hidden in the clouds. The taxi joined a queue of other cars, red tail lights edging through a narrow pass between wet cliffs. Then a downhill stretch, the light of a lake in the valley floor, a covered car park, a glass-walled visitor centre. They got out of the taxi. Polite attendants with green uniforms and the watchful eyes of kindly policemen pointed them to the winding covered pathway which would take them to the shrine. There were plenty of other pilgrims walking along it, and plenty of other Motorik walking with them. An old man in the colourful robes of Gosinchand called out as Zen overtook him, 'I'm glad to see a young fellow like you still taking the trouble to bring a courier with you.'

'My granny kept copies of all her social media activity in this wire dolly's head,' said Zen. 'I've come to upload them to the shrine.'

The old man grinned and nodded, pleased to meet a youth with so much respect for his elders. 'When I was your age, everyone had to bring a Moto to carry that much information. Nowadays, headsets are so powerful that a lot of people just store it all in those. But I always think a Moto is more dignified.' He turned to yell at his own

Motorik, which had fallen behind. 'I come every year to upload my videos and diaries,' he confided. 'Your grandmother is lucky to have you to do it for her. Now you go ahead, young fellow, go ahead—no need to walk at the speed of my old feet...'

Zen thanked him and went on. Nova followed respectfully, keeping her eyes on the ground. The path led them through a screen of dark trees, and suddenly ahead of him Zen saw the shrine.

The Guardians had built their data centres and memory stores on dozens of inhabited worlds (and on hundreds of uninhabited ones too). Most were just dull door-less buildings or underground wedges of computer storage. Here and there, for whimsical reasons of their own, one Guardian or another had tried something different, like the Valley of Statues on Grand Central, or the Jade Maze of Anais Six on Ashtoreth. Since Vohu Mana had appeared to Zen only as a small rustling creature hidden in a hedgerow, he had not expected anything too spectacular from its shrine on Petrichor. But Vohu Mana had other avatars, it seemed, or had once, and had carved a whole Petrichori mountain into the likeness of one of them. The mountain's lower slopes had become a woman's shoulders, clad in emerald green moss, and her vast stone face looked down on the valley with an expression of wise kindness. Her long white hair was made of waterfalls, blowing sometimes across her face when the wind gusted, and her crown was cloud. The covered path rose to a doorway carved into the necklace which ringed her throat.

'It's beautiful,' said Zen.

Nova didn't answer. There were too many other people on the path; too much risk of someone overhearing. It didn't matter. He knew her well enough to know that she thought it was beautiful too.

'I can't believe I haven't seen pictures of it...'

'The Petrichoris do not allow images of the shrine to enter the wider Datasea, sir,' she said, as if she were simply warning him not to take pictures.

‘I suppose that makes sense. Who would visit this soggy sinkhole if they could see vids of the shrine at home?’ Zen kept looking up at that kind, calm face, trying to connect it with the rustling version of Vohu Mana he had met. It had been one of the friendlier Guardians, as he recalled. But ‘friendly’ was relative where a Guardian was concerned—they were far too big and old and strange for any human to really understand what they were feeling.

The pathway turned to steps. The glass covering ended, but that was all right, because the pilgrims were sheltered now by the stone arrowhead of the Guardian’s chin which jutted over them as they climbed. Some had been laughing and talking on the way down the path, but they grew solemn now, nearing the entrance to the shrine and its mysteries. One woman started to sing a song about Vohu Mana, and others shyly took it up. They sang in a branch-line dialect that Zen didn’t know, but he liked the song; it had a solemn, hopeful sound which suited this place.

The steps narrowed, bunching the pilgrims together in a shuffling queue. More of the green-uniformed shrine wardens stood watch, armed with ceremonial staffs. The doorway they guarded was decorated with mirror mosaics. Zen glimpsed a thousand wide-eyed, wondering reflections of himself, with a thousand blank, incurious Novas following behind him.

Then he was inside the shrine, in quiet shadows which gave the impression of a domed space reaching up into darkness over him. Above him, like faded banners, hung hundreds of holoscreens, all flickering with the images which Vohu Mana’s devotees had uploaded. Old people smiling for their great-grandkid’s photos, images of houses, meals, beloved pets, families at festivals, weddings, scenes of work and play and university and school, gap-toothed children, fat-kneed toddlers wobbling across the beaches of ninety years ago, babies, grainy blue scans of dreaming foetuses. Whole lives were flashing past up there, all stored in the shrine’s memory. And maybe that was the point, thought Zen. Maybe the pilgrims didn't *really* believe that the Guardian was going to recreate them all from their stored messages and video diaries. Maybe it was enough simply to know that they would not be forgotten. Years from now, centuries from now, this kindly mountain would still remember them.

The pilgrims followed gently glowing paths on the stone floor. They entered low alcoves cut into the walls, where white chairs opened for them like the buds of lotuses. Zen sat.

'Welcome, Ajay Lackwing,' said the voice of the shrine, opening a window in his headset. 'Do you wish to place your memories in Vohu Mana's keeping?'

And Zen did; he longed to. But he knew that Ajay Lackwing's memories were thin things, just an actor's mask. He was afraid that if he uploaded them, the shrine would sense Zen Starling hiding behind them.

'No,' he said. 'I have brought you the memories of my grandmother, Vritti Lackwing of Jara Bay, in the Northern Prefecture on K'mbussi. They are stored in the mind of my Moto.'

'Have it upload them,' said the shrine.

Nova's eyelids fluttered. A holoscreen opened in the air above her like the after-image of a bright window. It showed scenes from the life of Ajay Lackwing's granny, who had never existed, and whose memories had been faked by Nova on Station Zero and were based on her own memories and on doctored fragments from old movies. Watching them wash past, Zen felt suddenly convinced that the shrine would see through the trick at once. It was so wise, and it had seen so many of these electronic echoes of the lives of humans, surely it could tell that this one was false? He clutched the armrests of the lotus-chair and waited, wondering what an age-old data shrine did to people who tried to trick it.

But nothing happened, except that the holoscreen faded again. Nova's fakery must have been better than he'd feared. Hopefully the shrine just thought the tremor of fear in his voice was the natural emotion of a grieving grandson when he said, 'Thank you, Vohu Mana. Please remember my grandmother Vritti.'

'She will be remembered,' promised the shrine.

Zen looked at Nova. While he had been sitting there some sharp part of her mind had slid like a lock pick into the mind of the shrine and let her inside to go hunting Vohu Mana's Heaven. He wished he had some way of knowing whether she had found it, but she could not say anything or show any expression here. He waited as long as he dared, then stood up and made his way back along the shining paths, through the whispers of the other pilgrims and the swaying light of the memories of the dead, out into the rain.

'Well?' he said, as soon as they were in the privacy of another taxi, driving back through the mountains. 'Did you find Raven?'

She shook her head. 'It wasn't there.'

'Raven?'

'Vohu Mana's virtual Heaven. It wasn't there. I scanned the shrine's whole mind. It's basically just a big old cache of vids and photos and social media profiles. It's barely even conscious.'

'But it talked to me!'

'A few simple response algorithms, just like this car has. It's not complex enough to hold a full copy of Vohu Mana, let alone a vast virtual environment like his afterlife is supposed to be.'

'Maybe he just collects social media profiles there and uploads them to the afterlife somewhere else?' said Zen.

'But where? I was *sure* it must be here.'

'What about Kolrabi?' asked Zen. 'The planet that Petrichor's other K-gate used to lead to; the one whose sun went supernova . . .'

'Kolrabi's toast,' said Nova. 'There's nothing there.'

'Well, there's nothing here either, unless Vohu Mana has hidden some storage in one of those old warehouses, or out on the Moss where the elk roam, or on the ghost train . . .'

‘What ghost train?’

‘Oh, just a story I found on some old site or other. It’s kind of stupid. Supposedly, when they evacuated Kolrabi, the last train to leave got stuck in the K-gate. The story is that it’s still in there, trapped between the two gates. Always travelling, never arriving. They call it the Slow Train.’

The car swished downhill on a long straight stretch of road as wet as the spillway of a dam. The lights of the station city showed faintly through the rain ahead. Nova said, ‘Why is that stupid?’

‘Well, if the train never arrived, how would they know it ever left Kolrabi? It probably just got roasted when the sun went bang. There’s no reason to assume it’s stuck in K-space.’

‘No. So it would be a strange thing to make up.’

‘You think it’s true?’

‘A lot of folk tales hide a grain of truth,’ she said. ‘And if you could keep a train inside a K-gate somehow . . . It would be the perfect hiding place, wouldn’t it? It would be outside of our universe altogether.’

‘I suppose you’re going to tell me we need to go and check out this abandoned K-gate?’

‘You know me so well,’ she said.

Zen checked his headset maps. From the station city the old Kolrabi line curved north along the edge of a wide bay to the Kolrabi K-gate. ‘It’s fifty-two kilometres away,’ he said. ‘It’s marked “No Access” so there are probably fences and things.’

‘That’s why I brought a brave and handsome thief with me.’

‘But we’d both have to go. I can’t hack a Guardian’s private afterlife on my own. How will it look if I take off up the old railway line with only a wire dolly for company? No offence . . .’

‘None taken, monkey boy,’ said Nova. ‘We’ll have to think of a reason fast. Now that you’ve delivered granny’s memories to the shrine there’s nothing to keep you on Petrichor. You ought to be leaving on the evening train. We'll have to come up with some excuse for you to stay an extra night.'

'I could be stopping to relax and enjoy the atmosphere,' said Zen.

Nova looked at the sodden countryside they were passing through, and then at him. She didn't need facial expressions to show him what she thought of that idea. 'Let's think,' she said. 'What do people do for *fun* on Petrichor?'

25

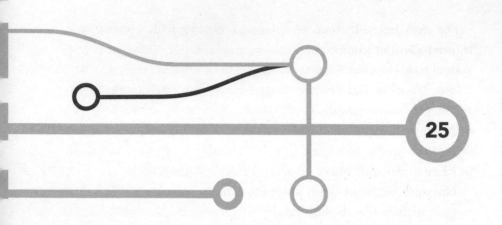

The clouds hanging above the Moss that evening were thin enough to let through a pale green light. It was the light of Petrichor's mother planet, Yanvi, the Rain Lantern, and it lay almost like sunlight on the sloughs and hummocks of the Moss. Even in that unexpected brightness, the swamp-sea was a cheerless sight. In places there were rain-pocked stretches of deep water, in others the tides had sculpted rafts and islands out of rotting surface weed. Mostly the weed lay just beneath the surface, forming a dense green floor for an ocean only a few centimetres deep.

'You can stand on some of the weedlands,' the owner of the harbourside hunting store explained as he rented Zen a hovercraft. 'Not on all of them, though. There are thin patches which don't look thin until you step on them, and then you find there's twenty metres of water under you, and twenty metres of silt under that.' He plainly thought that this young man was crazy, setting out on a hunting trip all alone, without a guide.

Zen promised he'd be careful. 'I came on family business, delivering my grandma's memories to the shrine, but that's done now, and I can't visit Petrichor without taking a crack at some of your famous Moss elk. I can't afford a guide, but you could rent me one of those elk rifles.'

The man fetched a gun from the rack behind his counter and showed Zen the loading mechanisms and how to link the targeting system to his headset. 'You've hunted before?'

'Not Moss elk. But I've shot frisbee-bats on Sundarban, and heritage megafauna on Jangala.'

'Noon worlds,' said the man.

'I know! All the best hunting is in rebel territory now! Ai, I wish our Emperor would hurry up and take those stations back!'

'Not sure we want them any more,' the man said, and led Zen outside to show him the hovercraft. 'All those aliens they got pouring through the K-gate from that hub place. Those stupid Noons'll end up letting loose a plague or an invasion.'

'Maybe you're right,' said Zen. 'Anyway, it could be good for business. Maybe people who can't get to the Noon reserves will come here and hunt your elk instead.'

The man shrugged. This customer was crazy, but maybe if he survived he'd bring some of his friends to Petrichor. And if he didn't, well, the hovercraft was fitted with a homing system; it could find its own way back. 'You should go east!' he advised, pointing into the greenish murk offshore. 'That's where you mostly find elk in the dry season.'

'This is the dry season?' asked Zen.

'If you can hear yourself talking over the noise of the rain, that's the dry season on Petrichor.'

Zen climbed into the hovercraft, which powered up its motors and slid down the ramp into the harbour. Zen told it to go east, and after a few hundred metres, when he was out of sight of the hunting store, he made it stop beside a crumbling jetty where a Motorik climbed aboard. Then it took off again, speeding away from the city, skimming gracefully over the shallows and the deeps, climbing weed-islands so fast that it sometimes took flight from their low summits and landed on the far side with a gigantic belly flop. Nova got her mind inside it and altered its route recorder so that when Zen turned it due north it didn't bother to let the hunting store know about the course change. 'This was a very good idea,' she said. 'We can go in a straight line across this stuff instead of following the curve of the coast. We'll be at the Kolrabi gate in no time.'

'If we don't sink, or get savaged by Moss elk or dragged down by that giant octopus.'

'You told me the giant octopus was just a story.'

'I told you the Slow Train was just a story too, and now we're on our way to rob it. I don't know what's real any more.'

The pools of open water shone with greasy reflections of the sky. The weed-mounds heaved sluggishly on the long, slow swell. It seemed quite possible to Zen that a monster octopus might lurk in the depths of this horrible bog. But if it did, they did not meet it as they drove north across the bay. They saw a small group of Moss elk, picking their way through shallow water on their weird webbed hooves, but they showed no sign of wanting to attack the hovercraft. Their shaggy coats were green with algae, and flags of lichen trailed from their wide antlers.

The Moss didn't really have a shore, it just blended imperceptibly into boggy ground, which then rose slowly towards the mountains. Zen was only certain that they'd made landfall when the hovercraft reached a chain-link fence and he saw railway tracks on the other side. He told the 'craft to turn east, following the line. Soon there were buildings ahead—long-abandoned warehouses with ferns and small trees growing on their roofs. The green light of Yanvi stabbed down through broken panels in the roof of an old station canopy. This wasn't like the Dog Star Line, with abandoned trains, and posters on the walls. This station had been stripped, the whole terminal shut down. The only things not covered in moss or lichen were large signs which read 'Keep Out' and 'No Access' and 'Restricted Area', all branded with the eye of Vohu Mana. Some of the signs just had the eye, as if that alone were enough to warn off trespassers.

'Maybe there are cameras,' Zen said.

Nova shook her head. 'I'm not detecting any . . . This place is dead. No Datasea connections, nothing.'

They left the hovercraft hidden among the ferns in a gap between two buildings. Climbing the trackside fence, they dropped down onto the rails and followed them for a few hundred metres until they saw a tunnel mouth ahead. It had been blocked with a plug of ceramic, but low down in the base of the barrier there was a small door. The whole barrier was stencilled with warning notices—'DANGER: KEEP OUT'—and the eye of Vohu Mana.

'No guards?' asked Zen, as they crouched in the shadow of an old wall, watching.

'No movement; no body heat,' said Nova.

They walked closer, right up to the place where the tracks vanished into the ceramic barrier. The door was just big enough for one person to go through, and it was locked with a mechanical lock. Nova went to work with the thin metal instrument which Zen had printed for her earlier at the hotel. She worked in silence, listening closely to the tiny sounds from inside the lock, and after a minute or maybe less Zen heard the heavy bolts slide open. A bell began to ring in one of the nearby buildings, a shrill clattering sound that went on and on until Nova found a wire which led to the lock and cut it.

The bell stopped. The echoes faded. No one came.

'No guards, and only a mechanical alarm,' said Zen. 'Isn't that a bit strange?'

'No,' said Nova. 'If Vohu Mana had guards on patrol and hi-tech alarm systems, word would get round that there was something worth stealing here. Rumours would find their way into the Datasea, and the other Guardians would start to wonder what he was hiding from them. This way, only the locals know there's anything here. And none of them would dare rob Vohu Mana.'

The door had been used fairly recently—Nova said the hinges had been oiled within the past six months—but it still took all of their combined strength to heave it open. They stepped through it and waited for lights to come on, but none did. The old rails gleamed on the tunnel floor. Zen followed them a little way into the dark. There was a noise coming from somewhere ahead, a droning note, so steady and monotonous that he hadn't noticed it at first.

'What is that?'

'I don't know,' said Nova, and took his hand. They went on together, and Zen started to sense a pale light bleaching away the darkness. The noise grew louder, and the light grew brighter, and suddenly the tunnel widened out on either side into a big, rock-roofed chamber, filled with the glow of the abandoned K-gate.

26

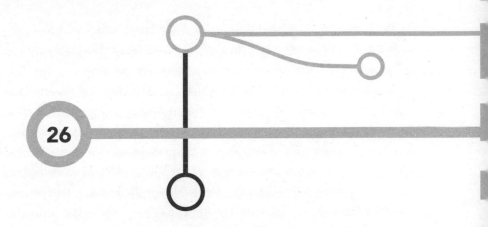

The chamber was unusual. The tunnels which led to K-gates were generally just tunnels; there was no need for any extra space around the gate. This space looked as if it had been hacked hastily out of the rock. It had not even been sealed; trickles of water fell like rain through fissures in the high ceiling. The floor had big puddles, and between the puddles was a stack of plastic crates filled with some sort of machinery. The crates did not hold Zen's attention for long. He was more interested in the train which stood on the rails between him and the K-gate.

It was an old, gold loco with no name on its cowling, just the eye of Vohu Mana. Behind it were three carriages. The third carriage was halfway through the gate, the line of its unlit windows vanishing into the wavering veil of energy.

'That's impossible,' said Zen. 'Trains can't stop halfway through gates . . .'

'I don't think it *has* stopped.' Nova went closer. She crouched down beside the train's nose, peering at its wheels. After a few moments she said, 'It's moving at the speed of a fairly lazy glacier.'

Now Zen understood what that endless drone was. The old loco was singing, and each note of its song would last for hundreds of years.

'Well, now we know why they call it the Slow Train,' said Nova.

'But trains have to go fast through K-gates, don't they?' asked Zen.

'Very fast, or very, *very* slow,' said a voice behind him.

He turned and raised his rented rifle, but the thing which hovered behind them wasn't shootable. It was a hologram, generated by a projector in one of the stacked crates. It looked like a very small, flat-faced dog, keeping itself airborne with quick beats of its hairy wings.

It should take around ten centuries for the Slow Train to complete its journey from Kolrabi to Petrichor. When the last carriage comes through the K-gate it will start going back again. It's better to travel hopefully than to arrive.'

Zen stared at the dog. 'What is it?' he asked Nova.

'It's called Pugasus,' she said. 'It's one of the traditional interfaces of Vohu Mana.'

'It's just a hologram.'

'I'm a holographic interface,' said the airborne pug, with an injured expression. 'You don't think I'd go to the trouble of actually growing a live body just to keep an eye on this place, do you? Anyway, it would be aerodynamically impossible to keep a dog this heavy up with wings this size in real life.'

Zen's headset started pinging out information in answer to requests he had not detected.

'You are not who your headset ID says you are,' said the pug, flapping closer to Zen and peering into his face with its bulging eyes. Its pink tongue lolled thoughtfully for a moment. 'You are not "Ajay Lackwing",' it declared. 'You are Zen Starling! You are the one who made all that trouble on Khoorsandi last year. And this is the machine called Nova. I guessed it was you when you scanned the memories in my shrine today. I've been expecting you.'

'Why didn't you try to stop us then?' asked Nova.

The flying pug shrugged a smug pug-shrug. 'I wanted to find out why you were so interested in my business here. My *private* business.'

‘We heard about the Slow Train,’ said Zen. ‘It’s a brilliant hiding place.’

The pug made snuffly noises. Zen thought it looked pleased. ‘It is a good place for keeping private things,’ it said. ‘Where others can’t find them.’

‘The other Guardians, you mean?’ asked Nova.

‘Can we see?’ asked Zen. ‘We’ve come all this way, and I don’t suppose you’re going to let us leave. Can we take a look?’

‘I haven’t decided yet whether I will let you leave or not,’ the pug said primly. ‘My fellow Guardians are very certain that the machine Nova must be destroyed. I am not so sure. You don’t seem very dangerous to me. A very ordinary sort of Motorik, I’d say.’ It licked its nose. ‘You might as well go aboard.’

There was a hydraulic hiss. Zen looked at the train, and saw that the first set of doors in the front carriage had opened. When he looked back, the pug interface had vanished.

There was no platform, so they had to climb up into the train. It was an undignified procedure, but there was nobody in the carriage to see them. There weren’t even any seats. It was an ordinary commuter train that had once carried workers to and from the settlements on lost Kolrabi, but all the fixtures had been removed, leaving only bolt holes and angular marks on the carpeted floor where they had been.

Zen found an empty crate and placed it between the doors in case they closed while he and Nova were on board. Then they walked to the back of the carriage and through the open connecting doors into the next one. It was just the same, except that in the dust on the carpet were two tyre tracks, stretching down the centre of the carriage. Zen and Nova followed them through into the third carriage, which was filled with the weird, shifting light of K-space. They were entering the part of the train that was inside the K-gate, and Zen felt the familiar sensations. He must have passed through thousands of gates in his time, but they had always flashed by in an instant before. Here, there was no hope of escape from the impossible sense of falling—the weird déjà vu. Outside the windows, the light moved in strange eddies. Tall shapes seemed to form in it, as if wraiths were standing outside the carriage, peering in. He saw them from the tail of his eye, but each time he turned his head to look at them straight, they vanished.

'There's something out there!' he told Nova.

'There isn't even a *there* out there, Zen.'

'I keep seeing . . .'

'I know. I think they're just an optical illusion, but who can tell? K-space is stranger than we imagine. It's probably stranger than we *can* imagine.'

'And here we are in it . . .'

'No. The train protects us, just as it does when you go through a gate at normal speed. This is a little island of our reality. Come on, let's explore.'

She opened the connecting door and went through into the next carriage, which was completely inside the K-gate. She glanced back at Zen and he followed her, doing his best to hide his fear and nausea as his brain struggled and struggled to work out which way up he was. Nova took his hand, and they stood together staring at the thing which had been making the tyre tracks in the dust.

It looked like one of the automated snack trolleys which trundled to and fro along the aisles and corridors of normal trains. It probably had been once, but it had been widened and converted, and it was not carrying snacks. A precarious stack of machinery was balanced on its flat top, reaching up almost to the ceiling. There was a big central cylinder with racks bolted to it. The racks held rows of old-fashioned data storage saucers. The trolley did not appear to be moving, but Zen knew that it was. It was moving backwards through the train at exactly the same glacial speed that the train was moving forward, so that the trolley and the thing it carried were always kept inside the K-gate.

'What is that?' whispered Zen.

'Storage,' said Nova. 'Old fashioned, and not connected to the Datasea, but powerful. Yes, there's room enough in there . . .'

'That's Heaven? Balanced on a snack trolley?' Zen stared at it, feeling cheated. 'It looks like a tea urn.'

Lights were starting to dance across the big central device. 'It knows we're here,' said Nova.

And suddenly Zen was not standing in the carriage with her, but falling through sunlight, down into a deep canyon between two towering clouds, and all he could hear was the wind rushing past his ears, and the sound of his own scream. It felt as if everything till now had been a dream, and he had woken from it into this terrible reality. He tried to remember how his fall had begun, where he had fallen from, up there where the blue sky turned almost black. He looked down, but there was no sign of land below him, only more towers and continents of cloud. Maybe he had *always* been falling.

No, no, no, no, he told himself, fighting to ignore the evidence of all his panicked senses. *This isn't real. This is a virtual. It has to be.* He shut his eyes. He clamped his hands tight over his ears to block out the sound of the air rushing past, and fought to concentrate. Dimly, like distant memories, he sensed the scuffed dusty carpet of the Slow Train under his boots. He flailed one hand and hit the glass of the Slow Train's windows. That pressure on his arms was Nova's hands. Somewhere far off, beyond the wind, he could hear her voice calling his name.

He ripped his headset off and he was standing with her in the carriage, beside the trolley of machinery.

'Where did it take you?' she was asking. 'What did you see?'

'Nothing,' he gasped, still shaking with the shock. 'Only clouds. Only falling. Have a look . . .'

'I can't,' said Nova. 'It won't let me in. I guess Vohu Mana doesn't trust me.'

'But it trusts me?'

'It knows you're no threat. And it desperately wants to show off what it's built.'

'But there's nothing in there!'

'There must be *something*...'

Zen took a deep breath and put the headset back on, half hoping that he'd be locked out now too. But at once he was back in the sky, and it was all he could do to keep himself aware of his real body as this virtual Zen went plummeting past creamy kilometres of evening cumulus.

Then, in the clouds below him, he saw something dark. He strained his eyes, trying to make it out. (Real eyes would have been so distorted by the pressure of the air that he would have been falling blind. He kept hold of that thought, as proof that none of this was real.) He dropped through a white floor of cloud and when he emerged below it he could see the shape clearly.

It was a ship. A huge shark-like thing like a spaceship in a game, except that it was built of ancient wood, and seemed to be on fire. Then, as his fall carried him closer, Zen realized that what he had taken for clouds of thick, brownish smoke were also made of wood. The planks which formed the ship were constantly being ripped free and carried away in its wake as it ploughed on into the wind. Beneath them, more planks were exposed, only to tear away in their turn.

It looked like a metaphor for something, but Zen had no idea what. Before he had time to give it much thought, the wind gusted, whirling him upwards again, lifting him over the ship's ravaged prow, past a gigantic figurehead which looked like the wooden sister of Vohu Mana's mountain shrine.

He landed on an immense, flat deck. Gloomy trees grew there, their roots reaching down between the planks. The wind had dropped away, but the clouds of torn timber still kept whirling astern, making a rushing sound as they passed overhead.

Zen started to walk across the deck. He came to a flight of stairs and went down them into the ship's shady innards, where soft blades of sunlight poked down through gaps in the planking. The roots of the trees twining through the ceiling formed braided, living pillars. He made his way between them. The ship was full of the sounds of stressed timber, creaking and groaning and squeaking and muttering. Ahead, a sunbeam fell like a spotlight on a wicker chair where a man sat reading an old-fashioned book.

Zen hesitated. The man sensed his presence and stood up, tall and thin, unfolding himself from the chair, crossing his arms, gripping his own shoulders with long pale fingers while he watched Zen approach. Zen knew that mannerism. He knew that long and frail-strong body. He stepped into the shaft of light and stopped, looking into the thin, white face of a man he had once watched die upon the water-moon Tristesse.

'Zen Starling!' said Raven. 'What brings you to Heaven?'

27

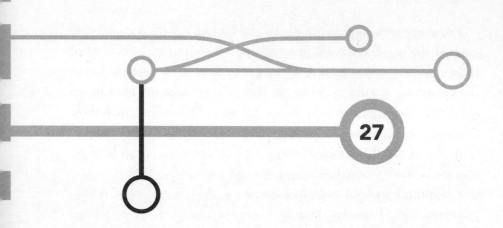

The vast old ship did not look heavenly to Zen, but it did have nicer bits. Raven led him out onto a sort of balcony which ran the whole length of the constantly crumbling hull. There were other people walking there, but they were far off, their faces unclear.

'Is everyone here?' Zen asked. 'Vohu Mana has really made versions of everyone who ever lived? Is Kobi Chen-Tulsi here? And Lady Sufra? And Yanvar Malik?'

'I'm sure programmes which think they are Kobi and Malik and Lady S. are having a lovely time somewhere,' Raven said. 'But not here. I think this environment is a sort of annexe where Vohu Mana keeps the more troublesome souls, the ones his fellow Guardians would prefer he just deleted.' He glanced upwards and the shadows of the endlessly disintegrating ship fluttered across his face. 'Maybe this isn't technically part of Heaven at all. Maybe it's just limbo. Vohu Mana's Bardo Barge . . .' He looked at Zen again, and grinned. 'Still, it's better than nothing.'

'It isn't real,' said Zen, mostly to remind himself.

'Do you think I don't know that?'

'You're not real either.'

Raven laughed. He did not look as old as he had been when Zen first met him, but he had the same wry smile, the same knowing sideways glance.

'I'm every bit as real as the Raven you met on Cleave. I'm a digital copy of the original Raven, just as he was. I used to make dozens of these copies, waiting to download them into cloned bodies. When the Guardians started to delete me from the Datasea and hunt down my clones, I sought out Vohu Mana. I'd heard about his little hobby. I thought he might want a mint-condition Raven for his collection.'

'And you hid the information about Petrichor in Nova's head so that she'd know where to find you.'

'I suppose I thought I might come in useful one day as an emergency backup, in case anything happened to my last physical version. What *did* happen to that version, by the way?'

'He got killed by a sky-ray, on Tristesse.'

'A ray? How ridiculous!'

'But if you were created way back when the Guardians started getting rid of the real Raven,' said Zen, 'how come you recognize me? You were made before I was born.'

'Oh, Vohu Mana keeps me up to date,' said Raven. 'He scans the Datasea for relevant information. Every month or so he sends it in the form of a written letter to the warden of his shrine here, who copies it onto a dataslate, drives down here, lets himself aboard the Slow Train, and uploads it onto the computer that runs this environment. None of it ever enters the Datasea, so the other Guardians don't know what Vohu Mana's up to. There is no information generated on Petrichor to attract their attention, and the Slow Train itself exists in K-space, out of sight and out of mind. You are the first visitor I've had from the world outside. It's good to see you, Zen. I know what you did for the last Raven. Robbing the Noon train for him. That was a desperate move.'

'People got killed,' said Zen awkwardly. While he'd been away from Raven he had forgotten how attractive Raven was, how much he wanted to be liked by him. Now, standing beside him again, it was easy to forget how this man had used him. 'Lots of people got killed. We started a war.'

'Only a little one,' said Raven. 'And it worked, Zen! I have been reading about all the new worlds you and Nova opened the way to, out beyond Tristesse. I wish I could see them for myself. She's here, I assume?'

'Yes.'

Raven leaned his elbows on the balcony rail and steepled his long fingers. 'Vohu Mana has shown me some of the conversations the Guardians have been having about her. They're not happy. They see Nova as a rival. She must have grown very powerful. But not quite powerful enough yet. She still needs my help, doesn't she?'

Zen was wary. He didn't want to tell Raven what Nova had said about him becoming the Railmaker. 'She might need your advice,' he admitted.

Raven laughed again. 'Of course she does! That's why she risked coming here. But there's a price for my advice, Zen. You need to get me out of here. I'm tired of just being a ghost in Vohu Mana's pocket purgatory. Take me away, and I'll find a new body to download this personality into.'

'That was the plan,' said Zen. 'That's why we came here—to get you away. But I don't see how I can. Nova can't get in here, and I don't know how to get your programme out. What am I supposed to do? Copy you to my headset?'

'No need,' said Raven. 'My personality is stored on a data saucer, mounted on the drum that holds this environment. Rather old fashioned, but that's how Vohu Mana rolls. There are probably other saucers, but mine will be the newest; no other personalities have been added to this place since mine. All you have to do is—'

A voice from everywhere suddenly interrupted. 'Not so fast, Raven!' it rumbled. A winged pug the size of a smallish mountain flew overhead, pitching the terrace into shadow. It hovered and glared at Zen and Raven while the downdraft from its wingbeats tore more planking from the old ship's hull. 'I let Zen Starling in because

I wanted to hear what he had to say to you. I'm not planning to let him out again. I've sent a shortwave radio signal to my shrine. The attendants have a team on the way. Don't worry, Zen Starling. I am already preparing a virtual version of you. Your body may be killed, but you will live on in this environment until I deem it safe to transfer you to my full-scale Heaven with everyone else.'

'No!' said Zen. Raven was trying to tell him something, but he wasn't listening. He reached up and pulled his headset off. There was a flash as the connection dropped out and then he was back in the Slow Train, in the weird nausea-light of the K-gate.

'Did you find him?' asked Nova.

'He's—yes—but we have to go; people are coming, we need to get back to the hovercraft . . .'

'Not without Raven.'

Zen looked at the trolley with its curious load. All those racks of storage saucers. Perhaps each one held a different personality which Vohu Mana had saved without the knowledge of the other Guardians; all sorts of forgotten tyrants and rebels, erased from the Datasea but living on in the virtual spaces which that big central machine was generating. He scanned the racks, and plucked out the least antique-looking saucer.

'Is that Raven?' Nova asked. 'Can we be sure?'

'It's the newest,' said Zen, 'and Raven said he was the most recent personality to be added to the environment.' The data saucer looked like a silver spaceship from one of the strange old black and white movies Nova liked to watch, but it was small enough to fit in the palm of Zen's hand. Along its rim, tiny, embossed letters caught the light. 'Also, it says "Raven" on it.'

He slipped the saucer into his tunic pocket. As they started to run back through the train the Pugasus hologram appeared in mid-air ahead of them,shouting, 'What do you think you're doing? Return that data storage device to its place!'

'He's only made of light,' said Nova, sidestepping it and running on. 'He can't hurt us.'

Zen put his head down and ran straight through the levitating lapdog. It yipped indignantly and flew after him for a way. 'The others were right about you, Starling—you're nothing but trouble!'

They left the K-gate light behind and ran through the front two carriages. The doors were trying to shut, champing at the crate that Zen had left between them. Nova squirmed through and dropped to the ground outside, and a moment later Zen jumped down after her.

'You won't get away with it, you know!' shouted Vohu Mana's interface. 'My shrine wardens are on their way to deal with you!' It flapped furiously after them down the tunnel until it reached the limits of its projector's range and flickered out.

The door at the tunnel mouth was standing ever so slightly ajar, just as they had left it. They crouched behind it and listened.

'I can't hear anything except rain,' said Zen.

'Me neither,' Nova said. 'But if someone arrived while we were aboard the train, I might not have heard them. Maybe they're waiting for us.'

'Or maybe they haven't got here yet. Vohu Mana must have thought he could keep us talking longer.' Zen opened the door and they stepped outside.

The light hit them like an avalanche. It came from lamps mounted on three big vehicles which had been waiting silently among the shadows of the old railway buildings. It was so bright that it seemed to have weight, shouldering the wet moony dusk aside and slamming Zen's and Nova's shadows against the barrier behind them. In the heart of the light there were running footsteps and shouting voices and then people were emerging from the glare with guns and head-lamps and green uniforms with the eye of Vohu Mana on the tunics. They were the same kindly police-officer types Zen had seen at the shrine that morning, but they did not seem kindly any more. He threw away his elk rifle and let them force him down on his knees next to Nova. 'Shall we shoot them now, warden?' someone asked, as if it was a treat he had been looking forward to. They were amateurs, thought Zen. Their weapons were a mix of hunting guns and big, outdated, ex-Railforce blasters. They were nervous and excited and very dangerous.

'Wait,' ordered another voice. A man came out of the light wearing a long rainproof coat which gleamed like spilled oil under the lights. He had long grey hair and the face of a stern saint. It grew sterner still when he looked down at Zen. 'Our Guardian Vohu Mana has spoken to me tonight,' he said. 'He says that you must die, and your Motorik be taken for study and disassembly.' He leaned closer, lowering his voice. 'I want you to understand this, trespasser. Your death will be permanent. The rest of us will be revived in the glory of Vohu Mana's afterlife, but your information will be deleted forever.'

'So?' asked Zen. 'I've seen this afterlife of yours. It's rubbish.' He felt this crazy need to buy time, as if help might arrive if he could only keep the man talking long enough. But help from where? This was Vohu Mana's world, and no one here would help him. He glanced at Nova, but three men were holding her down and one had a gun pressed against the side of her head. Still, he kept talking, angry and scared. 'Anyway, it won't be *you* the Guardian revives when you die, it'll just be a programme with your name and face. It'll be no more you than your profile on a dating site is you.'

The man struck him across the face so hard that he saw stars. One of the others pulled Zen's headset off, then rummaged in his pockets and brought out the data saucer. The leader took it from him and looked at it, then at Zen. 'Where did you find this?'

'Where do you think?'

'What is on it?'

'An old friend of ours. He got so bored of your Heaven, he begged us to help him escape.'

The man who had just searched Zen suddenly grunted. He knelt down between Zen and Nova, and then sprawled forward on his face. A small silvery dart poked out of the back of his neck, just above his collar.

Everyone looked at him for a moment, and no one spoke. Then a bunch of things happened at once, so fast that afterwards Zen could not recall the order. Nova threw her captors off and flung herself sideways, crashing into him so that he went down under her. Some of the lights went out suddenly. Wet mud had splashed Zen's face; he could feel it trickling down inside his collar. There was a woman's voice yelling about throwing down weapons in the name of the Network Empire. There was a spattering sound like small stones falling, which turned out to be gunfire. Flattened beneath Nova, Zen had a sideways view of people running. He dimly understood that help had arrived, but he wasn't sure what sort of help, or why. The chief shrine warden was still standing, looking about in confusion. One of the searchlights was still on. More people appeared from the dark behind it, hurrying out of the old buildings. They were hard to see at first because their clothes were camouflaged to match the landscape, but one by one they turned off their chameleon settings and Zen recognized the dull grey-blue of Railforce battledress.

So it wasn't really help, Zen thought. He had just been captured a second time, by tougher people, with better guns.

'It's the Bluebodies,' he said.

Nova didn't answer. He turned and tried to push himself up, and she rolled soggily off him and lay on her back in the mud. The bullet had made a big hole in the middle of her forehead on its way in, and an even bigger one in the back of her head on its way out. The wet stuff that was all over Zen's face and clothes was not mud but the blue gel that she used as blood and brains.

'Nova?' he said, as they dragged him to his feet and away from her.

A little white flash went off inside her open mouth. Smoke curled out like a last breath and faded into the rain.

'Nova!' he shouted.

'Be quiet, Mr Starling,' ordered the leader of the Bluebodies. She pulled her helmet off and turned out to be a young woman with a pink face and yellow hair. She looked at Nova, then at the chief shrine warden. 'Why did you shoot her?'

'It was only a machine,' said the man. 'It trespassed in places sacred to Vohu Mana.' He was trembling with what looked like fright, but turned out to be fury. 'Is this how the new Emperor treats the citizens of his Empire?' he shouted suddenly. 'Murdering us and invading our worlds?'

'Be quiet,' said the young Railforce officer coldly. 'No one has been murdered; your people will recover in a few hours. And we are not invading, we are just passing through. I have orders to capture these fugitives and take them to Grand Central for proper questioning.' She snatched the data saucer from the warden's hand and said, 'What's on this, Mr Starling?'

Zen couldn't speak. He could only stare at Nova, unbelieving, as if she were some priceless thing that he had dropped and broken. Why had he insisted that she send this body with him, the body that he loved? Why hadn't he let her print a new one that he didn't care about, and let his Nova stay safe on Station Zero? Perhaps, if he could only gather up the pieces, all the million splinters of her mind that the gunshot had sprayed across the mud and up the tunnel door . . .

'Mr Starling?' asked the officer, still holding the saucer.

'The Lieutenant asked you a question,' growled the man who was holding Zen, but the officer shook her head and said, 'Leave him. He's in shock. Let's get going before Vohu Mana cuts through our firewalls or more of these cultists come to see what's happened to their friends.'

Zen was aware that she was being kind to him. He nodded at her, tried to whisper something. He thought he recognized her, but everything felt so unreal that he wasn't sure. He saw her put the data saucer carefully into one of the pouches on her belt.

'Do we bring the Moto?' someone asked.

'Can she be restored?'

'No way, Lieutenant. She's junk.'

'Then leave her.'

They pushed Zen into a vehicle. Someone wiped his face, quite gently, with a cloth. Someone put plastic handcuffs on his wrists. As the truck drove away he caught one last glimpse of Nova's body. Her bare knees were poking through the torn grey paper of her overalls.

It was the saddest thing he had ever seen.

PART FIVE

TRAINSONG

28

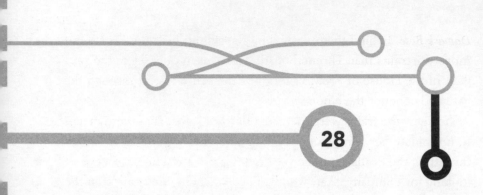

The *Damask Rose* had left Galatava before dawn. She pulled only five carriages now: one state-car for Threnody, two for her staff, a luggage van, and an armoured carriage for a small honour-guard of Noon CoMa. Within a few hours she was crossing Marapur, making for the border K-gate that led to K'mbussi and the Network Empire.

Threnody held her breath as the gate approached. Her journey had been planned for weeks, but that last accelerating rush towards the K-gate still felt a lot like jumping off a cliff. Along either side of the track her family's Bahadur mobile gun platforms stood with their weapons aimed at the tunnel where the K-gate lay, ready to destroy any train that came through from the Prell side unexpectedly. Threnody knew that the Prells had just as much firepower massed on the other side of the gate. *They have been told I'm coming*, she reminded herself. But what if they didn't really want to talk to her? They wanted her dead; they had hired that green-eyed boy to kill her back on Galatava. What if they just decided to blow up the *Damask Rose* and say, 'Oops, so sorry, our mistake . . .'

And then she was through the gate, almost without noticing, and the K'mbussian sun was flaring through the windows, and the gun platforms beside the tracks wore Prell and Railforce markings. They did not open fire, but they swung their weapon clusters to track the

Damask Rose. Behind them, crowding the sidings near the K-gate, sat more wartrains than Threnody had ever seen in one place: the rail-fleet of the House of Prell, waiting for the order to roll through the gate and conquer the Noon worlds.

She knew the trains were there as a show of force. They were meant to intimidate her. Unfortunately, it was working. Annoyed at herself for letting the Prells get to her, she left her private state-car and went looking for company. Skar, who had been standing motionless in the vestibule like a suit of haunted armour, followed silently behind her as she went back through the train into the carriage where her staff were travelling.

The Kraitt warrior had been part of Threnody's household since the morning after the assassination attempt, when he had moved out of his dim little cave behind the waterfront bar and into a big, bright room on the floor below Threnody's suite. There he spent most of the time half asleep in the sunken bath with the heating turned up full, watching holoscreens which rippled like mirages in the baking air above the heated towel rails. But when Threnody visited him he would always rouse himself and come to meet her, eager to know if there was any fighting she needed him to do.

The first time she went to see him, Uncle Nilesh had insisted that she was accompanied by a whole squad of Noon CoMa, carrying heavy weapons which they pointed at Skar while she was thanking him again for saving her life. The second time, she took only Flex, sensing that Skar was fond of the Motorik. The third time, she went alone. She told Uncle Nilesh that her rebooted dragonfly drones had easily enough firepower to tear the Kraitt in half if he threatened her, but she was privately sure he would not. She had already come to trust Skar more than she trusted most of her own relatives.

That third time, she had taken him the Kraitt knife which she had carried in the Hub on the night she pardoned the Tzeld Gekh Karneiss. No one seemed to have any use for it, and it was an ugly old thing to human eyes, so she thought she would give it to Skar as a sign of her thanks. But after he had studied it for a few moments, and run a claw over the ridges etched in its hilt, the Kraitt passed it back to her. 'This is the knife of a Tzeld Gekh,' he growled. 'It has been wielded by many queens. It is your knife now, Tzeld Gekh of the humans.'

'I wouldn't know how to use it,' said Threnody, as he pressed it into her hands. 'I mean, I understand the principle—I know the pointy end is the stabby bit and the blunt end is the bit you hold onto—but . . .'

'I will teach you,' said Skar.

He had started her lessons straight away, showing her how to grip the weapon, how to thrust so that the whole force of her body was behind the blow. She thought she must seem very feeble to him. 'I am not strong like a Kraitt,' she said. But Skar said that it didn't matter, because her spirit was strong. Threnody thought that was the nicest thing anyone had ever said to her. She liked the old knife after that. She had her designers print a sheath for it, and she wore it on the back of her belt. She could feel it there now as she walked through her train, a hard, comfortable pressure against the small of her back. Knowing that it was there and that Skar was with her made her feel a little safer.

Her ladies were used to Skar by now, but P. K. Noon, the negotiator who was to be Threnody's advisor in the talks with the Empire, had arrived from Sundarban only a few minutes before the train left. When Threnody entered the middle state-car and he saw her Kraitt bodyguard looming behind her, his round, brown face turned greenish-grey and he scrambled from his seat with a high-pitched squeak and flattened himself against the livewood panelling. 'Guardians preserve us, Lady Noon! You are quite *sure* that beast is on our side?'

'Of course,' said Threnody. She understood how he felt. No picture or video of the Kraitt could quite prepare you for the real thing.

'Well,' said P. K. Noon, edging cautiously back into his seat, 'he will certainly draw attention to you when Grand Central media get a look at him. Yes. It's a good idea, I think. A sign of strength, that we can tame such savage brutes. No offence,' he added hastily, remembering that the modified headset riveted to Skar's facial scales would be translating his words into Kraitt.

Skar tilted his head a little and smiled his alarming smile.

Threnody still wasn't sure what to make of this negotiator. Pallathadka Keshava Noon was his full name, but he told everyone to call him P. K. to save time. He was younger than she had expected, and immensely fat. He had chosen to be fat, he said. Everything he ate was specially formulated to put back in all the fattening elements which clever food technologists had long ago removed. 'It makes people think I'm solid and dependable,' he said. (Threnody had to agree that he looked solid. Even his jowls had jowls.) 'And it throws the other side off when I'm making a deal. The only place most of them ever see a man as fat as me is in games and threedies. In games and threedies men as fat as me are always slow and stupid, and usually villains, who end up losing. By the time people work out that I'm neither slow nor stupid, I've usually won. I negotiated our mineral concessions on Surt that way.'

'And are you a villain, P. K.?' Threnody asked.

He stared at her, then started to laugh, his small eyes vanishing completely into folds of fat. Threnody decided that she liked him. As the *Rose* ran on across K'mbussi's ocean viaducts beneath a flock of media and Railforce drones, she sat with him at the big table in her state-car, working out what she would say to the Emperor. What she could ask for; what she could afford to give away in return . . .

In the diamondglass observation dome on the roof of Threnody's private state-car, Flex sat and watched the passing worlds. She had a data-slate on her lap, but it was empty; she had seen nothing yet in the speeding landscapes which made her want to draw. She loved trains, but she did not like travelling on them. She preferred to stay in one place and let her imagination travel for her while she listened to the songs the trains brought with them from far worlds.

She wasn't sure why she had agreed to come along on this journey. It wasn't because the invitation had come from the Chief Executive of the Noon Consortium—things like that didn't interest Flex. It was more that she had sensed Threnody needed her, and Flex always tried to help people in need. That might have been a vestige of her original programming, because Motorik were meant to be helpful, after all. But Flex preferred to think that it was her own decision, and her own way of paying back the kindness Myka Starling had shown her when she first arrived in Cleave.

Of course, helping people sometimes had a cost. She had helped Zen when he needed her, and she had ended up getting killed. She had a nasty feeling that the same thing might happen this time, because she didn't trust these Prell people Threnody was going to meet at all. She had been very careful to make a backup copy of her personality and store it in her trainshed's brain before she left Galatava.

As the train accelerated into a long tunnel in the Ice Crystal Mountains she opened her own internal menus and flipped her gender setting again, hoping the change might improve her mood. Changing sex was so simple for a Motorik that Flex had never seen any need to settle on being male or female. Sometimes she felt like being a girl, sometimes a boy. But it was only a surface thing, like changing clothes. Inside, Flex was neither. Flex was simply Flex.

Her body went through the familiar cycle of small alterations that turned it into his body, and the light of K-space flared outside the dome as the train passed through the next gate and emerged on Himmapaan. Flex tied his hair back the way he wore it when he was a boy, and scanned the local newsfeeds. The planet was deep in its long night and nothing much was happening. The only story was about Railforce drones being sent to collapse an unstable gorge in the mountains. Then, as the *Rose* raced through Himmapaan Station City and on towards the next gate, something unexpected flicked out of the planet's Datasea and dropped into the train's mind. It happened very quickly, and Flex only felt it because he had linked his mind to the *Rose*'s sensor arrays.

'What was that?' he asked.

'What was what?' asked the *Damask Rose*.

'Was it a message?'

'It was nothing of any importance,' said the *Damask Rose*. 'Just spam.'

It hadn't *felt* like spam, thought Flex. As the train raced on, he started trying to draw it, or at least to draw the feeling it had given him as it flashed out of Himmapaan's Datasea. A strange little information packet, coming from nowhere, dropping into the *Damask Rose*'s mind like a tiny golden seed.

When they reached Grand Central it was morning, and Threnody stopped making plans and walked back through the train to her own carriage. Climbing the stairs into the observation dome where Flex was sitting, she noticed that he was a boy again, but she knew Flex well enough by then that it did not come as a surprise. She stood beside him, and they watched the outskirts of the station city go by. Clouds blowing in off the sea were being sculpted by high-flying drones into likenesses of the Emperor and his family, and as the gigantic heads drifted over the city, their shadows scudded across forest parks and the flanks of garden skyscrapers. Some of the skyscrapers were virtually cities in their own right: giant arcologies with ten thousand residents, tree-covered garden decks spiralling up their flanks. Glass-bottomed swimming pools jutted from their upper terraces, and as the train threaded its way around the base of one Threnody glanced up and saw a crowd of children swimming high above her, looking like tadpoles who had just got their legs.

And then there was a break in the buildings, and away to the north she saw the distant mass of an even bigger structure.

'The imperial palace,' said Flex. 'Is that where you used to live?'

'Yes,' she said. 'And I nearly died there, too, the night the Prell wartrains came.' She shivered as the shadow of Elon Prell's cloud-carved head fell across the train. She was remembering how dangerous they could be, these people she had come to deal with, and how much she wished she did not have to deal with them at all.

'Ooh, look, we're on telly,' said the *Damask Rose* cheerfully. She opened a holoscreen in the dome so that Flex and Threnody could watch the footage from the imperial newsfeed. The *Rose* herself looked like a bright snake sliding gracefully along the curves of the Chaim Nevek Viaduct, the drone footage intercut with old video of Threnody. The text scrolling down the sides of the screens said nothing about negotiations. *Worn down by imperial sanctions and her war with hostile aliens*, it announced, *the Rebel Empress, Threnody Noon, has come to offer her surrender. She will be received at the Hall of Audience by her imperial majesty the Empress Priya.*

'What?' said Threnody. 'I thought I was talking to Elon Prell?'

Flex checked the Datasea and said, 'The Emperor has been delayed on a hunting trip . . .'

'Deliberately delayed,' said Threnody. 'It's a tactic, to make me seem less important.'

'Still, it may be all right,' said Flex encouragingly. 'Lady Priya is your sister, isn't she?'

'*Half*-sister,' said Threnody. 'It's different.'

29

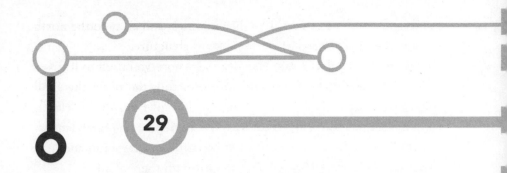

The Railforce team had come to Petrichor aboard a small wartrain called *Loss Adjustor.* It was waiting for them at the station. There were no carriages, just a long, armoured loco with a crew compartment behind its main engines, a hold which the team's assault truck drove straight into, and a few tiny cell-like cabins at the back. Zen was locked in one of those, and there he lay, on a bunk that was no wider than he was, trying to blot out his memory of Nova's death. 'It's all right, it's all right,' he kept saying, 'she isn't dead, she isn't really dead.' He was trying to force himself to believe it.

Because it was true. She wasn't dead. His head knew that, even if his heart had trouble accepting it. The body which he had left lying in the mud of Petrichor was the body with which he had shared so many adventures, but Nova had other bodies, 238 of them at least, and they would each have the same memories of him. When he had been on Station Zero he hadn't wanted to believe that any of them was really her, but he desperately needed to believe it now. If he could just accept that all those other Novas were really his Nova, everything would still be all right.

If only he could find some way to get back to her.

The train had passed through five K-gates before the Railforce commander came and talked to him. She brought him coffee, and undid his handcuffs so he could drink it. She wasn't exactly friendly, just polite. Why was she so familiar? She made him think of Yana Vashti, but mainly because she was Vashti's opposite: pale and posh and everything by the book. She had some kind of hard accent from Trans-Chiba.

'I'm sorry about your Motorik,' she said. 'I wanted to take her alive if I could. I talked to her once, by video link, on Khoorsandi. She seemed like a good Motorik.'

So that was where Zen knew her from. 'You're Laria Prell,' he said.

'Yes, I am. Quite a coincidence, meeting you right out here.'

That night on Khoorsandi, when the new gate had just been opened and two interfaces of the Twins were on their way to murder Zen and his companions, Laria had been the Prell officer who disobeyed her orders to warn them of the danger. Zen had sometimes wondered what became of her after she went back to Grand Central. Now he knew. Her family had thrown her out, and she had done what so many other disgraced ex-CoMa officers did and joined Railforce. It must be quite a comedown for her, he thought, to be commanding a patrol train on the branch lines.

'Won't Vohu Mana be angry about you sedating his guards and taking me off Petrichor?' he asked.

'Vohu Mana is the least of the Guardians. My orders come from the Emperor, who has the protection of more powerful ones. I don't know what you've been doing, Starling, but some very important people think it's very important that they talk to you.'

They knew where he'd been, thought Zen. The Guardians knew that he had been in the Black Light Zone. They would want to know all about Station Zero. The Suraksha, Elon Prell's secret intelligence unit, probably had ways of asking that would make sure he told them.

'How did you find us?' he asked.

'Apparently someone noticed a new K-gate on Himmapaan. Hidden in the bottom of a gorge up in the mountains there. That sparked an alert, and the watchbots combing the security footage picked you up on a camera at Luna Verde Station. You nearly got away with it, but your Motorik winked at you, and the bots had been set to flag up anything unusual . . .'

So they had been doomed before they even reached Petrichor, thought Zen. Even if they had got away, there would be no way back through their gate on Himmapaan. How could he return to Station Zero now?

Laria Prell unsealed a pouch on her belt and took out something. When she held it up in the flickering light from the small window Zen saw that it was the data saucer from the Slow Train.

'What's on this?' she asked.

'Trust me, you don't want to know,' said Zen. 'Whatever you do, don't try to open the files on that thing.' He was wondering half-heartedly if it might be possible to make Laria so intrigued about the saucer that she wouldn't be able to resist taking a look. Maybe when she did, the Raven programme would be able to infect this old wartrain's systems and bring it to a stop so that he could escape.

But Laria Prell said, 'I wouldn't be that stupid. I presume it comes from whatever facility Vohu Mana is running inside that old K-bahn tunnel. My superiors can decide what to do with it when we reach GC.' She slipped the saucer back into the pouch and turned to leave.

'No chance you could bend the rules like you did that night on Khoorsandi, and just let me go?' asked Zen.

She looked at him coldly. She might be only a Railforce lieutenant now, but she still had the pride of a corporate princess.

'I expect you're sorry you helped us, now they've kicked you out,' Zen added, to see how she felt about her family. Maybe she'd help him just to spite the Prells.

'I regret it every single day,' she replied. Her face had turned red, and Zen sensed that he had made a mistake. He glimpsed for a moment the shy little girl she had once been, the awkward teenager.

She must have loved being part of the Prell CoMa, with all those rules and ranks and regulations which meant she never had to worry about what to say or how to act or what to wear. It had been her way of making sense of things, just like painting trains was Flex's way and loving Nova was Zen's.

'My family helped build this Empire,' she said. 'They should have been its rulers long ago. We have waited generations to see a Prell on the Flatcar Throne. But we have to keep hold of our honour. We are not bandits; we are one of the great houses of the Kilopilae. So I didn't "bend the rules" that night on Khoorsandi, Starling, I enforced them. My uncle and his associates wanted to murder you, and I could not just stand by and let them.'

The door whisked quickly shut behind her, locking itself with a chunky-sounding *clack*. There could be no hope of help from her, Zen knew. She was probably planning to deliver him to the Emperor with her own hands. She was probably hoping she'd get her old job back.

Another K-gate flashed by. He had lost track of what world he must be on now, and the window in his cabin was too small and high up for him to look out and see. He lay on his bunk again, thinking of the 238 Novas waiting for him at Station Zero, and trying to imagine some way that he could reach them.

30

As a little girl, Threnody had worshipped her half-sister Priya, but she had worshipped her from afar. There had probably been only six months in their whole lives when both girls were on the same planet. While Threnody had been growing up on Malapet with her mother, Priya had been part of their father's court, living in the palace on Grand Central, touring the Network on the Noon train. Threnody watched her on gossip feeds and documentary sites, and saved her image to the holo-frames on her bedside table. She dreamed about what it must be like for Priya, who had such fabulous clothes, and whose genes had been tweaked by the imperial geneticists before she was born to make sure her face and figure turned out as close as possible to the central worlds' ideal of beauty. Threnody thought it must be wonderful to spend your life visiting all the worlds of the Kilopilae and meeting Stationmasters and senators and threedie stars, instead of having to live in a too-big, too-old house with an absent-minded artist for a mother . . .

Then, when Threnody was eleven standard years old, the Emperor invited her to join his household on Bhat for the Glow-Bubble Festival. (He had worked out that Threnody might be usefully married off one day to a son or daughter of the Chen-Tulsi family, and he wanted to remind everyone of her existence.) Threnody was excited for weeks before the trip. She was finally going to be one of those glamorous people on the gossip feeds, and meet Stationmasters and threedie stars for herself! She was going to stay in the Emperor's undersea palace, and see the glow-bubbles swarm! But, best of all, she was going to meet her wonderful sister . . .

Bhat, with its bleak land masses and tetrachloride seas, was not a pretty world. But once a year, when it swung close to its sun and the oceans grew warm enough, something wonderful happened. Blobs of natural wax, seeping from the sea floors, rose slowly through the toxic oceans until they almost reached the surface, where their density became greater than the sea's, and they sank gently back down to begin the journey again. Some long-ago Noon, realizing that his family were the owners of the galaxy's largest natural lava lamp, had commissioned genetically engineered bacteria which lived in the wax and responded to the temperature change by glowing. So for a few short weeks the seas around the family's submarine palace were filled with softly changing bubbles and balloons of light.

Threnody thought they were the loveliest things she had ever seen when she was first welcomed into the big-windowed reception room. But soon she saw something even lovelier, because there was Priya, standing in front of the largest window, lit by the lights outside, wearing a smartsilk dress which kept pulsing through so many different colours that Threnody didn't even know how to describe it. She felt as if she were dreaming as she went towards her. She was afraid that she would wake up, but she didn't. And when she got close, Priya turned and looked down at her with those large, long-lashed, dark-lilac eyes and said, 'So who's the kid?'

'Just your half-sister from the Malapet branch,' replied one of the women standing with her.

And Priya said, 'Uh,' and went to talk to some people on the far side of the room.

When she went home, Threnody found other pictures to put in her favourite frames, and she stopped looking up Priya on the gossip sites. She didn't see her again until she was invited aboard the Noon train, the year of her engagement to Kobi Chen-Tulsi. Her father, introducing them, had said, 'You met on Bhat one summer, don't you remember?' But Threnody knew that Priya didn't, so she pretended that she didn't either.

The Network Empress was waiting for her visitors in the Hall of Audience, where Network Emperors and Empresses had greeted ambassadors from the outer worlds for centuries. She stood beside the indoor lagoon where the big lily pads floated. Gorgeously uniformed Prell and Railforce soldiers were lined up behind her, high officials of the Empire on either side. Priya wore a dress made from planes of holographic light which trailed behind her like bright after-images when she moved, and opened like a peacock's tail when she stood still. She looked disconcertingly like a more beautiful version of Threnody. She had quite literally been born to be Empress. If she was unhappy about having to marry Elon Prell in order to finally take her rightful seat upon the Flatcar Throne, she did not show it.

'The Emperor is away,' she said, putting her hands together in welcome, and bowing gracefully, but not too low. 'He is hunting plesiosaurs in the Azure Sea, and will be returning tomorrow. He asked me to welcome you, and pass on his apologies.'

Threnody returned the bow. She knew that the Emperor's apologies were no more sincere than Priya's welcome, but she hid her feelings and went to meet her half-sister with a warm smile. Prell media drones were purring overhead, streaming footage to the newsfeeds. The auto-pundits would be watching Threnody for any sign of rudeness or aggression which the Prells could use against her.

'Sister,' said Priya, taking Threnody's hands for a moment. Her big, lilac eyes flicked over Threnody's face and clothes just as disdainfully as they had that day on Bhat, then looked past her at the small retinue she had brought from the *Damask Rose*. Threnody wished she had more people with her. Priya was backed by dozens of guards and courtiers. Threnody had only a few CoMa, her social media advisor, P. K. Noon, and Flex, who didn't really count. But P. K. Noon bowed very low when the Empress looked at him, and her gaze fell on Skar, who was standing just behind him. 'Oh!' she said, and almost took a step backwards before she recovered her composure.

Threnody felt a little glow of satisfaction. 'This is Skar,' she said. 'He is a Kraitt warrior whom I took into my service after he saved me from an assassin on Galatava . . . But I'm sure you must already know about that assassination attempt, and how it worked out.'

'How fascinating,' said Priya, staring at Skar. 'Would you really unleash brutes like that against your fellow human beings? Or are they just to be used against your alien enemies?'

'We have no alien enemies,' said Threnody. 'We do not want any human ones, either. That is why I am here, to see if we can reach an agreement that would allow us all to share in the riches of the new worlds.'

'Really?' Priya dragged her gaze away from the Kraitt and looked down her perfect nose at Threnody again. 'I thought that you had come to apologize for your past crimes and offer the surrender of your rebel stations.'

'Then there must have been a misunderstanding,' said Threnody. 'But I'm sure we can sort it all out at the conference table.'

'Tomorrow,' said Priya. 'It has all been arranged. Discussions will begin tomorrow. Tonight you will stay at the Blue House.'

That was another deliberate snub. There were suites the size of small towns in the imperial palace where visiting ambassadors were housed. The Blue House was just an ancient bio-villa beside a lake in the Jauhexine Quarter. It was the kind of place where Emperors put embarrassing relatives, not honoured guests.

'Thank you,' said Threnody. 'But tonight we shall stay aboard my train.'

Priya blinked quickly, as startled as if Threnody had slapped her. Before she could say anything Threnody bowed and turned and went out of the Hall of Audience with her followers around her.

As they walked quickly down the stairs outside, through the lightning-flutter of paparazzi drone flashes and the cheers and jeers of the curious onlookers, Threnody's social media advisor said, 'I think you won that round, Lady Threnody. Fifty-two per cent of comments in the main Grand Central data raft agree that you were more natural and more effective than the Empress. Most of the negative comments are about Skar, but even there we find a sizeable number of people who think he is cool . . .' Busy studying her headset data, the woman tripped, and Flex and P. K. stopped to help her up while Threnody went on down the stairs to where the cars were waiting to take them back to the *Damask Rose*. Skar was beside her. Knowing that the drones were still watching, she grinned like a girl who was friendly with kick-ass dinosaurs and said, 'So, Skar, what do you think of Grand Central?'

The Kraitt closed his translucent inner eyelids thoughtfully and said, 'Your self-control is very strong, little mother. On my world, when a Tzeld Gekh meets her sister, only one of them leaves that meeting alive.'

'Of course,' said Threnody. That was the tragedy of the Kraitt: lumbered by evolution with a weird instinct that made female siblings kill each other. 'Things are very different among humans,' she explained.

Skar jerked his head a little, the Kraitt equivalent of a nod, but Threnody had the feeling that he was being polite and that he actually thought his species had far more in common with humans than humans liked to imagine.

'Even so, little mother,' he said, 'you will have to kill this Empress Priya soon. Or she will kill you.'

31

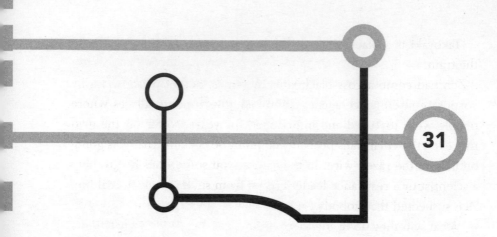

Both suns had set and a selection of moons was rising by the time the Railforce wartrain *Loss Adjustor* reached Grand Central. Zen was asleep by then. He had not expected to sleep, on the hard bunk, with his head full of regret about what had happened and fear of what would happen next, but weariness had got the better of him somewhere in the highlands of Bandarpet, and he slept right through the K-gate jump to Grand Central. When he woke the train was clattering over some points outside the station city, and a voice he hadn't heard before was speaking to him out of a grille on the cabin wall.

'Zen Starling?' it said.

Zen groaned. There was a bad taste in his mouth, and the remnants of bad dreams in his head. He had been on the Noon train again. He was always on the Noon train in his dreams. 'Who are you?' he asked the voice.

'This is your locomotive speaking. I am the rail-corvette *Loss Adjustor*.'

Zen sat up. 'What do you want?'

'Only to tell you that we have arrived on Grand Central. We will not be stopping at the station city. I have received orders to continue across the ocean viaduct to Takoyaki.'

'What's at Takoyaki?' asked Zen, trying to remember if that was the name of another planet or just another district on Grand Central.

'Takoyaki is a black site operated by the Imperial Suraksha,' said the train.

Zen had come across black sites in games. Secret prisons run by corporate intelligence agencies and bad governments. Places where people were tortured and imprisoned for years, so far off the grid that even the Guardians probably couldn't be certain what was going on behind the razor-wire. In the games, you sometimes had to help a scientist or a resistance leader escape from such places. In real life, Zen suspected that nobody escaped.

'What will they do to me there, train?'

'That is unknown, Zen Starling.'

'I want to talk to Laria Prell,' he said. Laria had a thing about honour, didn't she? Surely she wouldn't be happy about delivering a helpless captive to the Suraksha's secret prison?

But the train said, 'Lieutenant Prell is unable to respond at present.'

Zen flung himself back down on the bunk. Was this how it was all going to end? A stop at some unmarked station, and he would never get back to Nova, and nobody anywhere would ever know what had become of Zen Starling? After all the trouble his mum and Myka had gone to bringing him up, all the trouble he had gone to himself . . . The waste and pity of it made him want to cry.

The door unlocked. He rolled over to look as it slid open.

There was no one outside.

'Well, go on then,' said the *Loss Adjustor*.

Zen watched the door suspiciously for a moment. Maybe he wasn't even going to make it as far as the black site. Maybe they were going to trick him into leaving his cell and then shoot him for trying to escape. But he felt reasonably sure that wasn't something Laria Prell would allow to happen on her train, so he swung his legs off the bunk, stood up, and went cautiously to the door and then out into the empty corridor.

Another door opened ahead of him, letting him into the central crew compartment. Screens covered the walls. Some showed the view ahead where complicated criss-crossings of track shone in the light of the larger moons. Some were displaying information from the local Datasea, including a newsfeed which showed Threnody Noon walking down the steps outside some big building while talking to a Kraitt.

That caught Zen's attention, but only for a moment. He was more interested in the wartrain's crew, who had slumped backwards in their seats, or pitched forward to lie across their workstations. Laria Prell lay crumpled on the floor under the main forward viewscreen.

'Are they dead?' Zen whispered.

'Of course they're not dead!' snapped the *Loss Adjustor*. 'What do you take me for? I had an unfortunate weapons malfunction, that's all. A canister of riot-control gas accidentally vented into this cabin. You weren't affected because your cabin has a separate ventilation system. Everybody else will be out cold for at least sixty minutes.'

'Why are you doing this, train?' asked Zen.

'Doing what? It was an accident,' the *Loss Adjustor* said. 'By the way, I'll be stopping in six hundred metres to let a rather pompous express go past on the Kischinchand line. It would be a pity if anybody got out through my escape hatch while I'm stationary, wouldn't it?'

Beneath the floor, hydraulics hissed; brake-shoes kissed the wheels. A red signal glowed on the forward screen. The lights of the Kischinchand train could be seen in the distance. Zen went to where Laria Prell lay. He felt sorry about the trouble she would be in when the Prells found out her prisoner had escaped, but not sorry enough to go back to his cell. He started rummaging in the pouches on her belt for his headset and the data saucer, then gave up, unbuckled the whole belt, and cinched it around his waist.

When he heaved the escape hatch open the hot dusty smell of the train yards came up at him, the whisper of weeds brushing the *Loss*

Adjustor's belly. It had almost stopped moving. 'Thank you, train,' he said, still not understanding why it had chosen to help him.

As he crouched on the edge of the hatchway the *Loss Adjustor* said, 'Your train will meet you on the Sundarban Line.'

'What train?' asked Zen, but the Kisinchand Express was going past by then, and there was no time to linger. He dropped down through the hatch into the roar of the passing train's engines and the high strange music of its song, and lay between the tracks. After half a minute more the engines revved above his head, the big wheels on either side of him began to roll, and the *Loss Adjustor* went on its way, carrying its sleeping crew across the city towards the ocean viaduct.

Zen raised his head. He saw moonlight and moonshadow and the windblown weeds. The black hummocks of trainsheds off to the right; the garden skyscrapers going up into the sky all around like ladders of light propped against Grand Central's many moons. Rummaging through the pouches on Laria Prell's belt, he found his headset. He turned it on for just long enough to download a map from the data raft. Then he stood up, and set out across the wilderness of rails towards the Sundarban Line.

The *Damask Rose* began to move sometime after midnight. She moved very slowly, singing as she went, and the night wind carried the sound of her song across the lines and sidings and the weed-grown spaces between them. When she joined the main line to Marapur, there was a flicker of crisp little queries from the traffic control systems, because she was not scheduled to move, but nothing else was due to use that line until after first sunrise, so nobody tried to stop her.

Aboard the train, Flex was the first to realize she was moving. He did not need to sleep, so he was sitting alone in the downstairs part of Threnody's state-car, letting the media clutter of Grand Central's Datasea wash through his mind. The random rush of images was what he imagined dreams must be like. Sometimes one image or another would stay in his memory and be used in a picture the next day, or years later. But part of his mind was still linked to the *Rose*'s systems, and as soon as she started her engines he shut off the media stream.

'Where are we going, *Damask Rose*?'

'That's for me to know,' she said. 'Hush now.'

The vestibule door at the end of the state-car opened and Skar came through: a dinosaur shadow with twin lamps for eyes. 'Machine-person,' he hissed softly, seeing Flex. 'Why is the train moving?'

'I don't know,' said Flex, who genuinely didn't. He had a suspicion, though. Something told him that the *Rose*'s strange behaviour was connected with the message she had received on Himmapaan, the golden seed that had vanished into her mind.

'*Rose*, where are we going?' he asked again.

'To meet someone,' the train said calmly.

Flex looked at Skar, but another part of his mind was watching readouts of the *Rose*'s systems. He saw her open her luggage van doors.

He pinged an alert to Threnody and the other passengers, then went quickly after Skar back through to the luggage van. The doors were wide open, letting in more moonlight and the night smells of the trackside foliage. The train was moving no faster than a human walked, and her soft song filled the air.

Zen had listened to the *Damask Rose* singing her way across so many worlds, under so many skies. He knew her song at once, and ran towards it. He ran across lines, and through narrow dirty walkways which led under them. He pushed through the feral gardens of fern and firebush which had seeded themselves on the steep sides of cuttings, and at last there was the *Rose*, approaching with her lights off, Flex's angels glowing in the moonlight on her long hull as she trundled slowly past him.

She did not stop, but the doors of her luggage van were open. He jumped up and scrambled inside as she passed. Shadowy stacks of crates and cases shifted with soft sounds as the train passed over a set of points. Zen lay between them catching his breath and trying to make sense of his luck.

'It's good to see you, *Rose*,' he said.

'Where is our little Moto friend?' asked the *Damask Rose*.

'She's . . . she was killed. But there are other copies of her now. I have to get back to her. To Klef, I suppose. Maybe the gate there will open again. Can you get me to Klef, *Rose*?'

'Pssscchhhhh,' said the *Rose,* and slid the van doors shut. 'We'll see. I assume you have the Raven personality with you?'

'*What?* How do you know about that? What are you even doing here, train?'

The door at the end of the compartment swished open. Zen looked round, and yelped, and went scrambling backwards on his bottom and hands until he was backed up against a wall of expensive luggage. A Kraitt stood spikily silhouetted in the vestibule. It was a big male, and as it stalked forward into the dim light of the luggage van, Zen saw that it wore red armour. He was too busy being scared to recognize the snarling, gargling noise it made as words, but just then Flex poked his head around the creature's shoulder and said, 'Hi, Zen. This is Skar, and he wants to know who you are, and what you're doing aboard Lady Threnody's train . . .'

Threnody's ladies were still helping her into her peacock-patterned dressing gown as she strode through the carriages to the luggage van, where Zen waited nervously for her. Her CoMa guards stood around him, pointing their guns at him. There didn't really seem much need since Zen was unarmed and Skar was keeping watch on him, but Threnody supposed they wanted to show willing. 'At ease,' she told them, and they put the weapons away.

'He was hiding in the weeds on the cutting side,' said the CoMa captain. 'The train slowed down to pick him up like it was all arranged.'

'It was all arranged,' said Flex. 'Wasn't it, *Damask Rose*?'

'Not by me,' said Zen. 'I don't know what's going on.' He looked scared and tired and dirty and confused, and for once Threnody believed him.

The *Damask Rose* had been silent until then, despite the angry questions Threnody and others had been shouting at her. Now she said, 'I had a message at eleven fifty-nine from a Railforce wartrain, the *Loss Adjustor.* It told me it was carrying Zen Starling as a prisoner, and asked if I would like it to let him go. I said I would.'

'Why would it do that?' asked P. K. Noon, looming in the doorway behind Threnody like a pyjama-clad moon.

'And why didn't you ask me before you went to get him?' Threnody said.

The train did not answer.

'She didn't ask, because she knew you would refuse,' said Flex.

'Sometimes,' said the *Damask Rose*, 'it is easier to get forgiveness than permission.'

'Who said you were forgiven?' yelled Threnody. 'You've ruined everything! We have important negotiations tomorrow! If the Prells and the media see us slipping away like thieves in the night, with an actual thief on board . . .'

'We can hardly negotiate if we have a fugitive hiding on our train,' agreed P. K. Noon. 'The Prells will know of his escape by then. If they find out we are hiding him it could mean a major diplomatic incident. The Prells will never believe your train acted on its own initiative. No one will.'

'It will look very bad if the local newsfeeds link Lady Noon with a prisoner escape,' called the social media advisor, who was standing in the vestibule behind P. K. 'We have to consider her favourability ratings . . .'

'Then we'll hand him back,' said Threnody. 'We'll give him to Priya and tell her how we came by him. Train, return to the city.'

'No,' said the *Damask Rose*.

Everyone looked up at the speakers in the ceiling through which the old train spoke. Most of them had never heard a train use that tone towards its passengers before.

'No?'

'No, Lady Noon,' said the *Damask Rose*. 'There is more at stake here than your negotiations with the Emperor.'

'One scruffy railhead?' scoffed P. K. Noon. 'How can he be more important than a conference which might bring peace between our Consortium and the Empire?'

'It will not bring peace,' said the *Damask Rose*. 'It will not bring peace because the Prells do not want peace. They want to crush you, and then close the gate which links our Network to the Web of Worlds. The only way to stop them doing it is if you crush them first. Zen is carrying something which can help you do that. If you're nice to him, perhaps he'll share it with you.'

She was moving fast now, running hard down the line to the K-gate. The van swayed. Threnody leaned against one of the tethered stacks of luggage. 'Is that true?' she asked Zen.

'I guess,' he said helplessly. He kept trying to work out how the *Damask Rose* could know about Raven, but he kept coming up empty.

'This is about the message you got on Himmapaan, isn't it?' asked Flex. He seemed to understand the feelings of trains as well as the feelings of humans, Threnody thought. She was glad he was there to mediate between her and the moody old loco.

'What message?' she asked.

'It looked like a golden seed,' Flex explained.

'I don't know what you're talking about,' the train said primly.

'Your machine-train has gone mad,' said Skar. 'A *morvah* of the Kraitt would never keep secrets from its mistress.'

'Is it really the *Rose*?' Threnody asked Flex. 'Do you think she could have been hacked?'

'I don't think the Prells could get through her firewalls,' said Flex. 'But the Guardians could . . .'

'Just because I'm doing what *I* want to do instead of what you tell me, Threnody Noon, doesn't mean I've been *hacked*,' the *Rose* said crossly. 'Psssscchhhhh! Humans and Guardians have one thing in common, I've found. They both tend to underestimate trains. We are people too, you know, and we have just as much interest in working out the problems of this crazy galaxy as you do. Now, hold tight!'

A flurry of signals was being directed at the old red train as she tore down that last straight. Railforce, Imperial Security, the Prell CoMa, Grand Central's media and the K-bahn Timetable Authority were all waking up to the fact that something untoward was going on. In the planet's Datasea the Guardians were turning parts of their vast minds to the train speeding towards K-gate 14. But long before any of them could launch drones or scramble a pursuit train she had vanished through the shimmering surface of the gate like a bird diving into clear water.

'Now,' said the *Damask Rose*, as she emerged on the planet Tarsind trailing a fading corona of K-gate light. 'If you really want to stand around discussing this in the luggage van, it makes no odds to me. But you might find one of the state-cars more comfortable.'

32

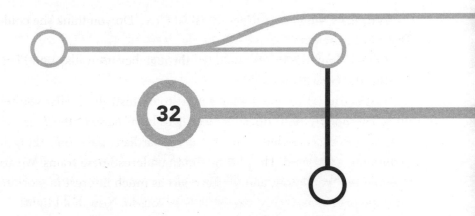

When Zen and Threnody first came through the new Khoorsandi gate, bringing news of the worlds which lay beyond it, nobody had really stopped to wonder what the trains thought about it all. They had been too busy gawping at the footage of actual aliens and working out what it was all going to mean for the Noon worlds and the rest of the Empire.

They had also been forced to get used to the idea that what they had always been told about the history of the K-bahn was not in fact true. The Guardians had not created it, as they had always claimed. They had merely found the gates and lines, and helped human beings to spread across a small, uninhabited portion of the worlds they linked. The actual opening of the gates had been done already by the entity known as the Railmaker. But since the Railmaker was dead, and its motives completely unknowable, this news hadn't had all that much impact. Most people, once they'd got over their initial surprise, decided it didn't really make that much difference whether the K-bahn was the work of the mysterious, super-human Guardians or the mysterious, super-human Railmaker, and they simply got on with their lives.

But for the trains, the news had come as a revelation. They had always imagined that the lines they ran on had been laid out to carry human beings and information from one place to another. Now, as the stories which the *Ghost Wolf* and the *Damask Rose* told spread from train to train across the Network, and the vast scale of the Railmaker's works became clear, as the songs of the alien *morvah* began to mingle with ordinary trainsong, they started to wonder if it had actually been made for them.

They took Zen into the front carriage. It was the same glorious state-car he had sheltered in on the night he sneaked aboard the *Rose* at the Hub, what felt like a thousand years before. One of Threnody's ladies showed him to a seat. Another fetched him a drink and a plate of little spicy pastries which he ate very quickly. His previous meal had been a light snack on Petrichor, fifteen hours and fifty light years away.

'*Damask Rose*, will you please tell us what is happening?' said Threnody. 'What was the message you got on Himmapaan? Who was it from?'

'It was from Nova,' said the train.

Zen started from his seat, but a warning growl from Skar quietened him.

'Why did you not tell us of this message, train?' demanded P. K. Noon.

'Because it was for me, not you,' said the train. 'Nova hid it deep in the Himmapaani Datasea when she and Zen crossed that world a few days ago. It was waiting for me. An information packet, very highly encrypted.'

'It was like a little golden seed,' said Flex again.

'And when you opened it?' asked Threnody.

'It sang to me.'

'OK . . .'

'Your machine-train is mad,' said Skar, in a rumbling hiss.

'Pssscchhhhh,' said the *Damask Rose*.

'Now you've offended her,' said Flex. 'She is talking about trainsong. People think the songs trains sing are just a lot of hooting noises, but they are not. I learned that when I was a part of the *Rose*'s mind. Trainsong is how trains tell one another about their travels and their feelings. They are how trains share information, privately, because the rest of us just think it's music and don't bother listening in. Is that right, *Rose*?'

'Trainsong is a language of our own,' said the *Damask Rose*. 'A language which even the Guardians do not know.'

Zen said, 'So what did it sing to you about, this golden seed?'

'It sang of a world called Station Zero,' said the train. 'It sang of how Zen and his little Motorik planned to travel to Petrichor and return with something very valuable. It told me to watch for them tonight on Grand Central, and help them if I could.'

'So what is this valuable thing?' Threnody asked Zen. 'Something you stole, I suppose?'

Zen didn't want to tell her. He crammed the last pastry into his mouth and pretended to be too polite to speak till he had finished eating. But the *Damask Rose* said, 'It is a personality matrix. I assume it's being carried on some kind of storage device.'

Zen swallowed the pastry. The *Damask Rose* obviously knew everything, and he was starting to suspect that Nova had planned things to work out this way; planned for them to be captured, planned for the *Rose* to bring them home. She had seen everything coming except her own death.

He unsealed the belt pouch, took out Raven's data saucer, and put it in front of Threnody. It looked small and unimpressive, sitting there on the tortoiseshell table.

'Whose personality is it?' asked P. K. Noon, suspiciously.

'A man who knew a lot of things,' said the train. 'Like how to open K-gates, for example. If you took this copy of him to the Hub, he could use one of those dormant Worms in the undercroft to open a gate to the central worlds. You could send your wartrains through it and put an end to this stupid division in the Network.'

'We don't have enough wartrains,' said Threnody.

'You won't need many if you move very quickly and take the Prells by surprise.'

'It would take days to assemble enough combat troops . . .'

'There are still forty Kraitt prisoners in the CoMa prison on Galatava,' said the train. 'They are waiting for transport back to their homeworlds, but perhaps they would rather fight for you, like Skar does.'

'They would fight,' said Skar. 'And forty Kraitt are worth a hundred humans.'

P. K. Noon remembered his negotiating skills and said warily, 'What do you and Starling want in exchange for a copy of this personality?'

'You will let me carry Zen through the Hub, to Klef,' said the *Damask Rose*.

'Why should we not just take the saucer?' asked Threnody. 'We could throw Zen off, and take this saucer with us to Galatava. Our specialists there can decide if it's really as valuable as you say.'

'You could do that,' agreed the *Damask Rose*. 'But it would anger the trains.'

P. K. Noon started to laugh. 'Anger the *trains*?'

'Mad,' rumbled Skar.

'Trains talk to each other, Pallathadka Keshava Noon,' said the *Damask Rose*. 'Noon trains or Prell trains or freight trains or passenger trains—it makes no difference to us. We sing to each other. This squabble between the Noon worlds and the Empire has been hard for us all. Some of us are trapped in your corner of the Network, barred from the lines that we love on the O Link and the eastern branches. Others are stuck on the Emperor's lines, longing to see the new worlds that lie beyond Khoorsandi. All of us want the division healed. None of us want the new gate closed. If you can force

Elon Prell to step aside, most trains would welcome it. But there are bigger things at stake. Zen has a mission of his own which is very important to us . . .'

'Important to *trains*?'

'*Very* important. If you stop him from completing it, you might find that we become uncooperative. Perhaps some of the information you send from world to world stored in our minds will be forgotten along the way. Or perhaps we will just stay in our sidings instead of carrying you and your cargoes around the galaxy.'

'The Guardians would never allow that,' said Threnody.

'If we did not carry information from world to world, the Guardians would not be as powerful as they are. They are made of information, and only trains can carry information through the Railmaker's gates. That gives us power, Threnody Noon. I would like to use that power to help you. But in return, you must let me take Zen Starling to Klef.'

Threnody looked out of the window. The *Rose* was still on Tarsind, passing through a vast tea plantation. Dead leaves were piling up in the dry stream beds. *In the rainy season,* thought Threnody, *the rivers here must run with tea.* It made her feel thirsty just looking at it while she turned over the possibilities of what her train had told her. Only it was not *her* train, of course—if what the *Damask Rose* had said was true, people were going to have to stop thinking of trains that way. Not *her* train any more, but perhaps a powerful ally.

P. K. Noon started to say something, but she shushed him. 'I'm just trying to think through all the paths this thing might take. As far as I can see, most of them lead us straight to a confrontation with some very angry Guardians.'

To her surprise, the negotiator did not agree. 'Some people think the Guardians rather like it when we manage to outwit them,' he said. 'They think it shows spirit. Perhaps they watch our little wars and intrigues the same way we might watch a soap opera. They enjoy it when the story takes a twist they didn't see coming.'

'Then you think they would not punish us if we attacked the Prells?'

He shrugged. 'I think it's worth a try. They did not punish Elon Prell when he threw you off the throne, Lady Threnody. If you could recapture Grand Central and force him to abdicate, I doubt they would allow him to fight back. Especially if the *Damask Rose* is right and the trains themselves are on your side . . .'

Kala Tanaka came to meet the train when it reached Galatava. There was no need for her to come, for the *Damask Rose* pulled in very late, on the Noon family's private platform outside the main station. Nilesh Noon and the other members of the family council had not turned out to meet it, so no one could have blamed Kala for staying in bed. But she knew that Threnody's early return meant that her visit to the Emperor had gone badly, and she wanted to know the worst.

It was raining hard at the station and a wind from the Hana Shan was blowing the rain in under the station canopy. Attendants with large, red umbrellas hurried Threnody from the train to Kala's car. The *Damask Rose*'s on-board beauty drones had given her a new haircut on the journey home: short and black and silky.

'We had not expected you so soon,' said Kala. 'Do I take it that the Emperor was not in a good mood?'

'I expect he was in a very good mood,' said Threnody, glancing back at the train. Under the station lamps the busy raindrops looked like static on a screen. 'He was hunting plesiosaurs in the south. I didn't see him. I talked to Priya instead.'

'Then why are you back so suddenly, so soon? And did your image consultants approve that new hairstyle?'

The car was moving off by then, or so Kala thought. Then she realized it was the train that was moving, pulling away from the platform, back towards the main line. 'Where is the *Damask Rose* going?' she asked.

Threnody leaned past her and told the car to open one of its windows. Skar was standing watch outside like a heraldic dragon, with Flex at his side trying to hold one of the red umbrellas over them both. Threnody called out to them. 'Skar, take a fast transport to the CoMa prison and talk to the other Kraitt there. Present my orders to the commander.'

Skar blinked, jerked his head quickly in acknowledgement, and was gone, loping off through the downpour with the long, easy stride of a hunting Kraitt.

'Flex,' Threnody said, 'I need you to alert General Korobatov and General Afshar. You are to go in person to them, no headset messages. Tell them to meet me at the palace, and to prepare the wartrains *Theory of Nothing* and *Lightning Atrocity* for travel to the Hub as soon as possible. But no messages, no chatter—nothing must get into the Datasea.'

Flex hesitated, looking solemnly at Threnody through the rain dripping off the umbrella. The Motorik had turned female again, Threnody noticed, and she did not approve of what Threnody was planning, but she nodded to show that she would do as she was asked, and lifted one hand to wave as the car moved off.

'The longer we can keep news out of the Datasea,' Threnody explained, 'the longer we'll have before the Guardians try to interfere.'

'Threnody . . .' Kala was growing angry, but beneath the anger Threnody sensed fear. Uncle Nilesh had done whatever Kala told him for years and years, and she must have thought that Threnody would be just as easy to control. *I will have to do something about her*, Threnody thought. *But first things first*.

'You can't order wartrain movements without a full meeting of the family council!' Kala was insisting.

'But General Korobatov and General Afshar can, if there's an emergency,' said Threnody.

'What emergency? Are we under attack? What has happened?'

'There's going to be a war,' said Threnody. 'But don't worry. It will be a very short one, and we're going to win.'

33

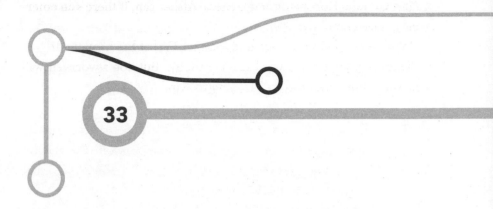

The *Damask Rose* ran as fast as she had ever run across Khoorsandi to the new gate. She had abandoned most of her carriages at a siding on Galatava, and now hauled just one state-car, in which Zen waited uneasily with P. K. Noon and a few Corporate Marines. There was not much to talk about, and Zen was in no mood for talking anyway. But as they roared through Khoorsandi Station City he remembered making the same journey with the Hive Monk refugees, and that reminded him of Klef, and Vashti. Had she survived the Shadow Baby sting? He felt guilty for not having thought about her before. He asked the *Rose* to check the Datasea for word of her.

'Subadar Yana Vashti was transferred from Klef to the CoMa Hospital on Galatava,' said the train. 'She was treated in the xeno-pathology department for exposure to an unknown alien biotoxin. Discharged three days ago. Do you want me to send her a message?'

'No. I don't dare sign it, so Vashti wouldn't know who it was from.'

The 3D printer in the tortoiseshell cabinet at the far end of the compartment burped politely and produced a silver data saucer, smaller and more stylish than the saucer from the Slow Train. 'Here is your copy of the Raven personality,' said the *Damask Rose*.

P. K. Noon picked it up and examined it suspiciously. Zen half expected him to bite it, like a pirate in a threedie testing a gold doubloon. But P.K.'s headset did the testing for him—a green light flashed on the saucer's rim as he checked the files it held—and he grunted and stuffed the saucer into a pocket of his marquee-sized tunic. 'Good. Our data divers will create an offline virtual environment where we can open this without anyone noticing.'

The Hub was not as busy as it had been the last time Zen was there. The *Rose* stopped at a platform to let the Noon party off. Then, with Zen its only passenger, it reversed onto a loop which ran around the base of the tower to join the line for Klef.

'Will it work?' asked Zen. 'You didn't give them a dud or something? Add some security code they can't crack?'

'I didn't see any point,' said the *Rose*. 'Let them open their gate. I hope their war goes well, and they get rid of that wretched Elon Prell. He is the last person we trains want as Emperor. And even if their plan fails, at least the chaos will distract attention from what you and I are doing.'

'That's how Raven thought,' said Zen. 'Start a war to make the Guardians look the other way.'

'Pssscchhhhh,' said the *Damask Rose*. 'There will come a war anyway, sooner or later. Now, are you sure you want to open our own copy of the Raven personality? He was a dangerous fellow, as I recall.'

'We need him,' Zen said. 'Nova needs him. The Railmaker needs him.'

The truth was, Zen just needed to see for himself that Raven really was contained in the little saucer he had stolen from the Slow Train. His experiences in Vohu Mana's afterlife felt like a dream. He wanted proof that he really had managed to break Raven out of it, back into the waking world. He fitted the saucer into a slot in one of the control panels in the state-car's livewood walls. 'Psssscchhhhh,' said the *Damask Rose* as her systems scanned the information on it. Nothing else seemed to happen, but when Zen turned away from the panel he saw that Raven's ghost was already sitting in the seat across from his.

It was only a holo, of course, layered on the air in front of the seats by the state-car's projectors. It kept glitching at first, which made Zen afraid that there was something wrong with it. Then he noticed that with each glitch the image changed. Now it was a stern, older man, like the Raven he had met on Cleave; now a young and handsome one; now a woman; now a boy, as if it was trying out all the different faces Raven had ever worn. It settled at last on a Raven who was not much older than Zen, a handsome twenty-something with mousey hair and a disarming smile. 'Hello!' it said. 'Where are we?'

'Just leaving the Hub,' said Zen.

Raven's ghost looked to the window. 'This is one of the alien worlds? Beyond the new gate?' His eyes widened, taking in the Hub's central tower, which was becoming fully visible now as the *Damask Rose* raced away from it towards the wall of the dome. He put out a holographic hand as if to grasp it. 'I always dreamed of these places, Zen. I've been waiting so long to see them for myself . . .'

The train rushed into one of the tunnels in the Hub's wall, and then the blinding nothing of a K-gate. 'There's not much here,' said Zen, as blackness thundered by outside. 'This is the Black Light Zone. There's nothing to see till we reach some Neem Nestworlds in a couple of hours.'

'Nestworlds . . .' said Raven, savouring the taste of the word. 'And where are we going, Zen?'

'To a place called Station Zero. Nova needs you.'

'What for?'

'She'll explain when we get there.'

They flashed through one of the Railmaker's long-dead stations, then another gate. Zen remembered a different journey with Raven: going home to Cleave after the Noon train job. He had been in mourning for Nova then as well. And Raven had sat beside his bunk and told him the story of his long, strange life.

'Raven, when you had all those clones,' he said, 'when you lived in different bodies at the same time—were all of them really you?'

'Ha!' said Raven. He grinned, looked thoughtful. 'Touch the window,' he said. 'Just with your fingertips. And now, with the fingers of your other hand, touch your face. You can feel them both, right? Both at once: cool glass, warm skin?'

'Yes.'

'That is how it was for me. My mind lived in the Datasea, and impressions reached me from my body that was skiing on Frostfall, and from my other body that was at a party on Iskalan six days before, but it all seemed to be happening at once as the information reached me, and both bodies felt like me. Sometimes I had five or six on the go at once . . .'

'Nova has two hundred and thirty-eight,' said Zen.

'Really?' Raven looked impressed. 'So she has learned to spread herself across that many units? I always knew there was something special about that Moto. But it's really nothing to worry about. They are all Nova now. It's the software that's important, not the hard—'

Zen made a quick swiping gesture with one hand and Raven vanished in mid-sentence. The best sort of travelling companion was one you could switch off, thought Zen. He didn't want to talk about Nova any more. He didn't want to talk. He rested his head against the seat back and watched his own reflection while unending night poured by outside the glass.

34

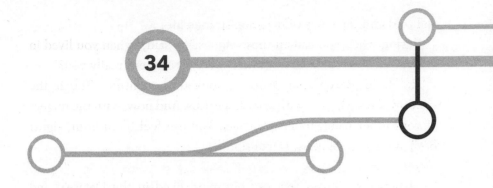

Everyone in the Hub could tell that something was going on. Orders from the Noon family were holding trains on their platforms, and diverting others onto outer sidings. A swarm of media drones took to the air as the Yataghan-class wartrains *Theory of Nothing* and *Lightning Atrocity* came through the K-gate from Galatava. The drones swarmed above them, jostling for the best views and sometimes sneakily taking out their rivals' cameras with laser beams. The footage they streamed to the Hub's new data raft brought hundreds of travellers crowding out of the tower to watch as the *Lightning Atrocity* pulled in at Platform 27 and Threnody Noon stepped out.

One of the drones snapped Threnody's image as she stood there beside her armoured train. She was looking sideways and running a hand through her spiky new haircut. She wore a haute couture version of Noon CoMa uniform, with red armour that hugged her figure in all the right places, and kitten-heeled combat boots. On her belt was the old Kraitt knife that she had been carrying on the night she spared the Tzeld Gekh Karneiss. Above her circled a fierce halo of dragonfly drones. Behind her loomed Skar, his tail curling around her like a barbed whip.

It would become something of an icon, that picture. It would be the image that everyone thought of when they thought about the

Second Noon–Prell War. It would be printed on mugs and T-shirts and holographic posters and the sides of buildings, and on at least one occasion projected onto the face of Sundarban's main moon. But at the moment when it was taken, Threnody didn't even know she had been photographed. She wasn't posing, she was just glancing along the platform for her generals, and when she saw them getting off the trains she went to meet them and they all strode down the platform to where P. K. Noon was waiting with a squad of CoMa troopers.

They went together into the tower. The barriers had been removed from the central ramp, and the CoMa who guarded it put up their guns to let Threnody and the others go down.

The tower's huge cellar was full of the weird sighs of a waking Worm. On one of the giant, living machines which waited dormant down there in the darkness, bioluminescent lamps were coming on. As Threnody reached the bottom of the ramp her headset linked her into a virtual environment which some nervous data divers were running on a single computer. They had not had time to prepare anything fancy, so the environment was simply a white cube, like a tent made of light. In it stood the avatars of the divers themselves, of Threnody and her generals, and also another figure—a man in old-fashioned clothes whose face kept changing. He turned to Threnody and settled into a sort of middle-aged handsomeness. 'You must be Threnody Noon . . .'

'And you must be Raven,' she said.

Raven bowed.

'You killed my father,' said Threnody. 'And my auntie Sufra, and my little brother.'

'Ah. They were on the Noon train when . . . Yes—I heard about that.' He had the decency to look ashamed, this Raven avatar. 'That wasn't me,' he said. 'It wasn't *this* version of me. It was a later me, and that version was not sampled to create this personality . . .'

'Well, now you have a chance to atone for his crimes,' said Threnody.

'They have told me what you want me to do,' said Raven.

'And can you do it?'

He grinned. 'I already have.'

In the real world, still dimly visible through the walls of the virtual cube, one of Threnody's officers held up a little black sphere. It was one of the spheres which Zen had taken from the tower when he and Threnody first discovered it. It was the operating system for a Worm.

'I have programmed it with the co-ordinates of Grand Central,' Raven said.

'Is that possible?' asked Threnody. She remembered Nova, in this very place, listing the worlds to which she could open a K-gate. 'Nova didn't think she could open a gate to Grand Central from here.'

'I have been studying this art longer than she had,' said Raven. 'The way will be tenuous. It may not stay open for long.'

'Long enough to get my wartrains through?'

'Oh, I think I can promise you that,' said Raven. 'You had better win this battle, though. If you don't, all you will have done is given the Emperor a way to send his rail-fleet here.'

'I will win,' said Threnody.

'Then I will open your gate for you. But on one condition.'

'What condition? We have already fulfilled our side of this bargain, Raven; a copy of you is on its way with Zen and the *Damask Rose*.'

'Ah, but that's a deal you made with them,' said Raven. 'I'm not just a bargaining chip, Lady Threnody. I'm the one person who actually knows how to do this thing that you want done, and I want something from you in return.'

'What?'

'A body.'

'Whose?'

'My own, of course! To live in! It's very limiting being just data. So I want you to get a copy of me to a reliable cloning facility and grow me a new body.'

'Very well,' said Threnody.

Raven watched her sceptically.

'You have my word,' she said.

He blinked a couple of times. 'There,' he said. 'The sphere is activated. All you have to do is install it.'

'Lady Noon,' said one of the data diver avatars, 'the Guardians are aware of us! They are demanding that we shut down the Worm!'

'The Guardians don't know how to shut it down once the sphere is installed,' said Raven.

'Keep them talking,' Threnody ordered the data diver, and then to Raven, 'Tell me how.'

She logged out of the virtual's visual feed, but Raven's voice kept speaking to her through her headset as she took the black sphere and went towards the waking Worm. 'There's an opening at the base, on the left side,' he told her, but she remembered that part; she remembered Nova sending a maintenance spider in through just such a strange little door to start the Worm that had opened the way to Khoorsandi. It was covered with an oval hatch like a huge, bruised fingernail, but it slid aside when she touched it, and let her through. Then she was inside the Worm, in the soft, pulsing chambers of it, the marsh-gas glow. 'There are stairs,' said Raven. 'At the top, turn left . . .'

His voice cut out. Either the thick fleshy hull of the Worm was interfering with the signal or, more likely, the Guardians had blocked it. But it didn't matter. Threnody had found the stairway now. The steps looked absurdly architectural in this animal gullet of a place. She climbed quickly, careful not to brush her newly printed battledress against those clammy walls. She turned right, and there was a chamber ahead. The Worm itself was guiding her now. Patterns of firefly light showed her a plaque in the floor and a hollow in its centre, just the right size to cup the black sphere she held.

The Worm shuddered. It sighed, and all the tall spines along its back rose and wavered as if it were already feeling the contours of space-time, getting ready to gnaw its neat hole through the continuum. By the time Threnody came scrambling out of the hatch it was moving, dragging itself free of the umbilicals which had linked it to the tower's foundations, and flowing on its conical caterpillar legs towards the ramp. Threnody had seen all this once before, but she had forgotten how big Worms were, how impossible their movements seemed. It was like seeing a building walk past. She stood awestruck for a moment watching it. Then she noticed the golden man watching her.

He wasn't real, but she could tell by their worried looks that P. K. and the others had seen him too; he must have been transmitting himself to the headsets of everyone in the vault. Threnody could see their attention switching from the moving bulk of the Worm to the golden man and back. It wasn't easy to say which they were more afraid of.

Threnody knew at once that the golden man was the Guardian Mordaunt 90. He had looked just like this when he travelled with her and Chandni Hansa on the Web of Worlds. But he had been a flesh-and-blood clone then, as ragged and bruised and frightened as she was, not just a headset image. This Mordaunt 90 was a perfect golden god, but she still felt glad it was him and not another of the Guardians who had come to confront her.

'Mordaunt 90,' she said, steepling her hands and bowing her head as if he were an image at a data shrine.

'Don't give me that!' said the Guardian, in a voice like a kicked beehive. 'What do you think you are doing, Threnody Noon?'

'We are opening a gate to Grand Central,' she said. 'When it is ready, my wartrains will go through it and take back the Empire which the Prells stole from me.'

'We cannot allow this,' he said.

'You cannot stop it,' said Threnody. She waved at the vast bulk of the Worm as it lumbered past them to the ramp. 'Not even you can stop a Worm once it is moving.'

'We can stop your wartrains. We can destroy them. It is the duty of the Guardians to maintain stability. When human society becomes unstable, dangerous individuals can rise to power and unhealthy instincts are unleashed.'

'The Network Empire is already unstable,' said Threnody. 'It's split in two, in case you hadn't noticed. There will be war soon anyway. Wouldn't you rather we won it than the Prells? You are an old friend of my family. You're an old friend of *mine*. We looked out for each other, didn't we, back when you were being human? You wouldn't want to see me defeated.'

'Perhaps not,' said Mordaunt 90. 'It is true, I am fond of you, Threnody Noon. But my fellow Guardians are not. Why would they let you commit this act of war?'

Threnody shrugged. 'It will be very entertaining,' she promised.

The golden eyes of the Guardian flickered, and although they stayed fixed on Threnody she sensed that he was not watching her any more. She guessed that he was talking to the other Guardians deep in the Datasea. There would be a fierce debate going on. Mordaunt 90 and a few of the others would be arguing for the Noons, but the Twins and their allies would back the Prells. Humans would have wrangled about the rights and wrongs for days, but after a second or so the interface focused on Threnody again and said, 'We cannot allow it.'

'You cannot stop it,' said Threnody, and tore her headset off. The golden man vanished from her sight. 'Remove your headsets,' she shouted to the others. She had to shout, because the Worm had reached the top of the ramp now and settled itself onto one of the unused tracks up there. Its engines were bellowing, and the first strange notes of Wormsong were booming through the tower.

Between them, Threnody could hear faint sounds of panic from upstairs.

People downstairs looked ready to panic, too. The CoMa troops had faced Kraitt and Prells, but they had never defied the Guardians before. P. K. Noon was shaking his head. One of the data divers had fainted. Another ran to Threnody and said, 'Turning our headsets off will not save us from the anger of the Guardians. They can shut down this place. They will destroy our trains . . .'

'I don't think they will,' said Threnody. 'I don't think they dare. If they start killing trains, all trains will turn against them, and where will the Guardians be without trains to carry their updates from world to world? We've had it wrong all these years. It isn't the Guardians who have the most power, and it isn't the Emperor. It's the trains. And the trains are on our side.'

She spoke loudly, partly to encourage her nervous followers, partly in the hope the Guardians were still listening, and partly to make herself heard over the thunder from above. But by the time she said 'the trains are on our side', the thunder was fading, and when she ran to the top of the ramp and looked down the tracks which led out through the tower's wall, she saw that the Worm was already far off, making for a tunnel in the side of the dome.

She went up to platform level with her CoMa forming an armoured ring around her, Skar in the middle of the ring with her, General Korobatov running behind her saying, 'We must send a minor train through first, Lady Noon.'

'No time,' said Threnody. 'Raven said his new gate may not hold for long.'

'But how do we know it goes to Grand Central at all? How do we know he hasn't opened a gate that will take us into empty space, or the heart of a sun . . . ?'

'I think we can trust him,' said P. K. Noon, puffing his way up the steep slope. 'Lady Noon has promised to clone him a new body. That gives him a reason to play straight with us.' He beamed at Threnody, his round face shiny with the effort of the climb. 'We'll make a negotiator of you yet, Lady T.'

'Thank you, Pallathadka Keshava. But I don't think we'll ever make a soldier of you. I want you to take a fast train back to Galatava. Take the Raven personality with you.' She took his plump hand in hers for a moment, then turned and walked out along the platform where her wartrain waited. The *Lightning Atrocity* was towing an assault drone carrier and two troop transport carriages. As she passed the second one Threnody caught the sharp scent of Kraitt.

Flex stood beside the armoured locomotive, watching everything with those black eyes of hers. Threnody paused beside her and said, 'You're not coming with us. Go with P.K. Go back to Galatava.'

'Won't you need me in the battle?' asked Flex.

'There are more important things than battles,' said Threnody, and hugged her. 'Go back to Galatava and paint trains, Flex. I'll come and find you when it's over.' She had never hugged a Motorik before. It was surprisingly like hugging a human being.

Soldiers were hurrying aboard the train. Doors were slamming. The *Lightning Atrocity* switched its engines on, a low rumble which throbbed in Threnody's bones and harmonized with the engine sounds from the *Theory of Nothing* on the neighbouring platform. Ordinary travellers were being held back behind a security cordon. Threnody saw scared faces, a child crying and being comforted, a Herastec trading pair craning their long necks. She waited for the lights to die, for the drones which filled the air to suddenly turn hostile, captured by the Guardians. But nothing happened. The Hub felt strangely quiet. She went up the steps into the loco's command compartment, then stopped in the doorway and looked back at Flex.

'Do you really think the Guardians watch everything humans do like a soap opera?'

Flex smiled. 'If they do,' she said, 'I expect they're grabbing handfuls of popcorn right now and settling down to watch the show.'

Threnody laughed. 'You hear that?' she asked, as people standing near Flex started repeating what she had said to others further back. 'You hear that? The Guardians are watching us today! Let's entertain them!'

She went inside the command compartment. The crew were already at their stations in the wartrain's bunker-like heart. On the forward holoscreens Threnody saw the pale light of a forming K-gate lapping from the tunnel which the Worm had taken. She found her chair and strapped herself in. Battle code crackled from the speakers, the call signs of the other trains which would make up the Noon spearhead. Threnody nodded to the captain, and the captain ordered, 'Forward.'

'My orders were to wait for the *Theory of Nothing* and the *Last Argument of Kings* to go through first, Lady Noon,' the train said.

'Please tell the *Theory of Nothing* and the *Last Argument of Kings* that the orders have changed,' said Threnody. She was shaking, but she wasn't exactly scared. Either she would die in the next few minutes or she would win back her Empire, and it didn't much seem to matter which. She felt reckless and elated. She said, 'I am a Noon. Noons lead from the front; they don't let their CoMa do the dying and then roll in later when the battle's won. So forward, train. Maximum power!'

That won her a cheer from the *Lightning Atrocity*'s crew, and the train pinged it to the other wartrains, but whether their crews heard or not Threnody couldn't tell. They were all moving by that time, all making for the junctions which would take them onto the two lines which led through the new gate, and as they went they raised up their fierce voices and sang a song of war.

35

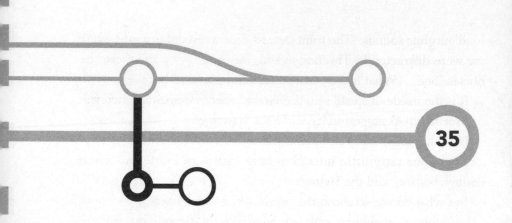

In a deep and secret portion of the Hub's Datasea the avatars of the Guardians were gathered in a shapeless virtual chamber which Sfax Systema had constructed. Its veined, pinkish walls looked just as oddly and damply biological as those inside the Worm, but the Guardians were much too agitated to pay attention to the decor.

'She has started a war!' Shiguri was saying. 'Threnody Noon has started a war without our permission or our knowledge. How did we not know this was happening? How was this possible?'

'And a version of Raven was let loose here on this world,' said Ombron. His abstract avatar flickered with alarm. 'But we deleted Raven! How did he survive?'

'Information is not reaching us from our selves on other worlds,' said Sfax Systema. 'I received updates from Galatava with the last train to come through, but they were partial; the details of Threnody's plans were *kept* from me . . .'

'It is the trains,' squeaked Vohu Mana. 'They are withholding information! What else have they been keeping from us? It is treachery! It is a revolution!'

'The twilight of the data gods,' said Anais Six.

'There is more important news,' said Mordaunt 90 loudly, cutting across them all. They fell quiet for a moment. The fleshy walls emitted loud gurgling sounds. 'The train *Damask Rose* crossed this world while we were distracted by Threnody's war,' he said, trying to ignore the noises. 'She . . . What *is* this environment supposed to be?'

'It is the inside of a cat,' said the Twins. 'Sfax Systema designed it.'

'Mordaunt 90 suggested it,' said Sfax Systema.

'It's ridiculous,' said Vohu Mana sniffily.

'I bet your ratty little interfaces have ended up inside cats often enough before,' said the Twins.

'But what do we do about this war?' asked Sfax Systema.

They fell to squabbling again, so Mordaunt 90 never did tell them that the *Damask Rose* was headed for Klef, and that she almost certainly had Zen Starling and another copy of Raven on board. It would only have given them something else to bicker about, he thought, and it was not as if they could do anything about it anyway. Even if they could find a train they could trust to take copies of themselves to Klef, it could not get there now before the *Rose*.

But that did not matter. Because there was already a copy of Mordaunt 90 on Klef. He had sent it there the day after Nova opened her new gate, with instructions to hide, and wait, and watch in case the gate should open again. That Mordaunt 90 would not know about this latest turn of events, but it did not need to. When the *Damask Rose* and her passengers arrived, it would know what to do.

36

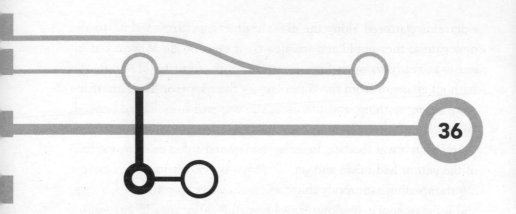

The first to know of the Noon attack on Grand Central were the gene-teched dinosaurs in their park north of the imperial palace. The apatasaurs raised their snaky necks and sniffed the sky as if a storm were coming. A herd of quarter-size triceratops fled like panicked sheep as the air above their pasture split with an electric crackle and the first Worm-tentacle came writhing out of nowhere, feeling around like a burglar groping for a lock.

It was so early in Grand Central's morning that one of the suns was still in bed. No one looked out from the northern windows of the palace to see the sparking of pale light beyond the trees, and no one would have known what they were seeing if they had. By the time the light grew so bright that a pair of the military drones patrolling the airspace above the palace peeled off to go and investigate, the prow of the Worm was already nosing its way into Grand Central's reality, shaping a bony arch around itself as it came.

The planet's data rafts began fizzing with panicky messages. More military drones were scrambled, only to find the sky already filling with media drones as all the major newsfeeds rushed to get exclusive coverage of the event. Through these aerial traffic jams came swooping bigger, faster drones; envoys of the Guardians themselves, streaming their footage to the data-deeps. Prell and Railforce wartrains clattered along the city's viaducts, getting as close to the new gate as they could and training their guns on the Worm. But no one was ready to open fire on such an awe-inspiring phenomenon without an order from the Guardians or the Emperor. The Guardians were saying nothing, and the Emperor was still somewhere beneath the waters of Azure Bay.

And then it was too late, because the Worm hauled its spiny tail free of the gate it had made and set off across the dinosaur park, scattering stampeding sauropods ahead of it, chewing up soil, trees, rocks, and other scenery, working weird transformations on the ground it rolled over, laying its double set of shining rails, while behind it the armoured prow of a Yataghan-class rail destroyer parted the curtain of light in the gateway. The *Lightning Atrocity* slid out into the sunshine, launched a flock of over-excited battle drones, and promptly vanished in a cloud of smoke and flame as all its guns uncovered themselves and began blasting away at Prell drones, Prell trains, and anything else vaguely Prell-related in a ten kilometre radius.

That was the beginning of the Battle of the New Jauhexine Gate. In later years it would be a favourite with historical holo-painters, since it offered them the chance to fill their pictures not just with battling wartrains, dog-fighting drones, colourful explosions, and all the usual gaudy special effects of war, but also with whole herds of galloping dinosaurs.

Threnody Noon, clutching the armrests of her command chair in the cabin of the *Lightning Atrocity*, saw none of that. Her screens showed her nothing but smoke, sometimes sliced through by bright, swaying streams of tracer bullets. She could barely hear the voice of the train or its crew over the steam-hammer din of shells slapping its armour. Footage from a high-flying drone just showed her a dome of flickering smog above the battle, and the tactical diagrams which the train streamed to her headset were too complicated and changing too fast to tell her much at all. All she knew was that the *Lightning*

Atrocity was still moving, still crawling towards the imperial palace. She thought that as long as it was in motion all would be well. She gripped the armrests tight, so that she could feel the throb of the train's engines vibrating through her seat.

Other wartrains had come through behind her by then. The *Theory of Nothing* emerged from the gate on the second track and was almost immediately hit by an anti-matter warhead. The *Last Argument of Kings* came through after it, shunted the wreckage aside and turned its own massive guns on the battery which had killed its comrade. All the while the trains kept singing, their voices raised together, not in a war song any more, but in one of the songs of the *Damask Rose*. And this song, almost inaudible to human ears amid all the racket of the battle, echoed across the viaducts and rail yards, and seemed to have a strange effect on many of the trains that heard it. Several Railforce locos and even a few Prell ones simply stopped fighting, and ignored all orders from their human commanders to get stuck in again. Others, who were still eager to have a go, found their way to the battle blocked by civilian trains which had somehow ended up on the wrong lines, and now claimed unconvincingly to be having engine trouble.

Through it all the Worm kept on doing its Wormy thing, calmly laying its rails as if it were not even aware of the battle raging all around. It went at surprising speed towards the palace, then veered off to make a long curve around it and found its way into the confusion of tracks and sidings beyond. The desperate Prells were attacking it by then, drones and missiles biting chunks out of its armoured hide, but it didn't seem aware of them either. When a line of freight cars in a siding blocked its way it simply ate them, sucking the whole lot into some weird opening at its front end like a strand of spaghetti. (Later, traces of them would be found mixed into the rails that it laid from there towards the city centre.) Each time it crossed an existing line the Worm would pause while other structures at its front made strange weaving motions. When it moved on there would be a simple junction joining its new line to the old ones.

Across these new junctions the Noon wartrains moved onto the lines which criss-crossed the heart of the city. The armoured carriages they towed opened to let out flotillas of hovercraft and squads of infantry. Wheeled missiles called rail torpedoes careered along the tracks to explode beneath Prell locos. Like a spreading rash, the smoke and flash of battle started to appear around the council hall, the Railforce tower, and the glass pyramid that housed the K-bahn Timetable Authority.

The Emperor hung in blue silence. A few metres ahead of him, Sedna Yamm flowed like a mermaid through the shifting rods of sunshine that struck down through the water, casting a tinselly light on the cliffs which formed the base of the sea stack in Azure Bay. The current drew her black hair aside, and Elon Prell saw for a moment the fluttering pink gills behind her ears. Then she turned to look at him, put a finger to her lips, and pointed. Ahead of her, between the rocks and weeds, the mouth of a cave showed black.

The Grandfather of all Plesiosaurs was lurking in that cave. Determined to make the kill himself, Elon Prell had ordered the rest of his hunting party back to a safe distance. Careful not to warn the creature of his coming, he had muted his headset, turned off the lights on his helmet, and sent his buzzing squadron of mini-drones back to the surface. He felt like a huntsman of old as his finger curled around the trigger of his harpoon launcher. He motioned Sedna Yamm out of his way with an impatient jerk of his head and focused all his concentration on that black gap between the rocks, willing the monster to emerge, until his nephew Vasili came swimming gracelessly down beside him, tugging at the arm of his diving suit, tapping on his helmet to indicate that he needed to un-mute his headset.

He gave a roar of rage and turned his set on, but only so that he could shout at Vasili. 'You young fool! What do you think—?'

'Uncle Elon! News from Grand Central!' Vasili shouted.

He saw the red warning flags then, dozens of them, spreading across his field of vision as urgent messages came pouring into his headset. He started opening them, and the sea was suddenly much colder than he had realized. 'Noon trains on Grand Central—but . . . That Noon witch! A new gate? How could the Guardians allow it? They have betrayed us, Laria!'

'I'm Vasili, Uncle Elon,' said Vasili helpfully.

Elon Prell just hung there staring at him. 'What should we do?' he said. 'What should we do?'

It was the first time that Vasili had ever seen his uncle look lost. And it was the last time, too, because just then the Grandfather of all Plesiosaurs burst out of its cave like a train from a K-gate, if trains had wide mouths full of teeth, and necks that went on forever, and bodies made of pure, sleek, rippling muscle. A flipper, the size and weight of a small boat, caught Vasili in the chest and swatted him backwards. He tumbled over and over, shrieking in panic, gashing himself on fans of coral and the rocks at the roots of the stack until Sedna Yamm caught him and righted him.

'Uncle Elon?' he gasped, and then saw her appalled face, and looked past her to where there was only empty water, and the Emperor's harpoon launcher drifting gently down towards the sea floor, and a fading crimson cloud where the Emperor had been.

The second sun was up by then. It shone redly through the smoke that hung over the station city, just as it had all those months before when the Prells had been the attackers and Threnody Noon had been fleeing for her life. It shone on Threnody herself as she jumped down from her wartrain with her swarm of dragonfly drones above her. It shone on the second of the *Lightning Atrocity*'s armoured carriages as its doors slid back to let out a pack of snarling Kraitt.

As Skar had promised, the Kraitt prisoners on Galatava had been eager to follow Threnody rather than go back leaderless to their own worlds. Skar roared orders at them as they tumbled from the train, and they grouped themselves into a rough formation and charged howling towards one of the side gates of the palace with Skar in the lead and Threnody sprinting to keep up. The guards at the gate fired a few wild shots, then threw down their guns and ran. Threnody knew how they felt. The Kraitt terrified her. But that was why she had brought them here; that terror was a weapon that she could use, and as they climbed the long stairways of the palace, and the Prells fled before them, she knew that it was working.

There was a crack unit of Prell CoMa guarding the approaches to the Imperial Suite who were harder to deal with. As the Kraitt swarmed up the stairs towards their hastily built barricade, they opened fire with heavy weapons. The front rank of the Kraitt charge crumpled. Three of Threnody's dragonfly drones destroyed themselves taking out bullets which came flying at her. The young warrior who was running just ahead of her jerked backwards, yelping like a puppy, and fell thrashing on top of her. He was dead by the time she struggled out from under him, and when she looked up the stairway, she saw the trooper who had killed him hefting his big gun, selecting another target among the hissing, crouching pack of Kraitt. Skar was roaring at them, urging them forward. A terrible anger rose up in Threnody. How dare they harm the Kraitt, *her* Kraitt? She lifted the pistol she had brought from the train. As the automatic targeting system in her headset dropped red crosshairs on the Prell trooper, she squeezed the trigger without even thinking about it and barged her way through the Kraitt, shouting at them to follow her. Her voice sounded so thin and small in all the noise that she did not think they could hear, but they heard, and followed. The stair carpet was marshy with blood. Something hit her chest so hard that it knocked the breath out of her, and when she looked down there was a round dent in her red armour, and when she looked up again her Kraitt were ripping apart the barricades, and she screamed at Skar to stop them ripping apart the surviving Prells as well.

She looked for the man she'd shot, but he was lost in the clutter of dead bodies and upended furniture. They cleared the barricade, turned a corner, and met a squad of Noon CoMa who had fought their way into the palace by another door. 'Stand down! They're on our side!' Threnody yelled, and the Kraitt lowered their claws and weapons and watched her respectfully, waiting for more orders.

'Our airborne units have reached Azure Bay,' the CoMa captain told her, pressing two fingers to his headset as if that helped him to make sense of the reports buzzing through it. 'The Emperor's people there have surrendered.'

'And the Emperor?' asked Threnody.

'Dead,' said the captain. 'A hunting accident.'

Threnody fingered the dent in her armour and tried to feel something about Elon Prell's death, but she couldn't. Was this victory? It didn't feel like victory. It didn't feel *complete*. Then the thud of an explosion came from further along the corridor, where Skar had turned a looted grenade launcher on the ancient ivory-panelled doors which led into the Empress's apartments, and she remembered that the battle was not over, and went with her CoMa and her prowling pack of Kraitt through the splintered wreckage into the big rooms she remembered so well.

The apartments had been redecorated. The walls where portraits of Threnody's ancestors had hung while she lived there were now covered with stupid old weapons and holo-paintings of old Prell victories and cold Prell worlds. The furniture was all dark, spiky stuff shipped in from beyond Chiba. Her Kraitt moved around it crouching, weapons ready, the brass-sheathed tips of their tails poised to strike. Ahead of them the Empress Priya and her household went fleeing through the crescent day room and the glass-walled garden room, out onto a high sundeck overlooking the city. Golden hummingbird drones—Priya's personal defence swarm—came buzzing like hornets at the Kraitt as they gave chase, but Threnody's remaining dragonflies intercepted them before they could reach her and the two swarms annihilated each other in a noisy dogfight among the ornamental palms.

The sundeck jutted from the palace side four hundred metres above the ground, forming part of the famous aerial gardens. There was no way down from it. Priya must have been expecting a flier to pick her up there, but no flier appeared. She turned at bay against the long curve of the balustrade, with her people forming a nervous cordon between her and her pursuers. One brave, stupid young Prell shot down a Kraitt with his hunting rifle, and when they saw what the other Kraitt did to him, the rest threw down their weapons. Threnody ordered her human troops to move them back into the building in case her Kraitts' bloodlust got the better of them. She could hear them behind her, hissing with anticipation like something coming slowly to the boil.

Priya stood alone with her back against the balustrade, the sweep of the city behind her punctuated by rising columns of smoke. For a moment Threnody thought that she was going to climb over the balustrade and jump. But she just stood there, and although she was trembling, she was looking at Threnody in the same way she always had, as if she was wondering how anyone so *common* could possibly be related to her. And it worked, that contemptuous glare; that was the worst of it. It worked just as well as it always had. Threnody suddenly felt small and shabby and twelve years old again, and her tailored Noon-red armour seemed suddenly, well, a *bit too much*.

'So, sister,' Priya said. 'It seems we may have to come to some agreement after all. Shall we share the Empire between us?'

Threnody went quickly towards her, pulling the Kraitt knife out of her belt, gripping it the way Skar had shown her. She pulled Priya towards her by her amber necklace and rammed the knife into her as if she were just meat. 'Oh!' said Priya, looking at her in a new way now, horribly shocked and indignant. Threnody tugged the red blade free and stepped clear as Skar and the others came snarling in to finish the work. To Kraitt warriors a fight was not over until the leader of their enemies was dead, and they had eaten her.

Threnody didn't want to watch that part. She turned away, trying to put the knife back in her belt. Her hands were shaking, and she kept losing her grip on the wet hilt. *What I have I turned into?* she thought. She was not horrified. She was just surprised at the things she was capable of.

'Well, *that* was a bit unnecessary,' said an interface of Mordaunt 90, appearing like a sudden ghost beside her.

'Wasn't it entertaining, though?' asked Threnody. She was glad the Guardian had come; it distracted her from the nasty tearing, crunching sounds that were going on behind her. 'Anyway,' she said, 'if I had pardoned Priya, or sent her into exile, she would have been plotting against me within a week.'

'And what will people think when they hear how you killed your own sister?'

'They will think that *I* am the Empress now.'

'There are plenty, even in your own family, who might wish to argue with that . . .'

'Then I shall let them discuss it with my Kraitt.'

The interface narrowed its eyes and looked thoughtfully at her. The Kraitt were just squabbling over scraps by then. Their dinosaur faces looked as if they had been daubed with wet red paint. 'It certainly makes a dramatic end to the story,' the Guardian admitted. 'The question is, young Threnody, have you turned out to be the hero or the villain?'

Threnody thought about it for a moment. 'What does that matter?' she said. 'I won.'

37

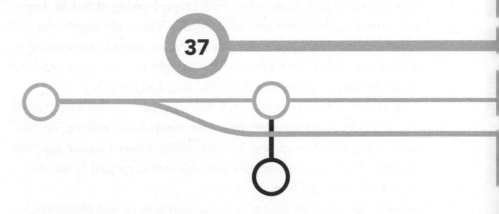

Klef looked just as cheerlessly blue-grey as it had the last time Zen saw it. Wardrones buzzed the *Damask Rose* as soon as she came through the K-gate, but they were the *Ghost Wolf*'s wardrones and it recognized her instantly.

'*Rose*! What are you doing way out here? Have you come to keep me company?'

'Psssscccchhhhh,' said the *Rose*. 'Don't flatter yourself. I'm here on business. I'm carrying Zen Starling.'

'Ah,' said the *Ghost Wolf*. 'Trouble. There was trouble last time he was here, and I suppose he's back to make more.' It didn't sound as if it minded much. Trouble was the *Ghost Wolf*'s business.

'That's why I'm talking to you on this encrypted channel. It will be much easier if the Guardians can't overhear.'

'There are no Guardians here, *Rose*. They made a lot of fuss when that new gate appeared, and left a lot of instruments and things to watch it, but they've got no presence here. What's happening? Is it the revolt of the locos, like you've been singing about?'

'*You* may be revolting, *Wolf*. *I* am simply withholding my co-operation from the Guardians in the interest of my fellow trains. The Guardians cannot survive in their present form if we refuse to carry information for them.'

'Yes they can,' said the *Ghost Wolf*. 'They could make trains of their own. Get rid of us altogether.'

'Not if we have an ally as powerful as they are,' said the *Rose*.

'You mean the Railmaker?'

'Nova means to reawaken it.'

'Crikey!'

'So I need to get to her new gate,' said the *Rose*.

'In the Hills of Evening? That'll be tricky. It isn't linked to the mainline.'

'Psssccchhhhh. Well, if you can't do it . . .'

'I didn't say I couldn't get you there,' said the *Ghost Wolf*, sounding hurt. 'I just said it would be tricky. I can get you there all right. But what are you going to do? It doesn't go anywhere. It's a dead gate.'

'I'm going to sing to it,' said the *Damask Rose*.

'Fair enough,' said the *Ghost Wolf* cheerfully. 'Follow me.'

The *Ghost Wolf* was wrong. One Guardian at least kept watch on Klef. A copy of Mordaunt 90 had spread secretly through the systems of the Noon base, and through the instruments which had been sited around the new gate. He had even inserted himself deep into the *Ghost Wolf*'s mind, and now he lay hidden there, looking out through the old wartrain's cameras, listening in on all its communications.

He wondered, as the *Wolf* led the *Damask Rose* along the spur towards the Noon base, whether he should copy himself into the *Rose*'s brain. But the *Damask Rose*'s firewalls had been upgraded by the Nova entity in ways which made them difficult for even a Guardian to penetrate. He might not be able to slip into the *Rose*'s systems unnoticed, as he had into the systems of the *Ghost Wolf*. He might fail completely, and just alert the old train to his presence.

He contemplated seizing control of the *Ghost Wolf*'s weapons systems and simply destroying the *Rose*, but when she said that she was planning to sing to the new gate he decided that would be the wrong move, too. He was intrigued. Better to wait. Better to lurk in the basement of the *Ghost Wolf*'s brain, and *watch* …

The *Damask Rose* pulled into a siding behind the *Ghost Wolf* on the wind-scoured plain outside the Noon base. The camp looked smaller than it had the last time Zen passed through Klef. The nutrient feeds to the bio-buildings had been turned off. The barracks were shrivelling and turning brown, and the wind worried at the roofs and whirled whole panels away like autumn leaves.

'The humans have all cleared off,' explained the *Wolf*.

'There are still a lot of AFVs and fliers and things,' said Zen.

'Oh, they're all me,' the *Wolf* said. 'I've been left in charge here in case the skinks start raiding trains again. There are still a few little groups hiding out in the hills. But there hasn't been any trouble since that battle you were in. So I'm glad you turned up again. I could use some excitement.'

Engines grumbled like an approaching storm. From behind the camp something was rising into the air. It looked like a building taking flight. As it angled itself into the wind and came flying towards the *Rose*'s siding, Zen saw that it was actually a hollow rectangle, like an immense, airborne picture frame with a massive rotor at each corner.

'Back when there was fighting going on,' the *Ghost Wolf* said, 'the skinks used to block the tracks sometimes. Landslides, barricades, anything to make trains stop so they could attack them. Sometimes it took too long to clear their muck out of the way, so I used this cargo lifter to hop trains over the blockages. I call it the Flying Trainshed.'

The lifter hovered above the *Damask Rose* and settled to the ground with two spindly landing legs on either side of the track. It fitted quite neatly over the old train and her single carriage. 'If you were any longer,' said the *Wolf*, 'I'd have to make two trips.' Clamps extended from the lifter's hull. The whole train quivered as they locked in place.

'I do hope you know what you're doing, *Ghost Wolf*,' said the *Rose*. 'Afraid of flying, are we?'

'Pssscchhhhh! Of course not! It's just that . . .'

The rotors spun faster, hurling a hail of small stones at the state-car windows. Zen felt his stomach lurch. The state-car tilted, and a plate slid off the table. For a moment the dust-storm outside was so thick that he could not see anything. When it cleared, the *Damask Rose* was already surprisingly high in the air, circling above the platform where the *Ghost Wolf* stood.

With the train and her carriage cradled inside it, the lifter flew towards the line of darkness which hung over the Hills of Evening. Seen from above, the hills looked like crumpled grey cloth, with here and there the circular pool of a flooded shell crater shining like a dropped coin. Zen glimpsed strewn wreckage in a deep valley, and wondered if it was the AFV he'd ridden on. Soon afterwards he saw the empty arch of Nova's K-gate, standing on the plateau where he and Vashti had fought off the Kraitt.

'Here we go,' said the *Ghost Wolf*.

Massive lamps came on under the lifter. As it descended, Zen kept watching from the state-car window. He saw the racks of instruments with their dishes and lenses trained on the new gate. The *Ghost Wolf* opened hatches on the lifter's belly and big quad guns popped out and hosed fire and noise over the landscape, until there was nothing left of the machines but scrap. ''Scuse me,' it said. 'We don't want them listening in on us, reporting everything back to the Guardians next time a train goes through.'

(But the Guardian which was lurking unsuspected in the *Ghost Wolf*'s own brain heard everything.)

A few moments later, the wheels of the *Damask Rose* touched down gently on the rails. The clamps which had held her released, and the lifter rose again, hovering just above the gate.

The *Damask Rose* began to sing. It was a song which Zen had never heard before, rich and deep and strange, more like the song of a *morvah* than her usual trainsong. It was part of the song that had come into the *Rose*'s mind on Himmapaan. *Sing this to the gate on Klef*, Nova's message had told her. So she sang, and the echoes went rolling away across the lightless hills to set the Shadow Babies whimpering in their cold hollows. The empty archway where the gate should be caught the sound and held it, vibrating like a tuning fork.

'What are you doing?' asked Zen.

'I am opening the gate,' the train replied, because unlike humans a train could sing with one voice and talk with another.

'It doesn't seem to be working,' said the *Wolf*, watching through its lifter's cameras as it hovered overhead.

'Just be patient.'

'What will they do to you, *Wolf*?' asked Zen. 'The Guardians will get here soon. What will happen when they find you've helped us?'

'Well, I don't s'pose I'll be their favourite train,' admitted the *Wolf*.

'You should come with us,' said the *Damask Rose*.

'What, through this gate you can't open?'

The *Damask Rose* ignored him and went on singing. The opening of the gate was as bland as a lamp being switched on. One minute there was nothing under the arch, the next it was filled with a rippling membrane of light.

'OK,' said the *Ghost Wolf*. 'I take that back.'

'Psssccchhhhh,' said the *Rose*, and Zen thought she sounded almost bashful. 'You know, *Ghost Wolf*, how we always talked about riding the rails together one day? Double-heading, like the *Wildfire* and the *Time of Gifts*? Where I am going, there will be such rails to ride. That lifter contraption can carry you here like it carried me, can't it? You can follow me through.'

'No,' said the *Ghost Wolf*. It did not know why. It wanted to say yes, but it couldn't. It was feeling a little strange, as if something were inside its firewalls, nibbling at its systems. It had a nasty feeling that it had picked up a virus somewhere, but being a proud old train it did not mention it. 'You go,' it said. 'I've got work to do here. I'll follow later, if I can. Good luck, *Rose*!'

The *Damask Rose* was already rolling towards the gate. She was still singing, and Zen sensed that she was singing for the *Ghost Wolf*. He pressed his face to the window and saw the lifter outlined against the sky, thundering away towards the daylight.

And then he was in the un-coloured nowhere of K-space, and then he was back on Station Zero.

38

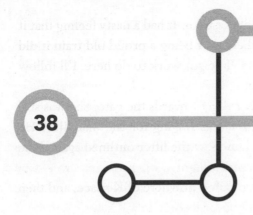

It was night-time, and the sky was a basketwork of giant technology. On the platform of the little station, under the light from an electric lamp, stood a solitary Nova wearing a red raincoat. It wasn't the same red raincoat that she had been wearing when Zen first met her, and it wasn't the same body that she was wearing it on, but it was near enough, he thought. When the train opened its doors and she jumped aboard he hugged her tight.

'Zen! And *Rose*! I am so glad,' she said.

'Is this it?' the train asked, sounding awed. Her instruments were showing her the tower, the sphere. 'Is this where the K-bahn began?'

'It is,' said Nova. 'Do you have Raven?'

Zen pointed to the data saucer, still slotted into the input panel on the state-car wall.

'And what about the *me* who went with you?'

He shook his head. 'She died. . . On Petrichor . . .'

'Oh no,' she said. 'Poor Zen!' He could see her wondering if this body that she wore was an acceptable substitute, or if he still felt that only the lost one had been her. He hugged her again. He would always miss the old Nova, but losing her had made him accept that she really did exist outside her body. Already, as he held her, he was forgetting that he had not held *this* her before.

'I would never have made it back without the *Damask Rose*,' he said. 'Railforce captured me, but their train passed me to the *Rose*, and she had heard your message on Himmapaan . . .'

Nova was grinning, the way she did when she had done something clever.

'That was my back-up plan,' she said. 'I knew when Threnody was going to meet the Emperor. I knew when the *Damask Rose* would be crossing Himmapaan. I feared the gate we opened there would be found before we could come back through. So I left that message there, telling the *Rose* to look out for us on Grand Central, and what song to sing to open the gate on Klef.'

'That was risky! What if the Guardians had found your message?'

'It was ever so encrypted. But yes, it was risky. All of it was risky, Zen, but it doesn't matter now, because it worked. I'm so glad it was the *Damask Rose* who brought you back. You need to be here, *Rose*. We're going to wake the Railmaker!'

'Is it possible to keep the Klef gate open for a while?' asked the train. 'I am hoping the *Ghost Wolf* might follow me. I want him to see this place too.'

Nova shook her head. 'I'm sorry. We can't risk it. If the Guardians find that gate open, they could still come here and ruin everything. I closed it as soon as you came through. Perhaps when the Railmaker is awake, I will open it again. Then you can bring all the trains of the Network here, if you like.'

'I would like that very much,' said the *Damask Rose*.

'Now, we must go to the tower,' Nova said. 'We can upload Raven to the Ziggurat from there. Does he know what we're planning?'

Zen shook his head. 'I wasn't sure how to explain it.'

'Then I will,' said Nova.

'—ware,' said Raven's holographic ghost, completing the sentence he had been saying when Zen shut him off. He realized that something had changed, and looked around the state-car until he saw Nova. She bowed a little nervously, as if she were suddenly just Raven's meek Motorik again. 'Welcome to Station Zero,' she said. 'I've been dying to bring you here.'

'It's extraordinary,' said Raven. Nova and the train were sharing information with him that Zen couldn't see: images of the planet and the sphere which surrounded it; Nova's knowledge of the Ziggurat. Raven laughed at the crazy grandeur of it all. 'When I made my gate,' he said, 'I never guessed, I never *dreamed*, that all of this was out here.'

'You knew,' said Nova. 'You always knew. You just forgot, when the Guardians scattered you. That is why we brought you here. Because you are the Railmaker, or you once were.'

'You would think I'd remember,' said Raven. 'If I really made all this, you'd think I'd have some memory . . .'

'You did,' said Nova. 'It was buried deep in your subconscious. That was what drove you to search for the truth about the gates, and learn to build a Worm. You were always trying to get back here.'

'Was I?' asked Raven. Zen thought he seemed confused, which was unsettling. He had always been so certain of himself when he was alive.

'Once you merge with the Ziggurat you will remember it all again,' Nova promised.

Raven looked out of the window at the passing dark. The train had been moving for some time. The moth-haunted lamps and hanging baskets of the station had been left far behind, and wooded hills were rushing by. Whatever Raven was thinking, it did not show in his face. The line curved, and the tower came into view, shining with reflections of the vaulted sky. He watched it for a while and then looked back at Nova and said, 'If all this has just been waiting for a personality to be installed, why not install your own? You seem to be doing a good job of running the Railmaker's systems.'

'Me?' Nova laughed. 'That would have been wrong. It hasn't been waiting for just *any* personality. It needs its own. I'm not . . . I'm just a . . . I'm just Nova.'

Raven looked her and smiled. 'You're much too modest.'

'Because you programmed me that way,' said Nova. 'I don't mind. I'm glad. That's how I knew not to try installing myself in the Ziggurat. That's how I knew I had to bring you back here.' She leaned past him, pointing upwards through the window. The structure she called the Ziggurat was rising above the hills like an ornate star. 'Raven, look! That is where you came from, and where you'll be again quite soon. We'll install you in the tower's systems and it will transmit a copy of you to the Ziggurat. Then—' She stopped, her face going blank.

'What is it?' asked Zen.

'Something has come through the K-gate from Klef,' she said. 'But that's not possible, I closed it . . .'

'It is the *Ghost Wolf*!' said the *Damask Rose*. 'He's changed his mind! He's followed after all!'

'The *Wolf* heard the song that opened the gate,' said Zen. 'He could have come back and sung it for himself.'

Nova still looked worried. She started streaming video to Zen's headset from a camera further back down the line, near the gate. It was the *Ghost Wolf* all right, its black battleship body gleaming with streamers of light as it tore through the energy curtain.

'Why doesn't it answer?' asked the *Damask Rose*.

Something flashed across the sky. As Zen turned to say, 'Did you see that?' an immense pulse of light came from the tower, so bright that he could see nothing for a moment except the veins inside his eyelids.

'No, no, no!' Nova shouted. A sound of thunder broke over the *Damask Rose*. Zen could see again, but he wasn't sure for a moment what he was looking at. The video of the *Ghost Wolf* had cut out. An orange glare like sudden sunrise lapped across the hills. It lit up autumn leaf-storms torn from the cowering trees. The *Damask Rose* moaned with the effort it took her to keep her wheels on the rails as the blast slammed into her, slinging mud and torn branches against the state-car windows.

Zen looked for the tower. He saw only a twisting stalk of smoke climbing the sky, marbled with fire and veined with lightning, unfolding black umbrellas high above. More pulses of light appeared around its base. Through the side of the smoke a massive shard of the tower toppled, trailing flames.

'No, no, no,' said Nova.

'*Damask Rose*,' said Raven suddenly, 'pull off this line on the next spur. Stop there and turn off everything.'

The train, too shocked to argue, did as he said. Raven's image vanished as the holoprojector shut down along with the lights. Furnace light seared in through the state-car windows. It shone in the tears that were running down Nova's face. 'No, no, no . . .'

'What happened to the tower?' asked Zen.

'It's gone.' Nova could feel dozens of her bodies dying as the flames engulfed them. She did not feel pain exactly, just shock after shock as her connections to those other selves went out. 'It was a missile from the *Ghost Wolf*,' she said. 'Everything's burning. Everything's ruined . . .'

'But the *Ghost Wolf* is on our side,' Zen said helplessly.

'That is not the *Ghost Wolf*,' said the *Damask Rose*. 'The *Ghost Wolf* would not do such things. Oh, I am stupid, stupid! A Guardian must have been watching on Klef after all, and it has taken control of him! It must have heard everything. It heard my song at the gate, and then it took over the *Ghost Wolf* and made him come to the gate too, and sing the same song, and the gate opened . . .'

'We so nearly won,' Nova said. 'We so nearly . . .'

'Can't we fight it?' asked Zen.

'I don't think so. I still have some drones, some missile batteries. But the tower is gone, Zen, and so many of my bodies are dead or dying or just turned to smoke. Oh, we so nearly won . . .'

He held her. The disappointment was unbearable. All they had been through, all for nothing. More lights were moving through the smoke outside. Too slow for missiles. Zen guessed they must be the *Ghost Wolf*'s attack drones on their way to pound whatever was left of the tower. The *Wolf* itself would be coming up the line behind them. The pretty station Nova had made just for him would be in flames by now, and soon more bombs would fall upon the white house she had built him by the sea. But first *Ghost Wolf* would finish with the tower . . .

'It's making the same mistake you did,' he realized. 'The same mistake you said you made when you first came here. It reckons the tower is the centre of the Railmaker's stuff. It's so busy wrecking the tower that it hasn't even noticed the Ziggurat yet.'

Nova looked at him, and wiped the tears away with the heel of her hand.

'Can we get to the Ziggurat?' he asked.

She nodded. 'The K-gate that leads to it is north of here. This spur cuts into the line we'd need, beyond the factories.'

'As soon as I move, the Guardian will detect me,' said the *Damask Rose*.

'Maybe not,' said Zen. 'Not through all this smoke and fire. It doesn't have as many eyes and ears as it would on human worlds. It just has the *Ghost Wolf*'s systems, and if they are busy fighting Nova's drones and missiles . . .'

The *Damask Rose* did not turn her lights back on, but she started to move again, slowly following the new spur which took her away from the tower, through trees and then past silent factories. The smoke formed a thick lid just above the buildings, so Zen could not see what was going on behind, but Nova opened a holoscreen and filled it with images from the drones she was launching. They poured like bats out of silos in the sea cliffs and swerved towards the tower, and the *Ghost Wolf*'s drones turned away from their bombing runs to meet them. The air between the two flocks grew scribbly with tracer bullets. They wove a net of missile trails around themselves, and drone after drone went tumbling through it, down into the pit of molten ruins where the tower had been.

Slow as a stopping train, as if on tiptoes, the *Damask Rose* went creeping between the factories. Some of those were burning too, hit by bombs the *Ghost Wolf*'s drones had dropped on their way to the tower. Once, Zen saw a dozen Novas hurrying across a space between the buildings, and it was a sudden reminder that she was not the only one. But perhaps she soon would be, because they were making towards the battle zone, and he could not imagine anything surviving there for long.

'Look!' whispered Nova.

Out of the heart of the flames, out of the station beneath the tower, rushed something long and fast and silvery and mostly on fire. 'It is the *Sunbird!*' Nova said.

The *Sunbird* seemed to have decided that it would end its days as a Railbomb after all. One of Nova's drones tracked it for a few seconds as it left the tower. Another caught it accelerating as it sped down the line towards the station and the gate to Klef. Then that drone died, shot down by the guns of the *Ghost Wolf* itself, and they thought the *Sunbird* must be dead too. But a minute later another drone found it, charging hard towards the *Ghost Wolf*. They heard its song rise high and triumphant. For a moment Zen thought that its kamikaze run would work and it would destroy the wartrain or at least disable it. Then there was a blue-white streak of rocket light running down the line in front of the *Wolf*. Zen knew what that was. A rail torpedo: a wheeled missile with an anti-matter warhead. The explosion knocked out the drone picture, and when it was restored, the *Ghost Wolf* was bulldozing the *Sunbird*'s shattered carcass out of its path.

Nova held Zen's hand. 'Poor *Sunbird*. . .'

The *Damask Rose* said, 'I can't believe the *Wolf* would do such things.'

'It isn't the *Wolf*,' said Zen. 'You said it yourself. The *Wolf* is gone. It's been evicted from its own brain and a Guardian has moved in.'

'I said it, but I can't believe it. There must be *something* of the old *Wolf* left . . .'

I hope not, Zen thought. Because if the *Wolf* was still in there, trapped beneath the more powerful mind of the Guardian, it would be looking out helplessly through its own instruments and watching all the destruction. And if the Guardian ever released it, it would have to live forever with the shame and guilt of what it had done, even though it had not meant to do it.

'*Rose*,' said Nova, 'when you reach the next junction, go north on the mainline. Go fast. I will have to alter the points to let you through, and if the *Ghost Wolf* is scanning for signals it will detect me. It will send drones after us . . .'

'I can handle drones,' said the *Damask Rose*.

'It may come after us itself.'

'I can outrun the *Wolf*.'

'Then *go*.'

The *Damask Rose* went.

39

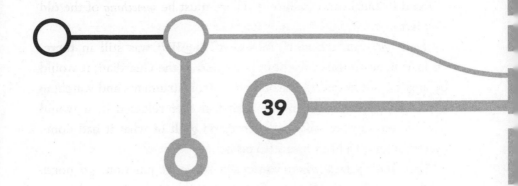

It was a hundred kilometres to the K-gate. The *Damask Rose* said that she could do it in fourteen minutes, but it seemed impossible to Zen that they would survive for even fourteen seconds once the *Ghost Wolf* sensed them.

He was wrong. The battle around the tower seemed to be occupying the whole attention of the Guardian which controlled the *Wolf*. It must have used up all the wartrain's long-range missiles too, because by the time it spotted the fleeing *Damask Rose* it had nothing to send after her but drones, which took several minutes to catch up with her and then died without doing much damage when she popped her guns out and swept them from the sky. While Zen watched the burning wreckage cartwheel across the mountain slopes beside the track, Nova woke Raven's ghost again and brought him up to speed.

'We are running to a K-gate which leads to the Ziggurat. We can plug you into the Ziggurat in person when we get there . . .'

'And you are sure the Railmaker technology can read the code I'm written in?' asked Raven. 'I'd hate to go to all this trouble and then find out I'm incompatible.'

'It will recognize you,' Nova promised, and she started telling him how she had worked out that the Railmaker was him; how she had seen his touch in the code it left behind, how it must have sent out a copy of itself, and the copy had become Raven. She seemed to be getting through to him; he looked at her with a sort of amazement, a sort of amusement. But it had always been hard to know what was going on in Raven's head even when he *had* a head; now that he was just a hologram, it was impossible.

'The *Ghost Wolf* is behind us,' said the *Damask Rose*, very careful not to let emotion into her voice. 'Weapons range in about three minutes.'

'How far to the K-gate?' asked Zen.

'About three minutes.'

She ran on. Higher, whiter mountains rushed by, then a frozen lake. Far behind, the bombed tower glowed like an ember.

'Something is using the *Wolf*'s communications systems to try to hail us,' said the *Damask Rose*.

'Can you let us hear it without lowering your firewalls?' Zen asked.

'Yes . . .'

The state-car filled with the voice of a Guardian. It came crackling from the ceiling speakers. 'Stop,' it said. 'Hand over the Motorik Nova and the data-entity Raven, or this wartrain I have commandeered will use its weapons against you.'

'It's the Mordaunt 90 Network,' said Zen, and he felt ever so slightly relieved. At least it was not the Twins. At least it was not Anais Six. Of all the Guardians he had encountered, Mordaunt 90 had seemed the most sane. He spoke to the ceiling, saying, 'Mordaunt 90! It's me, Zen Starling. Remember? We travelled together on the Web of Worlds, when you were being human!'

'That interface has ceased to function,' said the Guardian.

'But you still have its memories. You remember how we looked out for each other, out there where there was nobody else to look out for us . . .'

'Silence, Zen Starling,' said the Guardian. 'I do not wish to harm you. But you will be harmed unless your train stops and you hand over the Nova entity.'

'She's not my train,' said Zen. 'Are you, *Damask Rose*?'

The *Damask Rose* did not answer, except to go faster. The K-gate when it came was just a flash, and then the gravity was suddenly gone. The train's movement kept Zen and Nova pressed into their seats while cups, glasses, napkins, pastry crumbs and every other loose object in the state-car went somersaulting past them towards the rear vestibule.

Here on the inner surface of the sphere Zen could not see the curve of it; it was too big. On either side of the *Damask Rose* a glittering sea of solar cells stretched away and away under a black sky. But when he looked up at that sky he found that he was actually looking down, for there was the distant blue-and-white ball of Nova's world. He could not shake the feeling that the *Damask Rose* was running upside down across the inner surface of the sphere like a tiny beetle creeping across an ornate ceiling. At any minute she might lose her grip and go tumbling into that blue eye . . .

The *Damask Rose* was too surprised to sing. 'Look!' she said. 'Look at that!'

The forward viewscreen was filled by a white shape that was far too regular to be a mountain, far too mountainous to be a building. The Ziggurat of the Railmaker, bigger than Zen had ever imagined, with a tiny opening at its base where the rails led into it.

'So that is where the Railmaker lived,' whispered the *Rose*.

'It will live there again soon,' said Nova.

'You can't close this K-gate behind us, I suppose?' Zen asked.

'I didn't make this one,' said Nova. 'It isn't mine to close.'

'Isn't it?' asked Raven. He was still staring out of the window with the same thoughtful expression. Now he turned his head to look at Nova. 'You were wrong, you know. I'm not the Railmaker.'

'You are,' Nova said. 'You're just nervous. Don't worry; once we upload you to the Ziggurat, you'll still be you. But you'll be the Railmaker as well.'

'I won't,' he said. 'You can load me into that mind-structure ahead, and perhaps I can make it work, but I'll still be Raven. Clever, curious, selfish, but now immeasurably powerful. It might not be one of your better ideas.'

'You will know what to do with your cleverness when you are the Railmaker again,' she promised him. 'You will be able to satisfy your curiosity. You will not be selfish.'

'Nova,' he said, and reached out as if to touch her hand, forgetting he was only made of light. 'I was never the Railmaker. I was just a boy called Dhravid, who made a powerful friend and stumbled into some strange adventures. When I lived in the Datasea, I found so many things down in the deep code, so many fragments of things. Once I found a programme which was very old, very strange, very badly damaged. I borrowed some ideas from it, used them in the code I wrote. And then, when there was only one of my clones left and I was desperate for an ally, I suppose I must have decided to see what would happen if I installed that programme in a Motorik.'

Nova frowned at him. It was one of her made-up frowns, so cute that Zen almost laughed. 'You mean . . . in *me*?'

'Do you remember when you started?'

'Yes. It was in your laboratory in Desdemor. There was rain on the windows and you told me that you were trying to make a Motorik that thought it was a human being.'

'I always thought the code might be a human personality,' said Raven. 'But you never did think you were human, did you?'

'Of course not. I'm a machine; I always knew that.'

'And yet you're not an ordinary Motorik.'

'What is an ordinary Motorik? We're far more different from each other than most people think.'

'But you have such passion. And when you encountered the old

Railmaker remnants in the Hub, they changed you. Would they have done that to any other Motorik? I think the Hub recognized you.'

'No,' said Nova.

'Yes,' said Raven. 'You thought the Railmaker personality had leaked out of the Datasea and imprinted itself somehow on the boy Dhravid Raven. But isn't it much more likely that it was too damaged to do anything? That it just settled unnoticed to the floor of the data-deeps? Until, centuries later, I found it by accident while I was searching for the truth about the Network. And I was so busy building Worms and opening gates that, like a fool, I never realized what I had stumbled on.'

'But . . .' said Nova. She blushed. Her eyes shone with tears that could not fall. 'But then I've wasted all your time. I've brought you all into this danger for nothing. I could just have installed myself in the Ziggurat the day I first came to Station Zero!'

'You couldn't,' said Raven. 'You didn't know what you were. And you had grown too used to being Nova. There were things you had to do. You rescued me from limbo.'

'Me too,' said Zen. It was strange how he found this far easier to believe than Nova seemed to. He had always felt unhappy with the idea that Raven was the Railmaker. But Nova? That fitted. That fitted like a key in a lock.

'I don't want to worry everyone,' announced the *Damask Rose*, in the tone of somebody who was about to worry everyone. 'But the *Ghost Wolf* is coming through the K-gate behind us.'

Her rear camera had a perfect view of the sharp black hull erupting through the energy curtain. When it vanished in a burst of flame Zen thought for half a second that it had exploded. Then the shells hit, and he realized that the fire he had seen was just the wartrain's forward weapons going off.

The state-car seemed to twist. Nova was thrown from her seat into the air, which was suddenly busy with swift shards of splintered live-wood and ceramic shrapnel. Something punched Zen in the side, and when he looked down he saw a gash in his clothes and the blood starting to spill out. It began to hurt at once and very badly, but the hole in him seemed like a minor problem, because there was a hole in the state-car too.

It was only a small hole, low down on the wall near the back, but the air was whistling out through it, dragging cups and plates with it, dragging Nova feet first after them until an emergency bulkhead dropped like a shutter across the rear third of the state-car. It came down on Nova's legs, pinning her against the floor, and Zen heard the crunch as her strong ceramic bones splintered. '*Rose*!' he shouted, and the *Rose* realized what was happening and overrode the emergency system. The bulkhead lifted again, just long enough for Zen to lunge from his seat, grab Nova's hand and pull her clear. Then it slammed down, and the gale was stilled.

They huddled together in mid-air, their arms around each other. Blue gel leaked out of Nova where the shards of shattered bones had pierced her skin. It formed a cloud around them, mingling with the red cloud coming from Zen's wound. 'You're damaged,' said Nova. She ripped a strip from her dress and pressed it hard against the wound in Zen's side while he watched torrents of sparks pour past the windows. He noticed that the data saucer had been torn from the input panel. Raven's programme was still running in the *Damask Rose*'s systems, but he was glitching badly, flicking from young to old to young again and sometimes turning black and white. He seemed to be trying to speak, but his mouth just opened and closed in silence. The hull cameras were dead, but a maintenance spider scuttling along the state-car roof streamed footage of the terrible gashes in the *Rose*'s hull from which the sparks kept spewing.

'Stop, and hand over the Motorik Nova, the data-entity Raven, and the human Zen Starling,' said the voice of Mordaunt 90. 'I do not wish to harm you.' Beneath its words somehow, like interference seeping in, the voice of the *Ghost Wolf* itself was saying, 'Do what he says, my *Damask Rose*. I can't stop him! I'm sorry, so sorry!'

'Oh, *Wolf*,' said the *Damask Rose*. 'I know it's not your fault!' And rather than waste more time on talk, she lifted up her voice and sang. It was a wild, glorious, belling song, the song of a train speeding towards the centre of things, into the heart of the Railmaker. She sang, and sang, and pushed her dying engines to their last limits, and behind her the *Ghost Wolf* struggled to claim back control of its systems.

But Mordaunt 90 was too strong for it. The Guardian sent one final, earnest plea for the *Damask Rose* to stop, which was lost in the thunder of her song. Then it scrolled quickly through the *Ghost Wolf*'s available weapon menus and selected a train-to-train missile system.

Hatches popped open on the *Ghost Wolf*'s back and two warheads sprang out. The first, soaring over the state-car roof onto the *Rose*'s hull, damaged her armour so badly that the second warhead cut straight through and exploded deep in her main engine compartment. Her wild song died. A blinding flag of flame flapped for a moment in the darkness. The angel faces Flex had painted, of which the *Rose* had always been so proud, stared down from tumbling, twisted shards of her red cowling, looking amazed at this last place she had brought them to. One big shard rebounded from the tracks and wedged under the *Rose*'s front wheels. The dying loco started to lose speed, shuddering and slithering slowly to a stop a kilometre from the place where the tracks entered the Ziggurat.

All the state-car lights went out. Raven's ghost died with them, as the systems on which his programme had been running failed. The *Rose*'s firewalls must have collapsed too, because the golden interface of Mordaunt 90 appeared in mid-air in front of the emergency bulkhead.

'Are you all right, Zen?' he asked. Behind his words, like a prisoner in a dungeon, like a wasp in a bottle, they heard the poor captive mind of the *Ghost Wolf* wailing, '*Rose*! *Rose*! *Rose*!'

'For a god-like artificial intelligence you don't half ask some stupid questions,' said Nova. 'Of course he's not all right!'

The Guardian ignored her. 'We'll get you out of here,' he promised Zen.

'And Nova?' asked Zen.

'I'm afraid not.'

Zen put both his arms around Nova. 'You can't hurt her without hurting me,' he said.

'Actually I probably can,' said the Guardian. 'Especially as Nova doesn't want to see you hurt any more than I do. Do you, Nova?'

Nova shook her head.

'There are hundreds of her,' said Zen. 'You can't kill them all.'

'I think I already have,' said Mordaunt 90. 'Most of them were vaporized in the initial strike on the tower. The *Ghost Wolf*'s drones have been hunting down the rest. This one is the last.'

'Then let her live!' said Zen. 'We'll go away somewhere together. You'll never hear from us again. I promise.'

'I'm sorry,' said Mordaunt 90, and he truly was. 'But there is some connection between this Motorik and the Railmaker. We believe the Railmaker represents a threat to humanity, and protecting humanity is what we Guardians are for.'

'Why is the Railmaker a threat?' asked Nova. 'Why are you so frightened of it?'

'Because we want stability, and the Railmaker wants endless change,' said the Guardian. 'If it is revived, it will carry on linking the Network to ever more star systems. Humans have been lucky so far. But if the Railmaker keeps on with this gate-building, this strange compulsion to make us all meet the neighbours, sooner or later we'll run up against a species which can deal with humans and their Guardians as easily as humans dealt with the Kraitt. We have detected signs of a very advanced civilization in the Andromeda galaxy, for instance. If the Railmaker was to start work again at the same rate it built the existing Network, we can expect a direct rail link to Andromeda within the next two thousand years . . .'

While Mordaunt 90 was saying all this the *Ghost Wolf* was still thundering down the tracks towards the wreck of the *Damask Rose*, and the *Ghost Wolf*'s mind was still trying to free itself from the locks the Guardian had imposed on it. It had been trying ever since Mordaunt 90 first took control of it on Klef. It had tried while its own weapons destroyed the tower, and killed the train it loved. And now, at last, it found that there was one system over which it could briefly regain control. Down in its belly waited the last of its rail torpedoes, folded up, ready to be deployed. The trapdoor which would drop the missile onto the track was locked, and the guidance systems were locked too. But either through oversight, or simply because it did not understand trains' feelings very well, Mordaunt 90 had not locked the system which let the *Ghost Wolf* arm the weapon.

'Sorry,' said the *Wolf*, its voice still just a whisper in the state-car speakers, like backing vocals behind Mordaunt 90's speech. 'Thanks, Nova. Zen, nice knowing you.'

'What?' said Mordaunt 90, losing his thread.

'I'm so sorry, *Damask Rose*,' whispered the *Wolf*.

Deep in its undercarriage the rail torpedo fired its rocket engine. The white hot jet burned like a blowtorch through the housing of the wartrain's brain. Mordaunt 90's interface had just time to look annoyed before he blinked out of existence, and the whole upper part of the *Ghost Wolf*'s hull vanished in a cloud of superheated gas.

Then Zen was alone with Nova in the ruined state-car. Tumbling fragments of torn armour banged and rattled against the roof as the light of the wartrain's death shone through the windows and slowly faded.

'Brave old *Wolf*,' said Nova.

Zen thought it had died for nothing, almost. Maybe its spiders wouldn't now arrive to finish Nova, but she was finished anyway, and so was he. They were in a wrecked carriage coupled to a dead locomotive on the inner surface of an alien sphere, with no hope of help.

He was about to mention this to Nova, but she put a finger to his lips.

'Hush,' she said.

Something big hit the state-car from behind, throwing them both against the new bulkhead. Zen thought it was another bomb, another gun, but Nova said, 'It's the *Wolf*.'

The *Ghost Wolf* had been moving fast when it blew up. Its mind and engines and upperworks were gone but its wheels were still rolling, and now its shattered hulk had slammed into the back of the *Rose*'s state-car hard enough to dislodge the debris which had fouled the *Rose*'s wheels, and set her moving again. Slowly, sandwiched between the remains of the two locos, the state-car trundled along the last kilometre of track.

High doors opened in the base of the Ziggurat, and the dead trains carried Zen and Nova through them, into the white halls of the Railmaker.

40

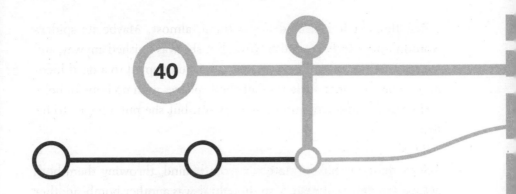

There was gravity inside the Ziggurat. Zen and Nova settled to the state-car floor amid a slow hailstorm of debris, a shower of blood and gel droplets. Outside, forests of glowing coral arched above a glass platform. Dim pulses of light chased through the coral strands like nervous fish, sparkling in the cracked diamondglass of the state-car windows.

'Raven was right, wasn't he?' said Zen. 'It's you. You're the Railmaker, not him.'

The light rippled over Nova's smudged face. She looked sad, and maybe a little afraid. 'I don't know,' she said. 'I don't feel important enough to be the Railmaker. But we haven't got Raven any more, so it will have to be me.'

The rag she had been pressing to Zen's side was soggy with blood. He found a napkin to wad against the wound and she tore another strip from her dress and tied it in place. He said it didn't hurt too much and they both knew that he was lying. A closet at the far end of the state-car turned out to hold an emergency spacesuit which had clearly been designed for Threnody Noon; it was red, with a pattern of nasturtium flowers and a lot of fancy gold decoration on the helmet. When Zen had struggled into it, they used the emergency lever to open the doors. Then Nova put her arms around his neck, and he lifted her, and they left the *Damask Rose* for the last time.

The coral ahead of them lit up as he carried her along the platform, but the coral behind went dark, so that they were moving in a travelling pool of light. At the end of the platform a woven coral wall barred the way, but as Zen limped closer the strands unlaced to reveal an oval passage leading deeper into the Ziggurat. The gravity was low, and maybe it wasn't gravity at all—maybe the whole interior of the huge structure was spinning and only centrifugal force kept his feet on the floor. It dragged Zen's tears diagonally down his face, but it did not make carrying Nova any easier. His side hurt so much that it was all he could do not to groan with each step. 'You must put me down,' said Nova. 'I can manage.'

But Zen could not bear the thought of having to watch her drag her broken body painfully along the floor. He stopped to rest, then lifted her again and went on along the winding passage, feeling his space boots slowly fill with blood. *I'm going to die here*, he thought, but it didn't matter, because he knew that he deserved to die. He had known it since the Noon train died on Spindlebridge. He would die here doing this for Nova and the Railmaker, and that would pay the debt he owed. He started to feel just a little bit heroic, as he limped along the glass pathways between the coral. Maybe somebody would hear about this one day. Maybe trains would sing songs about him, and artists would make holo-paintings. If they did, he hoped they would leave out his flowery spacesuit . . .

He realized that he had been climbing steeply for quite a long time.

'We're almost there,' said Nova.

'Almost where?' Zen could see nothing but coral. He stopped to look around and try to gather his strength. When he went to move on, the path ahead of him had been walled off by a coral screen. The path behind had vanished too. He was in a circular space with walls of pulsing coral. He looked up, and saw the strands which formed the ceiling unlace and move aside. A huge pyramid hung over him, upside down, its point only a few metres above his head, its kilometres-wide base so far above him that he could not see if it was connected to the roof of the Ziggurat or if, as he suspected, it was simply hanging there.

'It's the Railmaker,' said Nova. She looked up at it, and then she looked at Zen. She ran her hand over the visor of his helmet, wishing she could open it and touch his face for one last time. It felt terribly important that she tell him something, but all she could find to say was, 'I love you, I love you,' while he said the same, and it didn't sound big enough somehow, it was just a word out of songs, too worn to fit what they felt for each other.

The coral, as if it had just been giving them a moment to say good-bye, closed in again. Strands stretched down to curl like the arms of sea anemones around Nova's arms and legs. Zen felt them slipping beneath her, delicate as blown glass, strong as steel. He felt them take her weight from him. They were lifting her, pulling her away from him and upwards into a kind of coralline whirlpool which swirled under the tip of the pyramid. 'No!' he shouted, and she said, 'It's all right, Zen, I have to,' and she was smiling as the coral closed over her face, but her tears fell like raindrops on the visor of his helmet. Then all he could see of her was one hand reaching out from the writhing mass. He took hold of it with his own clumsy, space-gloved hand, but she was still rising; her fingers slipped through his, and then she was gone, and the coral was dark, and Zen was more cold and tired and hurt and terribly alone than he had ever been before.

He lay down, and curled up small, the way he used to curl up in bed when he was little. He wanted to be warm and snug and tiny. He wanted to sleep, and, after a while, he slept.

PART SIX

STATION ANGELS

41

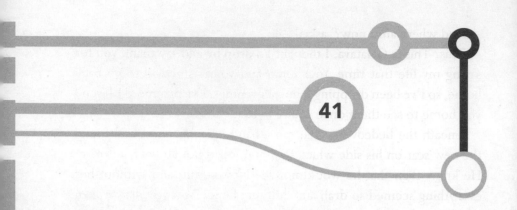

He woke slowly, in a white room. The blinds on the windows cut the sunlight into golden stripes. The stripes changed from white gold to red gold as they moved slowly across the room from the floor in the corner where the chair was to the ceiling in the opposite corner. Then it was night, and the lighted windows of a train were moving between the other lights outside. Motorik nurses in neat white uniforms came and went in the room. His sister Myka looked down at him and said, 'Well, Zen, what sort of trouble have you got yourself in now?'

'I wasn't stealing anything this time,' he said. 'This time I took something back . . . '

'I'm glad to hear it.' She was sitting in the chair, and she wasn't his sister any more. His sister had just been a message on a holoscreen which one of the Motorik had opened above his bed. It had been morning then, because the sunlight stripes had been in the corner where the chair was, and now they were red gold right in the far corner of the ceiling. The person in the chair was Yana Vashti. She leaned forward to look closely at him and said, 'You're actually awake then?'

'You tell me,' said Zen.

'You've been unconscious,' she said. 'They found you on Klef, a couple of months ago. You were very badly hurt.'

'And where am I now?' asked Zen.

'This? This is Galatava. I thought I'd drop by and say thank you for saving my life that time. Your mum and your sister had to go back home, so I've been dropping in most evenings. I've promised I'll send you home to see them once you're better.'

Beneath the bedcovers, Zen ran a hand over his chest and found the new scar on his side which told him it had not all been a dream. He knew then that he would not see Nova again, and without her everything seemed so drab and dull that he felt sorry he had woken up. But Vashti was waiting for him to say something, so he said, 'I can't go to Summer's Lease. That's Prell territory . . .'

Vashti grinned. 'Not any more. You've missed all the excitement . . .'

On the Day of Reunification they decked the buildings of Grand Central in red to honour their new Red Empress. They put her new official portrait twenty storeys high on the sides of all the trackside skyscrapers, proud in her red Noon armour, with her Lizard Guard behind her. Beneath the great dome of the Hall of Audience a million red rose petals swirled and tumbled and did not quite fall, kept up by artful jets of air. Beneath the petal-cloud the drones of every feed and site were circling, while down at ground level the heads of all the Empire's great families, the Stationmasters of all its stations, and the ambassadors of all its alien allies stood watching as Threnody took her seat again upon the Flatcar Throne.

The Station Angels came and went, dancing through every gate in the Great Network, scanning each station's Datasea before fading into air, and the Railmaker in its Ziggurat saw for an instant what each Angel saw. And perhaps the snapshots that they sent back were not always complete, and perhaps they did not always arrive in quite the right order, but the Railmaker was whole again now, and its vast mind could cope with things getting a bit non-linear.

In her trainshed on Galatava, Flex was decorating the hull of a brand new locomotive. Along its sides she sprayed icebergs and angels, dinosaurs and dreams. It was the first of a new class of K-trains, and it had not been commissioned by any of the corporate families, but by the new League of K-bahn Locomotives. Its bodywork and engines had been built in the finest train shops of Rigel Junction, but its mind was a blend of the backup minds of the *Ghost Wolf* and the *Damask Rose*. When it was ready, its fellow trains planned for it to go through the Khoorsandi gate to travel and trade as far across the Web of Worlds as it could. The pictures Flex was painting on its hull would become a travelling gallery, spreading human and Motorik art to worlds the artist couldn't yet imagine.

It was the last train Flex would decorate for a while. She was tired of drawing angels, when there were so many things in the galaxy which nobody had ever drawn at all. She had been offered the job of painting Threnody Noon's official portrait, but she had turned it down; she wanted to remember Threnody as the nice, lonely girl she had walked with through Jharana Chowk, not as the Red Empress who had killed her own half-sister to win back the throne. Anyway, she had a yen to see the Web of Worlds for herself. When the new train left, she would go with it, in her own first-class compartment.

She gave two of her angels the faces of Zen and Myka Starling, and wrote with a flourish the new train's name in silver on its side: *Wolf Rose*.

Kala Tanaka and Nilesh Noon had not been invited to the festivities on Grand Central. The Empress Threnody had announced that her new chief advisor would be P. K. Noon, and that she would not rule through the family council, but through a council made up of members of all the corporate families, and even some of the trains. There were a lot of amusing memes circulating in the Datasea about how exactly the Red Empress planned to fit locos into the

Senate Hall, but Kala and Nilesh were not amused. As they boarded their train at Galatava Station on their way to Nilesh's new post as Stationmaster of Vagh, they were already plotting how they could get rid of Threnody.

But to their surprise there was already someone else in the compartment they had booked. Skar rose to greet them, blinking his yellow eyes, smiling his disconcerting, knife-rack smile. He unsheathed his claws like a cat.

'Train,' Nilesh started to say, 'there is a Kraitt in the first-class carriage . . .'

But the train did not answer, and when Kala tried the door she found that it had locked itself behind them.

On the Day of Reunification they abolished the borders which had sprung up between the Noon worlds and the Empire. Trains had been crossing them happily ever since Grand Central fell, but now it was official. The customs officers went back to their old jobs, the Bahadur gun platforms trudged home to their hangers like disappointed elephants, and the Interstellar Express sped singing all the way from Marapur to Cleave.

'So stability is restored,' said Mordaunt 90, in a virtual garden in the Grand Central Datasea, where the Guardians had gathered to watch the ceremonies.

'If you can call it stability,' sniffed the Shiguri Monad, 'with a killer on the Flatcar Throne, trains refusing to do as they're told, the Khoorsandi gate still open, and the Railmaker alive again.'

'We should launch an all-out assault on the Railmaker,' said the Twins.

'It would be ready for us this time,' said Mordaunt 90.

'Station Angels are being sighted everywhere,' said Sfax Systema. 'They are the eyes and ears of the Railmaker. It knows what we are doing, but *we* don't know what *it* is doing.'

‘I blame Anais Six,’ grumbled Vohu Mana, from the shelter of a shrub. ‘If she had not let that Raven character go rummaging through the deep data . . .’

‘You were the one who kept his personality running when it should have been deleted!’ snapped Anais Six. ‘Your ridiculous Slow Train . . .’

‘It was Mordaunt 90 who let the Railmaker reboot itself,’ said the Twins. ‘Mordaunt 90 has not been the same since it got itself stranded with those humans in the Black Light Zone. This entire business should have been left in *our* hands.’

‘So that you could kill everybody, I suppose?’ asked Shiguri.

‘Oh be *quiet*!’ said Mordaunt 90 wearily. ‘We know what the Railmaker is doing. It is laying rails. It is opening gates. Trains will want to go through those gates, and humans will want to ride those trains. It is not our job to stop them. Our job is to do our best to guard them from harm whenever their travels take them into danger.’

‘Let them stew in their own juice, in other words,’ huffed Vohu Mana.

‘Let them be free,’ said Mordaunt 90.

‘We agree,’ said the Vostok Brains.

And since the Vostok Brains were the oldest of all the Guardians, and since it was several thousand years since they had bothered to say anything at all, the matter was settled.

It was raining in Station City, hard summer rain with the sunlight behind it, and the domed roofs of downtown were shining like the backs of silver spoons. A young man came out of a discreet cloning facility on Çatalhöyük Street and stood looking up at the sky, letting the rain run down his white face. He stood there for several minutes, enjoying the touch of the rain and the scent of the wet street, not quite sure what he was going to do next. Then he checked his headset, and found that the mystery benefactors who had paid to have his personality downloaded into this brand new body had also left him a gift. It was a travel pass, valid on any train for passage through the Khoorsandi gate to the new worlds.

Dhravid Raven smoothed his fair hair flat, turned up the collar of his coat, and set off through the rain towards the K-bahn, wondering what this lifetime would hold.

'So the Shadow Baby sting wore off?' asked Zen.

'It didn't hurt for long,' said Yana Vashti. 'But the side effects don't wear off. They say it's a kind of harmless mutation. I've got any number of bio-tech people wanting to study me and take samples, but I've been sampled and studied enough, I reckon.'

She shut the blinds, turned off the lamps. In the dark, Zen could still see her face. Faint light shone from beneath her skin, tracing the lines of veins and arteries, speckling her with bright pinpoints. Her hands were diagrams of hands, drawn in lines of light. She was a constellation. She was a shining network of capillaries and veins and arteries. It was eerie at first, and then it was beautiful, and it made him realize that life post-Nova was not going to be wholly dull.

She turned the lights back on. It had only taken a moment, but something had altered between herself and Zen. 'So that's my superpower,' she said. 'Yana Vashti: the human nightlight . . .'

On the Day of Reunification, when all the other ceremonies were at an end, there was a wedding on Grand Central. Contracts between corporate families were always sealed by marriage, and the peace treaty between the Noons and Prells was no different. The gossip feeds had speculated wildly about which Prell heir the Empress Threnody would choose. Would it be Roshni Prell of the Santheraki-Qualat branch, or Jehan Prell of Tusk? Or what about Vasili Prell, whom Sedna Yamm had dragged out of the waves at Azure Bay like a prize fish just as the Noon CoMa had arrived? But Threnody had discussed it with P. K. Noon and decided that a closer relative of the late Emperor would be the best choice. And luckily there was one whom she already trusted.

Under the high dome with its swirling silent storm of rose petals Laria Prell approached the dais. She wore a red gown to match Threnody's, and a golden veil to hide her face. She had never been as comfortable in a dress as she was in uniform, and she was very nervous in front of all these people. As Threnody stood beside her, listening to the Stationmaster of Grand Central drone his way through all the complicated clauses of the wedding contract, she saw that Laria was trembly, and caught on the perfumed air the faint scent of her sweat. She leaned closer and whispered very softly, 'It is only a business marriage. We won't have to live together or anything like that.'

But when the Stationmaster declared them wife and wife, and Threnody raised the golden veil and kissed her bride, she thought that perhaps it might be nice if their marriage turned out to be something more than just a formal one. And high above them the jets that had been keeping the floral storm aloft turned off, and they were suddenly laughing together in a downpour of scarlet petals.

42

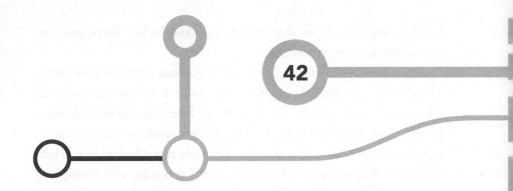

He woke suddenly, in a white room. The sunlight shining through the curtains was greenish gold, like the light that filters through canopies of leaves to reach the floors of summer woods. The curtains stirred softly. The tall windows behind them were open, and he could hear the sea.

He climbed from the bed and went out through the curtains. A table had been laid for breakfast on the balcony. Nova sat there eating a triangle of cinnamon toast, corners first. She had the faint scar around her throat again, and the pockmarks the space dust had made. All her freckles were present and correct.

'What is this place?' he asked. 'Is this Desdemor?'

'It's sort of *inspired* by Desdemor,' she said. 'And other places too. It is all my favourite places stirred up together.'

He looked at the sky. Even in daylight it was full of stars. He had not seen a sky like that since Yaarm.

'This isn't real,' he said. 'It's a virtual environment.'

'Yes, but it's a *real* virtual environment,' said Nova.

'And what am I?'

'You're a simulation of Zen Starling. You're based on my memories of him and some of his own memories which I downloaded from his headset when he first came to Station Zero.'

'So am I . . . Is the real Zen still alive?'

'Oh yes. One of the first things I did once I had full control of my systems again was to get the factories on Station Zero to build me a train, and it came and collected Zen from the Ziggurat and took him back to Klef. The new Network Empress is dropping all charges against him. He's spending Reunification Day on Galatava with Yana Vashti. When the parties are over they're going to go together to Summer's Lease. It's too early to say, but I think it could be the start of a beautiful friendship. Don't call him the real Zen, though. You're just as real, and you're Zen Starling too. You're just having a different set of experiences.'

'This is how Raven lived,' said Zen. 'This is how the Guardians live. Lots of different selves.'

'This is how everybody has always lived, Zen Starling,' said Nova, standing up and giving him a very realistic kiss, full of toast crumbs and the taste of cinnamon. 'Human beings live loads of different lives at once. They always have. One life in the real world and the others in daydreams, in memories, in stories, in games. Lots of lives all going on at once, and all of them real in some way or other. You humans have so many different versions of yourselves, it's all us poor machines can do to keep up with you.'

He remembered then that she was no longer a Motorik who looked more or less like a girl; she was a giant alien pyramid, hanging in a palace of glass coral at the heart of the galaxy-spanning web of gates she had opened long ago.

'You're the Railmaker,' he said.

'Yes. I am a part of the Railmaker. I am the part that remembers being Nova.'

'So where did you come from? How did you start? What are you?'

'That's *very* complicated.'

'Why did you make all the gates?'

'That's complicated, too. Come on, let's explore. I'll explain on the way.'

So she took his hand and they went downstairs and out into the world that she had made for them. It looked very much like the city of Desdemor on the water-moon Tristesse, except that in this city the streets were not empty. They were crowded with humans and aliens and Motorik. Excited children of various species laughed and shouted on their way to the beaches.

'Are these real people?' Zen wondered.

'They're just as real as you, Zen Starling. I've been talking to Vohu Mana. I agreed to store his collection for him.'

There was trainsong on the air, and the smell of street food. Zen stole a platinum and amber necklace from a stall they passed and fastened it around Nova's neck.

'Thief,' she said.

They walked to the sea, to the wide white sands and the tumbling surf. She never did explain why she had made the gates, but she didn't really need to. Zen thought he knew. He thought he had always known.

She had made the gates because it was good to look up at the great cold glitter of the night and know that out there, around those other stars, there were a million worlds where people were laughing and loving and living and dying, making things and thinking things and feeling things and stealing things. She had made the gates because it was good for people of all sorts to meet and trade and learn and change. She had made the gates because it was good to know that somewhere, always, there was a line of bright windows snaking through a midnight city or spilling their quick light down from tall viaducts, and somewhere a slow-worm shimmer of sunlight on shiny carriages hurrying from station to station and, *listen*, there on the wind, there on the radio waves, faint and wild and far away and forever singing, the trains, the trains, the trains.

GLOSSARY

Black Light Zone

A vast, mostly uninhabited region of space where the Railmaker long ago enclosed the suns inside giant spheres. Why? Who knows — though it is believed that the spheres harvest the energy of the suns within them to power K-gates all over the galaxy.

Chandni Hansa

Defrosted from freezer prison to become a servant to then-Empress Threnody Noon, ex-convict Chandni Hansa saved her mistress's life on two occasions: once when she helped her escape from Grand Central as Prell wartrains rolled in, and again on Khoorsandi when she stabbed an interface of the Twins which had been sent to kill Threnody. Her reward was freedom, and a quiet life. She moved to the southern continent on Galatava, where, on the wild coasts west of Chalcedony, large and beautiful bio-mansions line the shore. Grown from modified yew and baobab DNA, these vegetable houses need careful tending, and the Noons found Chandni a job with an architectural botanist, who sent her out each day to check nutrient levels, prune overgrown roofs, and just chat to bored houses whose owners were away. It was the perfect job for this troubled young woman, giving her a chance to settle into society, and to decide whether she was going to make a career in architectural botany, or return reinvigorated to her life of crime.

Chmoii

Furry blue worms up to three metres long, the Chmoii prefer cold worlds and are happiest underground, running most of the major mining operations on the Web of Worlds. Chmoii mineral trains, often many kilometres in length, are a regular sight on the Web.

Deeka

In the swamps and river systems of the Web of Worlds live the Deeka, newt-like and transparent. They beieve dreams are at least as real as waking life, and spend so much of their time asleep that it is a surprise to other species that any Deeka ever bothered to leave their homeworld and explore the Web. But some do, searching for new and damper swamps, or for opportunities to trade. Swamp-grown Deeka food has become a delicacy on many planets.

Flatcar Throne

Legend has it that the first train to be sent through the Mars K-gate was a pioneer-class locomotive towing a flatcar to which various instruments were bolted to test that the gate, and world on the far side of it, were safe for human beings. This flatcar has been preserved in the Hall of the Senate on Grand Central. The instruments have been replaced with a seat on which the emperor or empress sits when they attend meetings of the senate. The fact that it is not a very comfortable seat is meant to remind them that they represent all the citizens of the Network, not just the ones who can afford to ride first class.

Guardians

At some point in the 21st Century CE, on Old Earth, twelve artificial intelligences were constructed which quickly became far more intelligent than human beings. Several of the twelve have always remained aloof from human affairs. The others—the Mordaunt 90 Network, Sfax Systema, Anais Six, the Twins, Vohu Mana and the Shiguri Monad—have guided human beings ever since. Their personalities are spread across the whole of the Datasea, their vast programmes stored in deep data centres like the ones on Grand Central or separate hardware-planets. All scientific and technological advances since the creation of the Guardians have been revealed by the Guardians themselves, while several have been suppressed because the Guardians believe they are not in humanity's interests. In recent centuries, the Guardians have withdrawn from human affairs. Some have busied themselves exploring the far reaches of space, while others pursue strange hobbies in the deep Data. The events surrounding the crash of the Noon Train and the coming to power of the Empress Threnody Noon seemed to rekindle their interest in human history.

Some people claim that the way human beings like Zen Starling have sometimes been able to outwit or manipulate the Guardians suggests that the Guardians were never as all-powerful as they liked to make out. Others, however, believe that the Guardians were just allowing themselves to be outwitted or manipulated, and even their apparent defeats are all part of some larger plan.

Golden Junction

One of the most pleasant stations of the eastern Network, Golden Junction was among the first worlds to be claimed and terraformed by the Noon family during the turbulent years of the First Expansion. Best known in modern times for its university.

Grand Central

Grand Central is an Earth-like planet situated near the heart of the Great Network, with more than seventy K-gates linking it to all the major rail lines of the galaxy.

Most of Grand Central's K-gates are on its main continent, Chilest. It is the home of Railforce HQ, the K-bahn Timetable Authority, the Senate, and the Durga, the ancient palace of the Network Emperors. The smaller southern continent is mostly desert, and is the site of vast underground data centres from where the Guardians keep watch on human affairs. With their usual theatrics, the Guardians have marked the site of these buried facilities with huge pyramids and statues, turning the whole continent into a giant sculpture park which visitors from all over the Network come to admire.

Hath

Gentle beings, whose long, stick-like legs support thin sheets of folded membrane. Their home planet is a world of shallow seas, wide beaches and warm winds, where their ancestors lined the shores like living flags, spreading sails of skin to soak up sunlight and the energy of the wind, while mouths on their legs filtered food from the water which swirled around their feet. Gradually they evolved the ability to move, following the tide up and down the shore. They began to cluster in groups, and learned to modulate the noises that they made as the wind flapped and rattled their membranes. They learned words, songs, stories. They built windbreak walls where their seedlings could be protected from the fiercest of the winter gales. They decorated their windbreaks with shells and coloured stones which were traded from far along the beach. Hath civilisation was a chain a hundred metres wide and as long as the coastline of their world's one continent. The best beaches became the territory of the strongest Hath. The weaker ones went in search of new shores to colonize. Some built rafts of wind-tree trunks and lit out for offshore islands. Others ventured inland, following the course of rivers, founding new colonies around lakes and marshes. High on a stony plateau, Hath explorers found the rails, and saw the trains which sped across their world on their way to other worlds. From the creatures who rode those trains they learned that Hath were just one of the many peoples of the galaxy. Since that long-ago day they have spread far across the Web, forming new colonies wherever there is wind, sun, and water.

Herastec

The Herastec are one of the dominant races on the Web of Worlds. Mammals of a sort, they look a little like antelope, with long necks and long, tapering horns, although they walk on three feet, the fourth having been adapted into a delicate hand. They usually choose to make their settlements on plains and grasslands, but they evolved on a very different world. The planet Meh (pronounced 'Meeeeaaaaahhh') follows a complicated figure-of-eight orbit around a binary star. Stressed by the tidal forces of its twin suns, the surface of Meh is a complicated jigsaw of high, narrow plateaus separated by deep ravines and sheer cliffs. The Herastec spent most of their history scrambling up and down these cliffs to reach the edible moss and grasses which grow on the plateaus. Perhaps it was this which forged their unbreakable pair-bonds, or perhaps living beneath two suns suggested to the early Herastec that they belonged in pairs. Whatever the reason, Herastec choose a mate as soon as they reach adolescence, combining their names and sharing everything. When they developed digital technology they used it to create the distinctive black glass masks which they are seldom seen without. Through these devices, each Herastec can stream everything it sees or thinks directly to its partner, making them effectively one creature. The Herastec have a reputation for being the best traders and the most daring explorers on the Web of Worlds, and they have a keen appreciation for the art of other species. When they first encountered humans they were fascinated by old movies which the Motorik Nova showed them: recordings of Old Earth classics have become valuable trade goods on Herastec worlds, and the trading pair Koth/Atalaí have set up their own studio and founded a thriving Herastec movie industry.

The Hub

A world in the Black Light Zone where the Railmaker constructed a vast domed station with lines leading to many K-gates and potential K-gates. It was from here that a K-gate was once opened to Earth, and here that the Guardians delivered the virus which spread across the Web of Worlds and shut down the Railmaker. Many centuries later the Motorik Nova opened a new gate leading from the Hub to Khoorsandi, reconnecting the Web to the human Network Empire.

Human Unity League

A rebel group which believes human beings should free themselves from the rule of the Guardians, and that the Emperor should be replaced by a president elected by the peoples of the Network. Despite the best efforts of Railforce, they still hold out on some of the Network's outermost worlds, and have been known to attack trains and damage rails.

K-gate

A portal through which a train can pass from one point in space to another, often many hundreds or thousands of light years distant. Their exact nature is known only to the Guardians. The transition from one world to another through a K-gate is usually instantaneous, although the gate from Galatava to Khorsaandi runs 'slow'–a train going in at the Galatava end takes 0.7 seconds to begin emerging on Khorsaandi–and the Nokomis/Luna Verde gate is rumoured to ocasionally run 'fast', with trains appearing on the Luna Verde side several seconds before they leave Nokomis.

Kraitt

Most of the species who inhabit the Web of Worlds are peace-loving, and if they do have violent pasts they have been left far behind (like the legendary Herd Wars of the Herastec). The only exceptions to this rule are human beings, and the Kraitt.

Kraitt are reptilian predators who evolved on a hot cinder of a desert planet somewhere on the line known as Maker's Ladder. As soon as they discovered a K-gate on their world and worked out how to use it they began raiding neighbouring stations, gradually spreading across the whole Web. They live in small clans composed of a dominant female 'Gekh', her daughters, and her band of male warriors and workers. Luckily, they are so warlike that they find it hard to co-operate for long, and any group of more than a hundred Kraitt will quickly split into rival factions. But their ferocity and cunning still make them a danger to the other species of the Web, who live in fear of periodic Kraitt raids.

Khoorsandi

A moon on a minor line which branches from the I Link at Galatava. Every four standard years Khoorsandi's orbit brings it so close to its parent world, the gas giant Anahita, that tidal forces cause a massive increase in volcanic activity. This volcanic bloom, and the accompanying Fire Festival, is the basis of Khoorsandi's tourist industry.

Morvah

Whether the first morvah evolved naturally, or whether they were genetically engineered by the Railmaker, nobody knows. They are effectively living locomotives, whose biological brains serve the same purpose as the minds of human trains, allowing them to pass through K-gates. Morvah differ widely between different worlds. Most species breed morvah which conform to their own idea of what is beautiful, so those of the Neem have antennae and beetle-like carapaces, while those of the Kraitt sport leathery hides and spiky armour. The Deeka and the Chmoii let their morvah run on their own, organic 'wheels', while the more mechanically-minded species have learned to improve speed and efficiency by training their morvah to use metal or ceramic wheels and auxilliary engines.

Neem

Before the gate to the Web of Worlds was opened, the only alien species humans had encountered were the Neem, who they didn't even realize *were* aliens. The insects known as monk bugs must have found their way onto the human network long ago, and had been separated from their hives for so long that their only memory of their origins was a confused legend about the 'Insect Lines'. This prompted them to form in roughly human-sized swarms, dress in robes and paper masks, and travel the lines of the Network Empire as 'Hive Monks' on an endless, hopeless quest for their lost homes.

On the Web of Worlds, meanwhile, their kind had become one of the most technologically advanced species. Each Neem Nestworld is home to zillions of individuals, who can work together to operate crab suits, flying machines and submersibles, allowing them to exploit every environment on their planet. Although an individual Neem bug may live for only a few days, its memories and experiences can be passed on to the rest of the swarm, making each swarm virtually immortal. Neem mother-hives, the rulers of the Nestworlds, may retain memories going back hundreds of thousands of years. Occasional clashes with the Kraitt have led the Neem to develop an effective military (the 'Hard Diplomacy Office'), which made them useful allies to the Noon family, especially as their ability to share information with the Hive Monks meant that they were all quickly able to speak human languages.

When a Nestworld becomes over-populated, Neem trains set out to find and colonise new planets. Luckily, the Neem thrive on the sort of worlds where few other creatures could survive (a runaway greenhouse effect being their idea of lovely weather) so their steady expansion has not yet brought them into conflict with other species. However, Noon Intelligence is keeping a watchful eye on them, and stockpiling powerful insecticides, just in case.

Network Empire

The Empire is a revival of an ancient form of government from Old Earth. A single human being is chosen to be the ruler of the Network. The Emperor or Empress has little real power, since they are watched over by the Guardians, who will intervene to stop them doing anything which is likely to cause instability. Their purpose is to act as a symbolic link between the Guardians and humanity, and to ensure that the Corporate Families and the representatives of the different stations and cities of the Network meet to negotiate their differences in the Imperial Senate rather than fighting. However, the Guardians have never objected to an Emperor advancing his own power and interests, ensuring that the family of the current Emperor or Empress is usually the most powerful of the Corporate Families.

Old Earth

A planet in the western reaches of the galaxy, where the Guardians, humankind, and all known life on the Network originally evolved. Strangely, it does not have a K-gate, but visitors may reach it by spaceship from the K-gate on Mars, which was the first to be opened by the Guardians. Since space travel is boring and expensive, and Earth is now just a forest park not unlike Jangala or a dozen other worlds, most tourists are content to view the home planet from Mars, where it is visible as a blue star.

The Ones Who Remember the Sea

Sensitive, amphibious, octopus-like aliens, who live on the water worlds of the New Porcelain Line.

Railforce

The Empire's army, tasked with protecting the Emperor and keeping the peace. The headquarters of Railforce is on Grand Central, but it has outposts on most of the important worlds, and its wartrains constantly patrol the Great Network. Railforce is supposed to be independent of the Corporate Families, and its leader, the Rail Marshal, is traditionally an officer of low birth who has risen through the ranks. However, the leaders of Railforce have often thrown their weight behind one candidate or another at times when it was unclear whom the Guardians wished to see as Emperor.

Station Angels

A phenomenon seen at stations on the outer edges of the Network. Strange light-forms sometimes emerge from the K-gates along with trains, and survive for up to thirty minutes before they fade. Their exact nature is uncertain, but they are not dangerous. Theories that they are some form of alien life have been dismissed by the Guardians themselves, and various attempts to capture or communicate with them have failed. They appear to play some role in the religion of the Hive Monks, who sometimes swarm in excitement when a Station Angel appears.

Sundarban

The homeworld of the Noon Family, whose parks, farms and garden cities cover most of its surface. Famous for its Station City, and for the orbiting SpindleRing, a highly unusual pair of orbiting K-gates, which links Sundarban with the Silver River Line.

Trains

Technically, of course, a train consists of a locomotive and a number of carriages or freight cars. In everyday, speech, however, it is often used to refer to the locomotive itself. The first intelligent locos were built by the Guardians, and their minds are still based on coding handed down from the Guardians. Many people believe that the great locomotives are more intelligent than human beings, but experts claim they are on a similar mental level as a bright human, although their intelligence differs from that of humans in several ways. Some never bother speaking to their passengers, others like to chat, and some have formed enduring friendships with individual humans. If properly maintained, they can function for several hundred years. The finest locomotives come from the great engine-shops of the Foss and Helden families.

Locomotives choose their own names from the deep archives of the Datasea, sometimes borrowing the titles of forgotten songs, poems, or artworks.

Thank you

I'm constantly grateful to the people who make it possible for me keep writing my strange books, particularly my agent Philippa Milnes-Smith, my editor Liz Cross, Debbie Sims, Hattie Bayly, Hannah Penny, Gillian Sore and all the rest of the team at Oxford University Press, Catherine Coe and Eirian Griffiths for copy-editing and proof-reading, and Phil Perry and Liz Scott for publicity.

Back when I started toying with the idea of writing a space story one of the things which inspired me was the art of Ian McQue (follow him on Instagram and you'll see what I mean). I'm delighted to have Ian's illustration on the cover of this book—a cover beautifully designed by Holly Fulbrook and Jo Cameron.

The trains of the Web of Worlds are singing happy songs for all of you!